FULL STEAM AHEAD?

"General Beardsley," said the President of the United States loudly, "do you recognize that I am speaking to you as your Commander in Chief?"

"I do, sir," came the prompt answer over the protected microwave link. "I await your order, Mr. President."

"Then, General Beardsley, in accordance with the authority of the Aircraft Atomic Energy Act of 1963, order the *Langley*'s commander to start his aircraft's engines."

Beardsley looked impassively back out of the TV monitor, then snapped to attention and saluted. "The wing is ready, sir. We will not fail the country, Mr. President. *NOR THE WORLD OF STEAM!*"

"The world of what?" said a startled President.

Other Tor Books by Hilbert Schenck

Chronosequence (hardcover)

HILBERT SCHENCK

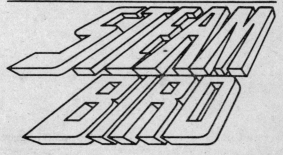

A TOM DOHERTY ASSOCIATES BOOK

STEAM BIRD

Copyright © 1988 by Hilbert Schenck

A TOR Book
Published by Tom Doherty Associates, Inc.
49 West 24 Street
New York, NY 10010

Cover art by Vincent di Fate

ISBN: 0-812-55400-0
Can. ISBN: 0-812-55401-9

First edition: August 1988

Printed in the United States of America

0 9 8 7 6 5 4 3 2 1

Dear Garret and Grant: Let a smile be your S.D.I.
H. S.

Contents

Steam Bird

AUTHOR'S NOTE

IN 1952 THE UNITED STATES AIR FORCE DECIDED TO PRESS ahead on the design of an atomic-powered bombing plane capable of attacking any point inside the Soviet Union from any other given point of entry, and able to stay aloft along the Soviet borders for long periods of time before attacking. Two engine companies, Pratt and Whitney Aircraft and the General Electric Company, were engaged to produce the power plant, working under the requirement that two entirely different engines must emerge from the two companies, and the Air Force would then choose the design on which to base the airframe. In fact, at least four different engine cycles were considered in the next six years, all of them operationally dangerous in various unique ways.

The supercritical-water, steam-turbine-driven fan-jet "Steam Bird" happened to be the weapons system on which I worked as a just-graduated mechanical engineer at Pratt and Whitney, specifically in the condenser design group. And though we got the big baby flying inside the computers, the whole thing was dropped . . . luckily for the country . . . in 1958 when the flight of *Sputnik* showed that intercontinental mass murder does

not require slow, vulnerable and crash-prone battlewag-
ons of the sky. This story, taking place more or less in
the present, assumes a world in which that decision was
not made and in which three such bombers were actually
built, to sleep forgotten awaiting some final purpose.

The flight of Steam Bird here, its multitudes of technical and operational problems, and the crew's and Washington's responses to these surprises are either my own
professional estimates or else the projections of other
engineers. The much-discussed problem of 'roll-up', for
example, was first pointed out to the Air Force by an
AEC consultant in 1950.

As to the Muth family, their friends, adversaries, and
co-conspirators, they are wholly fictitious and not based
on any real persons.

                                                    H. S.

Cuttyhunk, Mass.

THE FOUR-CYLINDER ARTICULATED Y6B, HER TWIN STACKS blasting, hit the sag at the base of Sherman Hill doing fifty scale-miles an hour, over a hundred loaded coal hoppers behind her drawbar and heading for Tidewater. Colonel Bob Muth, sweat already popping on his pink forehead, felt his train's momentum drop away as the big engine tackled the main grade and car after car came through the sag and started into the climb.

Colonel Muth's wife, Betty Lou, watched with frowning, critical eyes. "I told you to go in the hole at Newberry Junction," she said firmly. "The *Dixie Flyer* is only ten minutes back and running late!"

Colonel Muth was too busy to make a response. He gave the locomotive full regulator, then increased the cutoff to forty percent. The engine, now barking sharply like an enraged dog, slowed and fought the hill. On the tail of the kite, behind the caboose, was a single helper engine, an ancient Berkshire, also puffing and shouting hoarsely.

"Will you push!" said Colonel Muth tensely to the Berk's engineer, Major Fisk. "For God's sake, Harry, put it in full forward gear, please!"

Fisk shook his head. "My water's already down to the crownsheet, Bob. I can barely hold steam now!"

The drag slowed and slowed as the top of Sherman Hill came nearer. "More sand, Bob," said Betty Lou Muth quietly. "You're going to lose your feet!"

Colonel Muth pushed the sanding lever further over and shook his head. "I'll be out of sand before the top. How the hell can I stop her at Tidewater?"

Nobody answered. They were all watching the big engine begin to slip her forward drivers. The exhaust bark became uneven and, in desperation, Muth slammed the sanding lever way over and shoved the machine into full forward gear on both sets of cylinders. In a final ecstasy of rapid exhaust puffs and spinning wheels, the big engine topped the hill at no more than three scale-miles an hour and the hoppers began to come over the ridge behind her. Muth let out a great sigh, pulled back on his Johnson bar and, to show he had never really doubted the top, cut loose a triumphant, though brief, blast on his whistle.

"Lucky, Bob," said his wife, trying to appear unimpressed.

The long train slowly accelerated as each new hopper hit the level, and Colonel Muth finally whistled his helper off the train. The gasping Berkshire immediately dropped away and ran slowly backwards to the helper pocket at the base of Sherman Hill, her engineer still breathing deeply in relief.

The main line of the Tidewater Northern went to two tracks a scale mile beyond Sherman and Colonel Muth pulled into the passing track to let the *Dixie Flyer* go by. He steamed slowly along as the varnish suddenly appeared behind, two high-stepping Pacifics on the point, four head-end postal and express cars, twelve heavyweight eighty-footers, all ending in a handsome boattail observation lounge, the whole consist smoothly tearing by them at ninety scale-miles an hour. Both whistles broke into a continuous scream and after the *Dixie*

whirled away, Colonel Muth gave two cheerful toots
back and speeded up when his signal dropped back to
caution.

The rest of the run to Tidewater was on a descending
one-in-two-hundred grade, and Colonel Muth, now
quite low on sand, applied his air a quarter-mile from
the division yards so that his train might assist in
bringing the engine to rest. They passed the yard limit
signs doing seven scale-miles an hour and he put the
Y6B into reverse gear and quarter regulator, watching
the wheels slip and skid, then pulled his train air to full
emergency. The long train drifted neatly to a stop along
the arrival track of the rotary dumper and Colonel Muth
grinned, wiped his face with a red bandanna hanging
around his neck, and flipped up the long black bill on his
blue-striped engineer's cap.

Master Sergeant Stewart, whose six-wheeled switcher
began at once to break the coal drag into manageable
pieces, stuck up his right thumb. "A sweet run, Bob.
Lovely!"

Colonel Muth sat silent and grinning to watch the
northbound commuter, a small, ancient Prairie and
three open vestibule shorty cars, huffle busily by. Then,
just as the commuter pulled into Lakeview, everything
suddenly stopped and the room lights went fully on.

"Gentlemen," said Betty Lou Muth, who was Division Super for that session, "It is now twelve noon, July
fifteenth, nineteen hundred and forty-three. Next Thurs-
day we complete this day. Division Superintendant will
be Harry Fisk. The rest of your assignments are posted
on the call board."

Betty Lou looked up and down the sixty-foot length of
the HO train layout whose several levels filled the
gigantic basement of the Muth home. "Let's remember
next week that we're on wartime rules. We'll be handling
about one hundred and sixty percent of normal traffic."

Bob Muth poked up his hand diffidently, grinning at
his wife. "Super," he said in a respectful voice. "Can't

we get a better helper in the pocket at Sherman than that completely decrepit and useless Berkshire?"

Betty Lou shrugged. "You find it, Bob, anywhere on this division. The *Dixie* is running double-headed in both directions now. We've got two solid trains of troop sleepers coming south as extras during the next session and even the division's local peddler freight is so long it needs two switchers or else a decent road engine."

"On the other hand," stoutly answered Bob Muth right back, "if we have to split the coal trains at Sherman, we'll block the whole road for an hour or more at a time."

Betty Lou, shrugging again, turned toward the stairs. "As I said when we started the session, Bob, there's a war on." A smattering of laughter and applause greeted this firmly-stated announcement. "Okay," said Betty Lou, "you boys police up the butts and secure the layout while I go pour the cocoa."

The men soon straggled upstairs from the basement, chatting about the various problems of the just-ended operating session, to find hot cocoa and cookies laid out in the big living room. "The trouble is," said Bob Muth to Fisk and Stewart, as they sat down on the long sofa and sipped their cocoa, "the whole loco roster is stored right there in the minicomputer memory. The damn thing *knows* that Berkshire was supposedly built in 1917, hasn't had a major shopping since 1940, and leaks steam at every joint."

"It sure is a dog, all right," said Harry Fisk. "Good grief, the computer had me out of water after five minutes on full regulator!"

"Does the computer really know when you forget to stop for sand, Bob?" asked Sergeant Stewart, remembering the problem with stopping the Y6B.

Bob Muth shook his head in rueful remembrance. "You better believe it does, buddy! You weren't here three weeks ago, but I forgot to sand up the switcher I was running at Tidewater. I came down light off the dumper, going a bit fast, hit the brake and sander, and skidded into the drink. Five demerits!"

"You went into the water?" asked an unbelieving Stewart.

"Well, down on the epoxy, Jim. All the bumpers are set to give way if a train hits at over ten miles an hour, and I was well over that."

Stewart shook his head. Going onto the ground while driving on a crack model railway like the Tidewater Northern was humiliating enough. But to go over onto the epoxy ocean! "Boy, I'm never going to touch that regulator again before I check my sand!" said Jim Stewart fervently.

At that instant the phone began to ring. Bob Muth peered at his watch, noting it was almost midnight, then picked up the receiver. "Colonel Muth speaking," he said in a terse voice.

Conversation in the room abruptly stopped and everyone turned to watch Bob Muth speak into the phone. "Yes sir. I understand, General. Well, sir . . . all my crew is here except my copilot, Captain Jackson. . . . Ah, he's with you now then? Fine."

Muth hung up and turned, completely without expression, back to his wife and guests. "Gentlemen," he said in a calm tone, "the Soviet Union has refused to call back its two vessels taking missile bodies to Nicaragua. President O'Connell has placed the wing on a six-hour alert. General Beardsley suggests that everyone get some sleep. We have to be in the aircraft ready for takeoff at five A.M. Any questions?"

The Muth living room was absolutely still. Nobody moved a finger, a shoe, or a muscle, yet their eyes darted everywhere, each man staring in turn into the eyes of the others, and in each eye there was a single, burning hope. Rapidly and silently each man finished his cocoa and left the house. Bob and Betty Lou nodded their acceptances of thanks and said their good-nights in low voices at the front door, and soon the driveway was empty of cars.

Colonel Muth peered out past the neat lawn to the tall pine forests that surrounded the northern Maine town of Moosefoot. He sighed deeply.

Betty Lou suddenly put her arm around her husband, hugging him strongly. "You're getting your hopes up again, aren't you baby?" she said softly.

Colonel Muth bit his lip and grinned sheepishly at her. "It's got to be this time, Lou. If they don't use us now, the wing is down the chute."

"How many other times have you been on six-hour red alert, Bob?" asked his wife softly.

"Eight," said Bob Muth immediately and ruefully. He turned to look at his wife. "Oh, I know there's not much chance, but the pressure is stronger on them to use us too, each time we get called up."

Betty Lou hugged her husband tight. "You think I should call Uncle Nate, Bob?" Her level grey eyes looked lovingly and directly at him.

Muth shook his head. "There's no point getting Nate stirred up at this point. But if we should be ordered to go critical . . . then you better get him." He put an arm around her sturdy shoulder and gave her a squeeze back. "You've got to get us back, good buddy," he said suddenly. "You and Nate."

Betty Lou nodded and kissed her husband on the cheek. "You know we'll get you back, Bob," she said in a positive voice. "I just hope Steam Bird gets you up."

Bob Muth took a deep breath. "She'll do it. All she needs is a chance." His voice was positive and strong, and as he looked out over the dark, silent woods, then up into the cold air, he could almost see the huge bird lifting, up and up, her turbines singing a shrill song to the very stars.

II

THE MOOSEFOOT AIR FORCE BASE AND ITS ASSOCIATED TOWN were neighbors to such far-north Maine municipalities as Eagle Lake, Quimby, and Allagash. During World War II the long runway had been one of the American ends of that great bridge of aircraft that flew across the Atlantic to beleaguered England. Now, all that remained of those memorable days was the Third Intercontinental Bombardment Wing, USAF, consisting of three nuclear-propelled aircraft, the only three in the world.

None of these huge planes had ever actually flown. The original idea had been to use one as a trainer, keeping the other two unflown for combat. The difficulty was that once a flight, or even a start, was made, the plane's reactor became hot and deadly for all time to come, and since the aircraft could only carry enough shielding around the reactor to protect the air crew located forward, a working plane would have to be kept and serviced in a special place, the 'hot hangar'.

Inside this hot hangar, in addition to massive, moveable shielding walls, was planned a shielded diesel locomotive to move around the remote-servicing arms and servo-controlled TV cameras to check and repair the aircraft. This quarter-billion-dollar project had been traded off in a long-ago Congress for some other, and more interesting, weapons system, so that the Air Force had no choice but to save all its atomic airplanes for some future 'big show'.

Congress had eventually relented a bit and provided a few dozen million to train the three crews on a flying simulator, a gigantic, prop-jet, kerosene-driven copy of a nuclear-propelled bombing plane. Like the electrically-propelled 'steamers' on Colonel Muth's HO-gauge model railway layout, the response of this giant plane was filtered through a computer programmed to make it respond like a nuclear machine. Since fossil fuel gas turbines have a much more prompt response to environmental and control changes than a nuclear-heated cycle, the simulation was practical and readily carried out. The difficulty, of course, was that the assumed behavior of the atomic airplane was just that: assumed. Nobody really knew what the things might truly do, or fail to do, in an actual flight.

Colonel Muth, tall and stern in his bulky flight kit, stood at five A.M. with his silent crew under the wing of their gigantic atomic aircraft, the *Samuel Langley*. The machine was essentially a low-wing fan-jet, but with wing-root-mounted engines. The huge size of these ten shrouded-fans required a wing-fuselage junction over thirty feet thick, so that from the front the *Langley* seemed like one vast tapered wing with five insect-like eye complexes on each side of a stubby but huge nose. The many wheels and their complex of undercarriage structure created a sense of busy confusion between the *Langley*'s great bulk and the hangar floor, and a sense of her weight could be gained by noting how mushed flat were the many fat tires.

Behind, in the cavernous hangar, bulked the two other shadowy planes of the wing, and everywhere about them men prepared to move the huge machines out into the quiet dawn, should the order ever be given.

Major Peter Brush, aircraft commander of the nearby *Sir Hiram Maxim*, walked up to the *Langley*'s air crew, smiling crookedly. "You want to flip to see who goes first, Bob?" he asked with elaborate casualness.

Colonel Muth clapped Brush on the shoulder and grinned. "Sorry, buddy. Today I'm pulling rank and seniority. You can go first next time," but when he saw that Brush did not think this very funny, he softened his voice. "Maybe they'll fly us all, Pete," he said squeezing the man's arm.

"Look," said Major Brush, suddenly smiling. "If only you guys get up," and he looked around at them all, "well, Jesus, good luck! I just wish we could double-head this run, Bob."

"Me too, Pete," said Colonel Muth in a firm tone.

Suddenly General Beardsley's voice boomed within the gigantic hangar. "Aircrews, man your planes! Ground crews, begin the tow-out!" The *Langley*'s crew stared at each other, their eyes filled with a sudden, wild surmise. Sergeant Stewart shook his head and muttered to himself. "I am *not* going to get my hopes up," he said over and over.

Betty Lou Muth sat in her car outside the high cyclone fence with her younger daughter, Alice. They peered across the wide field into a distant corner of the huge, lighted hangar. Suddenly the girl pointed. "Mom, look! They're towing out the *Langley!*"

Mrs. Muth quickly lifted a pair of 7x50-power night binoculars to her eyes and focused on the distant activity. "You're right!" she breathed. "Lordy, here they come, Alice!"

The hangar doors came fully up in the predawn darkness and the inside light spilled out around the gigantic, slowly-moving form of the *Langley*. It took three D-8 Caterpillar tractors to move each huge flying machine on its ninety-six wheels, and these roaring, creeping monsters were utterly dwarfed by their load. Betty Lou Muth peered steadily through her glasses.

"They've gotten this far before," she said, half to herself. "Let's see if they start the fans."

The *Langley*'s flight office was an almost unnoticeable blister on the monster, bulbous nose of the plane. Colonel Muth sat in the right-hand or plane commander's seat, staring out and down at the distant, huffling tractors as they pulled with agonizing slowness out into a pink dawn. The wind was a modest ten miles an hour and blowing right down the runway toward them. They had only to turn the aircraft a few degrees to begin a takeoff run.

Next to Muth in the copilot's seat slouched Captain George Abraham Jackson, the only black in the *Langley*'s crew and generally regarded as the most skilled high-pressure steam man on the base. 'Gaby' Jackson had been raised as a youth in England, the son of a minor consular official, but while there he had come under the influence of the great model engineer Edgar Westbury, holder of many international hydroplane records and remembered as the poet of flash steam.

Although modern model hydroplane contests had become increasingly dominated by supercharged one-cylinder petrol engines, Captain Jackson had astonished and dazzled the model world by winning the Class D (unlimited) hydroplane classic at the Chiswick, England model basin that past year with a world record of ninety-two miles an hour, using his flash steam driven *Nickie XXII*.

Having nothing to do until the *Langley*'s engines were placed in start mode, even though surrounded by banks of instruments and controls, Captain Jackson was carefully reading his latest copy of *Flash Steam Monthly* and shaking his head over what appeared to be suicidally-thin bearings in a new impulse turbine design.

Colonel Muth turned to his introspective copilot. "Did you and the general get his flash steam outfit going, Gaby?" he asked, finding the tense silence suddenly too much to bear.

Captain Jackson looked up from his magazine and stretched. "We got thirty seconds, Bob. I told General Beardsley those two water pumps wouldn't be enough, but he was dying to try the rig out, so of course we burned out two feet of uniflow tubing at the hot end. That burner is really a screamer. Terrifying!"

Bob Muth grinned at his copilot. "If *you* say that, buddy, then it must be so! You think old Beardsley will ever get his car built?"

Jackson shrugged narrow shoulders and winked a big, brown eye. "He will if he doesn't kill himself first, Bob. The question is, who will drive the thing? You wouldn't get me in a sixteen-hundred-pound flash steam racer intended to go two hundred miles an hour."

Colonel Muth sighed. "I dunno, Gaby, about all this speed stuff. I think I'd just as soon be driving Nate's twelve-ton Shay, holding seven miles an hour up a four percent grade and puffing like it was doing two hundred."

Captain Jackson stuck out a large red tongue and made a rude noise. "Don't give me that 'speed is silly' stuff, Bob," he said at once. "You'd cut off your right arm if somebody would put you in *Mallard*'s cab with Driver Duddington when she came down Essendine bank doing a hundred and twenty-six."

"You're absolutely right," said Bob Muth cheerfully. "But then, I'd also give a right arm to be driving the lead South Park Consolidation with five engines behind me, ramming the push-plow through to Gunnison against fourteen-foot drifts."

Captain Jackson's large, dark face assumed a thoughtful cast. "Who wouldn't?" he said finally and almost to himself.

In the center of the control panels surrounding the two pilots were inset two miniature TV screens. Certain commands to the *Langley* could only be given by certain people, and it was essential that the *Langley*'s crew actually see who was issuing the order. Now these two screens were alight and showing the thin, patrician, white-moustached face of General Beardsley, and behind him the busy ops room of Moosefoot Airbase.

"Colonel Muth and crew of the *Langley*," he said from firm, narrow lips. "Commence the reactor and engine check-offs. You will start the criticality sequence on my order. We are towing the portable shields into place."

Colonel Muth and Captain Jackson stared at each other in total disbelief that immediately gave way to expressions of total triumph, as they simultaneously looked back over their shoulders and saw the big Cats, shouting in deafening bellows, dragging the immensely heavy rolling shields between the *Langley* and the open hangar. Since it had proved impossible to carry enough reactor shielding on board the plane to protect any ground crew at the rear of the *Langley* after the reactor start, they had to interpose a lead-concrete rolling wall between the airbase and the plane before she went critical. This distressing and onerous requirement had one silver lining; Russian jet fighters, which could move at five to six times the speed of the *Langley*, might be discouraged from pressing a stern attack when they realized they were tearing into a thousand-Rem-per-hour radiation field.

Betty Lou Muth passed the field glasses to her daughter and started the car. "They're pulling out the shielding!" she said in a tight voice. "I'm going to call Nate. If we hurry, we can get back here before they take off."

She floored it in reverse and spun the station wagon's wheels in the dirt shoulder as they jumped out on the highway. With a scream of tires, the Muth station wagon darted back toward the main street of Moosefoot and its single outdoor pay phone. Twelve-year-old Alice Muth peered out her side window with the big glasses, watching the distant *Langley* squatting like a winged spider on a planet a thousand or a million times bigger than earth, the crisp pink dawn showing through its multitudes of wheels. Even from two miles away it seemed to dwarf the trees and buildings.

"Mom," said Alice, "if Dad can get that to actually fly, well, he must be the best pilot in the world!"

"Amen," muttered Betty Lou Muth as the Moosefoot city limit signs went by them at eighty miles an hour.

III

THE PRESIDENT OF THE UNITED STATES FACED HIS DAY AHEAD with both annoyance and disquiet. For one thing, it seemed obvious to him, though he readily admitted he was no military expert, that firing a few ballistic missiles from Nicaragua, over Costa Rica, to hit the Gatun locks on the Panama Canal, was about as unlikely a way of actually hurting the damn thing as he could imagine. The trouble was that the canal kooks, for whom any threat to their beloved waterway was more to be resisted than a landing of Russian tank forces at New York's Battery Park, had their damnable wind up.

President O'Connell shook his head sourly at a room heavily dotted with uniforms. It seemed especially ominous to him that he had never heard, after two years in office, about the Moosefoot Airbase and his country's three nuclear aircraft. After all, they *were* a part of the United States nuclear deterrent, for which he was solely responsible. The President felt even more distress over the absence of his major domo and chief White House aide, 'Happy Jack' Hanrahan, the man who actually ran Chicago while Mayor Shamus O'Connell was striding about the South Side, tossing his white mane, wetly kissing tiny black children, and running for president.

Happy Jack was a thin, wizened Irishman with a mind so quick and all-encompassing that no computer data bank or newspaper morgue could ever compete with it. Happy Jack's memory for names, facts, and faces was more extraordinary than any mental freak counting a field full of cows in seconds. The President rubbed his hands and frowned. Jack would know plenty about Moosefoot and the nuclear bombers, probably the name of its Commander in Chief, how he voted, and who was in the Maine state legislature from Moosefoot Township.

The President steepled his hands, pursed his lips, and lidded his eyes, to imply deep thought. The longer he could stall them, the more chance there was of Jack getting back from California and keeping him out of trouble on this.

But General of the Air Force Mike 'One-Eye' Zinkowski was not prepared to wait any longer. "Mr. President," he said in a respectful but firm voice, "the first atomic aircraft is now prepared for engine start-up. Under the Aircraft Atomic Energy Act of 1963, *you* must issue the order. I now respectfully request such an order."

The President opened his eyes and cleared his throat. Well, they were pressing him, all right. He peered about the room, knowing that he had to say something incisive. "General, starting the engines does not commit us to takeoff, is that correct?"

General Zinkowski set his large jaw in a conciliatory position and nodded. "Takeoff is a second and entirely separate order that is transmitted directly from you to the plane commander."

The President sighed. "Very well." He turned slightly to face the TV camera. "Are we hooked into Moosefoot?" he asked his press aide as an aside, and when the man nodded, whispered, "Who's that general up there?"

"Beardsley," the aide hissed back.

"General Beardsley," said the President of the United States loudly, "do you recognize that I am speaking to you as your Commander in Chief?"

"I do, sir," came the prompt answer over the protected microwave link. "I await your order, Mr. President."

"Then, General Beardsley," said O'Connell, "order the *Langley*'s commander to start his aircraft's engines."

Beardsley looked impassively back out of the TV monitor, then snapped to attention and saluted. "The wing is ready, sir. We will not fail the country, Mr. President. Nor the world of steam!"

"The world of what?" said a startled President O'Connell, but the screen picture had dissolved to shards of blinking, bright lines. The President rubbed his nose slowly and let his eyes drift over the many men sitting at the big conference table, most of them watching him in a kind of attentive mindlessness or else peering blankly at papers that lay in front of them. O'Connell missed Jack more than ever, because now the President's sensitive political antennae were sending disturbing signals. Either somebody was planning some kind of weird coup or scam, or else the United States Air Force had turned into a kind of gigantic mental ward. Or perhaps both. My mother wanted me to be an accountant, thought Shamus O'Connell with a sudden, sweet sadness. I could be mowing a green suburban lawn somewhere, right now.

Following the full check-off of the pre-start settings and instrument readings, the crew of the *Langley* silently awaited the criticality order. Muth and Jackson peered at each other in suspended hope, their bodies stiff in their contoured foam seats.

General Beardsley's face reappeared on the TV screen and he spoke sternly. "The President has ordered the *Langley* to go critical and reach idling mode. I order you to start your engines at once, Colonel Muth."

Bob Muth pushed the radiation alarm button to warn anyone between the shield and the plane of a start-up.

"Okay, Harry," he said quietly on the intercom to Major Fisk. "Go."

Harry Fisk, the *Langley*'s chief flight engineer, was now responsible for starting the reactor, then the steam turbines. He unlocked the fuel-rod switches and set the automatic damper-rod servos on withdrawal for normal start. As the rods came out and the multiplication factor approached unity, Fisk intently watched his temperature gauges for the reaction chamber. One of the very many problems with the *Langley*'s power plant on start was that the reactor needed an immediate flow of water to prevent it from melting through the bottom of the plane and the asphalt runway as soon as the chain reaction was self-sustaining, but the turbines could not function to pump that water until they had steam. Furthermore, the gigantic steam-to-air condensers that made up much of the *Langley*'s wing structure needed air flow from the turbofans to condense the exhaust steam so it could be pumped back through the reactor as water. In essence, everything had to happen at once.

Fortunately, the cold condensers had so much metal that they could function for a few moments without any air flow. But the main and condensate pumps had to be bootstrapped from somewhere else, specifically a series of hydrogen peroxide steam generators that fed the pump turbines for the few moments it took to get the main turbines going.

Major Fisk continued to follow, second by second, the conditions in the reactor pressure vessel. They were now well beyond nuclear criticality and the temperatures were rising steeply. At twelve hundred Fahrenheit the pressure began to rise exponentially. Major Fisk pressed the ignition buttons on the peroxide units and muttered a brief prayer.

Immediately the peroxide steam began to blow through the pump turbines and out a number of bypass valves onto the tarmac under the wings and body, so that the entire huge space under the *Langley* was instantly filled with a dense white fog.

General Beardsley, watching all this from the shielded Operations office high above the field, smiled at his communications officer. "Kind of looks like a Virginian triplex blowing all her steam and drain cocks at once, eh, Captain Frothingham?"

"Wider than a triplex, General," muttered the officer, staring in wonder at the sight.

"Heavier, too," chuckled General Beardsley.

The sudden burst of steam brought the pump turbines and their directly-connected water pumps rapidly up to speed, and main-line water sluiced through the reactor vessel. This dropped the reaction temperature sharply, but Major Fisk skillfully caught the thermal sag by overriding the damper automatics and suddenly running out the control rods. The hot steam now entered the main fan turbines in abundance, then expanded to the lower pressures in the wing condensers. And this expansion began to turn the ten ponderous turbofans slowly around and drive air back through the wings.

Steam Bird was running.

Betty Lou Muth had managed to reach her brother, Nathaniel Hazelton, through his unlisted Washington number, rousing the sleepy congressman from his bed and the floozie with whom he usually shared it. Betty Lou then roared back out of town and skidded up to the fence just as the peroxide steam billowed out and up underneath the *Langley*.

"Say a prayer now, Alice," whispered her mother. "If Dad's crew mess up the start, they'll just wheel up another plane." She watched through the glasses, then let her breath out with a rush as the vast steam cloud suddenly blew backward and the *Langley*'s mass of spidery undercarriage stood once more whole and visible.

"Well," said Mrs. Muth in relief, "they got the fans going anyway." But she knew by a touch of coldness in her heart that there was still one more large hurdle: takeoff.

Colonel Muth felt the *Langley*, alive for the first time

in her existence, vibrate up to idling speed. The ten huge turbofans, five within each massive wing root, spun and drove the air streams backwards. Even at minimum idle, the huge engines developed some fifteen thousand pounds of thrust, and only the automatic chocks sticking up out of the tarmac prevented the *Langley* from starting to roll ahead.

"General Beardsley," said Colonel Muth, speaking steadily at the tiny TV screen. "The *Langley* is prepared for takeoff."

General Beardsley composed his expression to an iron rigidity and straightened to ramrod posture. He turned again to the communications console directly connected to Washington.

 IV

PRESIDENT SHAMUS O'CONNELL LEANED IN THE DIRECTION OF the Air Force contingent and swept out a stubby finger that encompassed them all. "You mean to tell me that we've gotten this far and the aircraft has no nuclear weapons aboard?" He said this sternly from a grim countenance, but inside the President felt suddenly much easier about the whole thing.

The impassive Air Force chief plucked at his large, bulbous nose, then adjusted his black silk eyepatch. "That is correct, sir. You remember back in the early sixties when that commission on nuclear proliferation said there were too many different bomb dumps? Well, we made a study . . . quite a few studies actually . . . and set a kind of activity-level criterion below which a base wouldn't store atomic weapons locally. . . ."

"And," said the President impatiently, "Moosefoot fell below this level?"

"Yessir," said General Zinkowski curtly. "With only three aircraft, we just couldn't justify storing any weapons on the site."

"Well," said the President, his eyes darting, trying to

watch them all at once, "do you think we should arm the *Langley* then, General?"

Zinkowski seemed genuinely shocked. "Sir, we're not claiming they're sending nukes to Nicaragua, just missile bodies. I'm not sure that would be appropriate . . ."

"Exactly!" said the President, stabbing at him with a finger. "Then why should we send up the plane at all?"

The general shrugged and blinked his one eye, looking, thought O'Connell suspiciously, like the damnable pirate he probably was. "The Russians don't actually know the on-board bombs are dummies, sir." He leaned forward and gestured with a thick, black stogie. "Mr. President, it was you who asked us to come up with what you called an 'appropriate response' to the two Russian ships and the missiles. If you want to try something else, well, we're ready to listen, sir!" The general adjusted his craggy features into an appropriately submissive expression and waited.

But President O'Connell's eyes were narrowing. Without Happy Jack whispering in his ear, he was lousy at spotting their multitudes of gimmicks, tricks, scams, and rip-offs, most especially the military and science gangs, the one simply venal, the other venal and damn smart besides. But now he suddenly seemed to see a glimmer of sense in all this. Okay, so somebody way down at the bottom came up with the *Langley* thing in good faith, but before the upper brass could squash it and think of something else, it arrived here at the White House.

The President cogitated furiously. Moosefoot AFB had been up there, a nuclear wing, ten or more years, eating up god-knows-how-much treasure just to heat the hangars. Never a mission. Never a purpose. So, how did he really *know* the base was all that ready, engines running, all that stuff? Was this really a part of his deterrent force? How could he ever know if they never went up? So, he decided, why not? Fly one plane and see how soon it gets into the air, if it ever gets up at all.

The President steepled his hands steeply and tried to

read their impassive faces. "No, General Zinkowski, I think this is an appropriately measured response. I suppose the canal lobby would prefer all three, but I think one aircraft is fine for the moment."

O'Connell pointed up at the camera. "Connect me with the *Langley*'s commanding officer," he said in a strong voice.

"You're hooked in, sir," whispered the press aide, shoving a scrap of paper into the President's hand bearing the words, "Colonel Robert Muth."

The TV screens now showed Bob Muth's large head and keen eyes to the President and the others, while on board the *Langley* Colonel Muth now looked back into the face of his Commander in Chief.

"Colonel Muth," came the mellow Irish voice, "do you recognize me?"

"I do, Mr. President. I await your orders, sir." Colonel Muth locked his face into its sternest mold, although under his thighs, out of sight of the camera, he had his fingers crossed on both hands.

"Then Colonel Muth, I order you to take off at once!"

The onboard TV screens blanked as the *Langley* instantly went into takeoff mode. "Operations," said Muth rapidly, "drop the chocks."

Immediately the hydraulic chocks that had blocked about a third of the *Langley*'s ninety-six wheels sank into the ground, and the huge airplane began to drift forward.

"Ramp us to full power, Harry," said Colonel Muth. "Now. Go!"

Major Fisk immediately began control-rod pull-out, and the turbine whine became a scream of slowly-increasing pitch. The *Langley* began to lumber ahead, drawing more and more air into her fans as she accelerated. And as more air came through, so Major Fisk was able to condense more steam and thus develop more power.

Takeoff with the *Langley* raised a number of special problems because of condenser lag during acceleration.

Reactor power was actually limited by water flow and thus by condenser operation. Condenser operation, in turn, was governed by reactor power as it drove the fans, accelerated the plane, and brought in more air. The only way the machine could theoretically accelerate was if the condensers were sufficiently overdesigned at lower speeds so as to handle excess water, and it was at this point in the operation of the power plant that theoretical anticipations and practical results had their most important confrontation. For the long-departed design engineers of the *Langley* had regarded the takeoff problem as the thorniest of all—thorniest, that is, until someone attempted to land a plane that had jumped this first, essential hurdle.

But at about this moment in Washington, Happy Jack Hanrahan, his dark, trim silk suit rumpled by a hard run in from the helicopter on the South Lawn, burst into the President's conference room and stared at them all. The tiny, wrinkled man walked rapidly around the table and bent over the President, cupping both hands around O'Connell's large, right ear.

"For God's sake, Shamus," he said in a harsh whisper. "Stop them! That crazy thing will roll-up and blow up!"

Shamus O'Connell jerked around, staring at his wizened aide. "What the hell is 'roll-up', Jack?" he said from behind a hand.

Happy Jack took off his pearl-grey homburg and held it between their faces and the others at the big table. "If the airplane crashes, the whole damn reactor, shield, and pipes will tear out and roll along the ground. The shield is so heavy that it can collapse the reactor core in on itself. Jesus, Shamus, it's possible the thing could become a nuclear bomb with as much as a twenty-kiloton yield! Furthermore, the damn planes have never flown before! Nobody is sure how long a runway they need to take off!" This last seemed to frighten even thin-lipped, deadpan Happy Jack, and he fiercely rubbed one lined cheek, his eyes wide.

President O'Connell stared, shocked, into his old friend's dour face. "What if they don't get off, Jack?"

Hanrahan flipped his hat on the table and twirled his two forefingers around each other, making a smaller and smaller twirl. He suddenly popped his two hands apart, all the fingers flying out in an explosive gesture.

A dismayed President O'Connell turned again to the room. "Get me General Beardsley in Moosefoot, at once!" he said in a hoarse voice.

The TV screens flashed up and they again saw part of Moosefoot ops room with General Beardsley's mask-like face staring at them. The President breathed more easily. At least communications seemed to be pretty dependable today. "General," he said in a level voice, "abort the takeoff. Order the planes towed back into their hangars. I've decided on another response to the Nicaraguan missiles."

General Beardsley snapped to attention, staring straight ahead. "The *Langley* has begun her takeoff run, Mr. President. At her present speed over the ground it will be considerably safer to let her reach flying speed and take off. Otherwise there's a remote possibility of what we call 'roll-up'. . . ."

President O'Connell's mouth flew open. "You've started the takeoff already?" He peered down at his watch. "What the hell are you doing up there, General?" he snarled.

General Beardsley's face remained graven rock. "You ordered the *Langley* to take off, Mr. President." He paused, then more stiffly, "I think the taped record will show that . . ."

President O'Connell finally lost his temper. "Listen, you son-of-a-bitch, I know I ordered the damn thing to take off. Four minutes ago I ordered it to take off! General Beardsley, if I ask the CIA for a report on oil reserves or the State Department for an opinion on West Africa, do you know when I eventually get it?" He shook his fist at the TV screen. "I usually get it when one of my

aides reads about the conclusions that have been leaked
to the *Washington Post* or *Aviation News* six months
later! It took *four months* to hire and clear a swimming
instructor to teach my kids two hours a week in the
White House pool. I can't usually get a helicopter on the
lawn or a limo at the door in less than forty-five minutes!
And now you're telling me that in bloody Moosefoot,
Maine, wherever that is or isn't, you began a mission *ten
seconds* after I gave the order?!"

The President's eyes narrowed and he drew his upper
lip back from large, fang-like teeth. "I don't know what
you're pulling up there, General Beardsley, BUT YOU
WON'T GET AWAY WITH IT! I've taken enough from
you uniformed phonies! Your butt is now mud, General!
MUD! This is your Commander in Chief talking! I'll
break you for excessive zeal, General. And if that crazy
damn airplane . . . what the shit did you call it, Jack?
. . . *rolls-up,* I'll see that you're shot!"

In the brightly-lit ops room at Moosefoot, the uniformed staff stood or sat, transfixed with horror, as
President O'Connell's large, white-maned head con-
torted from fury to rage to cruelty and back to fury
again. But General Beardsley, standing stiffly at attention, was actually paying only partial attention. Even
though Steam Bird had not quite left the ground, he was
already framing his communication to *Modern Steam
Power,* a magazine that listed him on the masthead as
Consulting Editor. He would write it as a simple letter to
the editor, but he knew they would set it in a special box
on the first editorial page and follow it with long,
thoughtful, and supportive comments.

"Gentlemen," he would begin it, "It is my great
pleasure to inform you that the first steam-propelled
airplane ever flown by mankind, the *Samuel Langley,*
piloted by fellow steam-enthusiast Colonel Bob Muth
and other highly-motivated men under my command,
took off from Moosefoot Air Force Base at . . ."

At the instant that the *Langley* had begun to move

forward the Muth station wagon tore off down the
two-lane road bordering the runway outside the fence.
Betty Lou knew that seven miles further on there was a
broad open space in the forest that gave a view of the
final two-thirds of the runway.

A few minutes later she slammed on the brakes and
careened off the road up to the fence, stopping with a
jerk. In moments, Mrs. Muth and Alice were standing on
the roof of the wagon, peering back down the way they
had come.

The huge *Langley* grew larger and ever larger approaching them, but with a sullen, agonizing slowness.
There seemed no sense of lightness about her, no evident
desire to rise and lift. Looking through the glasses, Betty
Lou Muth could see that many of the huge tires were still
bulged out from the vast weight of the thing. The several
acres of wheels and undercarriage structure rumbled,
vibrated and mushed along the asphalt runway. The
gigantic plane now seemed to Alice like a weird insect,
perhaps a sick, giant wasp with masses of eggs hanging
off her trailing feet and trying, with no real hope, to
achieve a moment of flight. But this was no Japanese
monster flick! The thing was HERE!

"Oh, Mom," said Alice in a small, frightened voice.
"It's going so *slowly.*"

Betty Lou put her arm around her daughter and pulled
her close. "It takes a hell of a long run, Alice. Oh, Bob,"
she breathed in a tense whisper. "Move it now. Put it
into full forward gear, baby!"

The *Langley* trundled along the ten-mile-long runway,
gaining speed with dignified deliberation. At mile-five
they achieved sixty-two miles per hour, still just barely
within the acceptable speed-distance takeoff envelope.

Bob Muth gently tested the wheel in front of him and
scanned the reactor monitor instruments. "How's our
lift, Sergeant Stewart?" he asked in a tight, low voice.

Master Sergeant Jim Stewart's takeoff station was in
the little undercarriage office deep inside the *Langley*,

where he was responsible for the complex retraction procedures required to bring the *Langley*'s many wheels up into her wings and belly. "Sixty-four percent now off the wheels, Bob," he said promptly.

Captain Jackson, who was continuously tracking and projecting the aircraft's speed-lift-distance behavior, shook his head in bitter frustration. "Bob, she's not picking up fast enough! We're going onto the abort side of the takeoff specs!"

Colonel Muth peered straight ahead through narrow eyes, watching the huge ribbon of runway unfold in front of him, seeing in the far distance a first sense of the fringe of trees at the end. He had spent ten years thinking about this moment.

"Steady," he said sharply to them all; then, "Major Fisk, two-minute maximum override on the reactor. Now."

"Done, Bob," said Fisk at once, grimly watching his dials begin to swing into their red zones.

"Sergeant Stewart, prepare for a phased undercarriage retraction. I'm going into partial rotation."

With this, Colonel Muth pulled back on the control wheel and the *Langley*'s huge, blunt nose slowly raised up and up, lifting about half the wheels off the ground. "Jim!" said Colonel Muth, "bring up all the unloaded wheels. Now!"

And that was what it took. As the spidery undercarriage structures began to disappear into their housings in the wings the *Langley*'s aerodynamic drag-shape improved dramatically and continuously. This, plus the extra power from the reactor override, brought her quite smartly up to flying speed. At mile-eight-and-a-half Colonel Muth spoke again, this time brisk and cool. "We are now in ground effect. All remaining wheels up, Jim. I'm completing rotation for takeoff." He eased the wheel back and, as her angle increased again, the final sets of wheels began to lift into the plane's belly.

Steam Bird was flying.

Captain Jackson, his jaws still aching from minutes of tight clenching and his eyes wide, watched the end of the runway pass at least two hundred feet below the climbing *Langley*, then let out an explosive breath. He turned an awed face to the plane commander. "Jesus, Bob. Even Driver Duddington never pulled anything like that! Beautiful, baby!"

Colonel Muth took one hand off the wheel and seized his copilot's hand tightly. His eyes were bright. "Gaby, we're up! Look! Ground speed is one hundred miles an hour!"

This announcement elicited a round of cheers from the other crew members, followed by various shouts of,

"*Nine-nine-nine!*"

"*City of Truro!*"

"*The Morning Hiawatha!*"

"*Flying Scotsman!*"

The magic century mark handily behind her, the *Langley* bored upward into the cold Maine air, her turbines spinning with that splendid, solid whine of machinery that knows itself to be cherished.

On top of the station wagon, Mrs. Muth and her daughter watched these final evolutions of the *Langley* clutched tightly in each other's arms. When the last undercarriage began to come up and the first line of light showed completely between the *Langley* and the ground, Alice Muth gave a triumphant shout. "He started retraction while they were still heavy . . . to cut down on the drag! Oh, Mom, isn't Dad just super!"

Betty Lou Muth was busy wiping her eyes and taking deep breaths, her wide, full mouth now set in a massive grin. "Your father is a nut, Alice, but oh, what a *dear* nut! Come on, let's go find out when Uncle Nate is coming up."

And as the Muth car drove, rather more sedately, back toward Moosefoot, Betty Lou noted with satisfaction that in addition to several dozen private cars parked and watching the takeoff, there were two white, remote-

broadcast TV vans with their rooftop cameras continu-
ing to follow the distant, rising, but still impressive form
of the *Langley* as it began a wide, shallow turn toward
the north.

V

THE PRESIDENT, HIS STAFF, THE JOINT CHIEFS AND THE REST of them watched the *Langley*'s takeoff as transmitted from a Moosefoot chase helicopter in total and pregnant silence, and when the gigantic plane finally lifted up and up over the thick, unbroken forest, President O'Connell exhaled in an explosion of compounded relief and disgust and turned flinty eyes on General Zinkowski. "Well, General," he said in a barely-civil tone, "having put the *Langley* in the air, it seems to me that you have certain problems with making a landing anywhere . . . and especially in Moosefoot, Maine. The basic mission of a nuclear deterrent force, General Zinkowski, is to bomb, or threaten to bomb, the *enemy*, that is, *some other country!*" He said these last words in a carefully-enunciated snarl such as one might take with a four-year-old having a supermarket temper-tantrum. The President showed his fangs again, then gave them a mock-innocent look. "If I'm being too difficult for you gentlemen, using too many big words, I hope you'll catch up with me."

"Mr. President," said Zinkowski in his most responsible-sounding voice, "we have a number of options regarding the *Langley*'s landing. Moosefoot AFB is only one of them."

"And why, General," said O'Connell in a voice now silky with rage, "weren't all these difficulties . . . for example, roll-up, too short a runway, no place to land, and no place to put the thing after it lands . . . why weren't these all at least *mentioned* before we committed ourselves to takeoff?"

Zinkowski lifted his eyebrows and pointed with the most unobtrusive of gestures. "It's all in the Mission Profile and Command Decision write-ups in front of you, sir."

"Ah yes," said President O'Connell, as though seeing the two thick, thousand-page, secret-stamped documents for the first time. "It's all here someplace, isn't it? . . ." He began to shout. "Listen, you bastards, I've got more things to do than read through ten pounds of horseshit science fiction dreamed up by you and your paid Ph.D. whitecoats to con a bunch of brainless, fat-assed congressmen into spending money so you can have a new chopper to take you to your golf games! Two rusty tramp steamers with tin missile bodies that are probably actually stuffed with cases of vodka and we send up a flying nightmare that can actually crash at any moment and produce a new Hiroshima in Maine! Talk about curing the common cold with cancer!"

But at this point the President's National Security Advisor, Professor Andrezoti Bzggnartsky, his large, thick glasses reflecting odd circular rainbows in the brilliant fluorescent blast of the room, interjected a loud, thick, Slavic, "Come, come Mr. Prezident, Zir. Calm yourzelf. Zere iz an entirely oppozite vay to view ziss zituazion."

"Ah, yes, Professor," gritted a now-blazing O'Connell, partly out of breath from shouting, his eyes as thin as a snake's. "Do tell us how to correctly view Armageddon, I insist!" Following a long-established yet obscure tradition set by his predecessors, Shamus O'Connell had reluctantly appointed an Eastern European, thickly-

accented hawk from Cambridge, Massachusetts as his
Security Advisor instead of his real choice, an old WWII
buddy who was a major general in the Illinois National
Guard. He had never regretted that decision more than
at this moment.

Professor Bzggnartsky swiveled his pointed bald head,
his glasses glinting balefully at everyone. "Firzt," he said
in his heavy, penetrating voice, "Can ve underztand zat
ze *Langley* iz not likely, az you feared Prezident
O'Connell, to roll-up on takeoff? For one zing, if ze pilot
remained vizzin ze zpezificazionz, he vould have
ztopped ze plane or reverzed it before ze danger point
vas reached. Alzo, ze treez in ze voodz at ze end of ze
runvay vould have prevented ze rolling mozion
nezezzary to produce ze roll-up phenomenon. Zere iz no
gazoline aboard ze *Langley* zo zere can be no fire or
explozion."

The professor paused and flashed a shark-like grimace
at the President. "Zome treezzz might have zuffered,
Mr. Prezident, but apparently, Maine haz many treez.
Ze *Langley*'z flight pathz and mizzion profilez in zoze
bookz keep ze *Langley* over ocean or ze polar vastes
unlezz, of courze, zhe iz ordered to attack Ruzzia."

"Wonderful, wonderful," said Shamus O'Connell, his
voice fruity with sarcasm. "We didn't need to arm the
plane after all, eh, General Zinkowski? Just flying it
around over Russia should frighten the bejesus out of
them, I should think! And even though the *Langley* can
barely make three hundred miles an hour and MIG
twenty-fours can go Mach 2, they'll really have to think
twice before they press an attack—right, General?"

General Zinkowski shrugged his large shoulders. "I
don't think anyone is suggesting sending the *Langley*
into Russia, sir. The mission we're suggesting is an
extended patrol north of Severnaya Zemlya, then . . ."

But at that instant the private White House phone at
O'Connell's elbow gave a discreet buzz. The President
knew that these high-level emergency get-togethers often
served to divert his attention from other activities, and

so he always had his most trusted people watching the world, and the bureaucrats, with special care while he was closeted away.

"Yeh?" he said quietly into the phone.

"Chief! We're catching a shit storm at the switchboard!"

"What the hell, who?"

"The whole goddamned eco-lobby, Chief. Green Earth, Inc., Seal Watch, Whales International, the Arctic Protection Society, Friends of Polar Bears, the Northern Littoral Guardians, Sea Mammals Forever, the Alaska Club, Save the . . ."

"What in hell is their beef now, Dave?"

"The *Langley*, Chief. They think we're going to dump it in the Arctic and irradiate a walrus or something."

"How did they get that idea? The damn thing's only been in the air for thirty minutes."

"The networks shot film at Moosefoot of the takeoff and played it ten minutes later on the *Good Morning Breakfast Show*. But the Arctic thing was in last week's issue of *Aerospace News*. They had a story on Ice Island Three and mentioned how it might handle a nuke airplane with shielded tractors, and not even bother with a hangar. You could just cut a big hole in the ice."

President O'Connell shut his jaw with a crunch. "For God's sake, Dave! Ice Island Three was supposed to be a top secret concept. Furthermore, we don't *own* the damn . . ."

"Then why did you mention it to those four congressmen two weeks ago, Chief? You know this is an election year!"

Shamus O'Connell sighed heavily. "Why *did* I tell those congressmen, anyway?" he muttered half to himself. "Well, look, Dave, you guys cook up a response over my name, okay? Something to the effect that the *Langley*'s flight path is being rigidly controlled to prevent even the most minuscule environmental impact and that no danger . . ."

"What should I tell the Sea Bird Watchers of America,

Chief? They claim the *Langley*'s tail-cone of radiation will be cooking the frigate birds."

"Tell the idiots that when they find a damn frigate bird that will fly three hundred miles an hour at twenty thousand feet, I'll order them to shut down the *Langley*'s engine and teach it to flap its wings!"

"Righto, Chief. Oh, I almost forgot. The Russian freighters have stopped."

Shamus O'Connell blinked. "Do you mean to say the *Langley* has had an effect, Dave?"

"Doubtful, Chief. That raving queen on the Russian desk at State tried to sell me that con, but we looked at the latest spy plane pics under magnification and I figure one of the boats has engine trouble and the other one has gone alongside to assist. . . . One of the crews is all women, Chief."

O'Connell really chuckled for the first time that day. "Maybe they all got horny and decided to lay up for a party and a screw. Ha! No wonder that limpwrist at State couldn't figure it out. I'll get back, Dave. Bye."

The President drew himself up and fixed General Zinkowski with a fierce stare. "The *Langley* is kicking up an environmental hurricane, General. Although I'm not yet too familiar with these most interesting and obviously complete documents,"—he contemptuously indicated with a thumb the two huge books in front of him—"I assume that that important aspect of the missions and the landings is dealt with somewhere?"

Before the general could reply, Professor Bzggnartsky had straightened up and was now pointing a nail-bitten finger at the president. "Zir! If I may zpeak! Ve are looking at zis completely backvardz. Vat are minor, low-level environmental rizkz compared to ze triumph, ze unique technical marvel itzelf! Zir! Ve are flying ze largezt aircraft ever zent aloft! Driven by ze mozt advanzed propulzion zystem in ze hiztory of aeronauticz! An aircraft zat can ztay in ze zky for many dayz, go anyvere ve chooze! Zeze affluent midget mindz viz zier prezzure groupz! Zese effete dezpoilerz of zeir own livez and zitiez telling ze vorld how to live! Zey muzt not detract from zis achievement! Mr. Prezident! Ztand before ze vorld, Zir, and proudly zay, Now, nozzing iz denied America!"

That was quite enough for Happy Jack, and he did something most unusual for him. He spoke up in a dry, brittle, penetrating voice edged with contempt and menace. "Let them eat neutrons! Is that it, Professor?" Happy Jack dropped his fist heavily on the table with a deadly thud and the room became very still.

"You . . . you from Snotsville-on-the-Charles." Happy Jack's thin, ice-blue eyes fixed on the Professor. "They're still holding your tenure, aren't they? You can go back to slicing up your friends and screwing the coeds any time you want." His eyes turned like twin cannon on the Air Force group. "And you bespangled bus drivers have those wonderful pensions, a main contribution to the present bankruptcy of the United States, not to mention the one-hundred-K jobs in missile plants whenever you decide to leave us . . . well . . .," he thumped the table again, "this administration has to get *re-elected* . . . with *votes* . . . and it may be true, Professor, that those environmental fruitcakes do filthy-up the suburbs and spend most of their lives screwing with their psychiatrists, but . . . gentlemen . . . they *vote*! So let's all understand one thing. We threw some red meat at the drunks in the VFW and Legion bars when the *Langley* went up. You boys are going to figure out how to get it down without a ripple, and that means that everyone, including the American Friends of the Snail Darter, are going to be smiling and happy! Is this all absolutely clear?"

It was, and President O'Connell gripped the little man's shoulder in gratitude. While Happy Jack had been delivering his floor talk, President O'Connell had slipped into reverie and briefly envisaged a large tumbler of White House crystal, half-filled with neat Jack Daniels, and containing exactly two, large, very cold, spring water ice cubes. But the thought of ice immediately called to mind Ice Island Three, and it was obvious now that his original naive theory that the *Langley* was some sort of mistake was no longer tenable.

He leaned back and put his mouth directly at Jack's ear. "The *Langley* is a scam to annex Ice Island Three," he said, emphasizing each whispered word equally.

Happy Jack pursed his lips in thought. Then he gave a single nod of agreement, but said nothing.

O'Connell spoke in icy tones. "General, the missile freighters have stopped. I want the *Langley* held on this side of the pole, if it actually ever gets that far, and in an environmentally-neutral area. Is that both clear and possible?"

General Zinkowski nodded.

"Now," said the President in a new, deceptively pleasant voice, "let's talk about those 'options' you mentioned in regard to landing the *Langley*, General, if you would be so kind?"

VI

COLONEL MUTH BEGAN HIS LONG, SPIRAL TURN TO THE NORTH and east as soon as the *Langley* reached two hundred feet of altitude. The geographic mission profile required them to leave the coast at Chaleur Bay, steering about northeast over the Gulf of Saint Lawrence, then out to the Atlantic over the Straits of Belle Isle. They would then turn more northerly, avoiding Greenland and keeping over Davis Strait and Baffin Bay until they came out over the pack ice to await further orders.

It was hoped by everyone that this three-thousand-mile climb would be sufficient for the *Langley* to reach its estimated service altitude of around twenty thousand feet. Climb presented many new problems for the *Langley*'s power plant since both the temperature and the density of the air changed continuously with altitude. These affected, in different ways, both the condensers and the fans, not to mention the aerodynamic characteristics of the plane itself. Since the continual reduction in temperature and density had exactly opposite effects on maximum fan horsepower, the *Langley*, in a more complicated but similar manner to the huge old dirigibles of other days, was at the mercy of local weather and the temperature lapse-rate through which it moved.

They had just left Dalhousie astern and come out over the water when Captain Jackson looked at the speed indicator and cleared his throat. "Friends, we are now moving over the ground at one hundred and twenty-seven miles an hour. Let me remind you that the only man to officially achieve this speed under steam, until now, was the great driver Fred Marriott, in a Stanley racer at Ormond Beach, Florida, in 1906."

The rest of the crew greeted this announcement with a good-natured collection of jeers, cheers, lip farts, and moans. The fact that the official 1906 Stanley record was only one mile an hour faster than the great effort of the London and North Eastern Pacific *Mallard* on Essendine bank was a constant source of irritation to the locomotive men. Jackson, of course, did not regard the margin as in any way indicative of what the car was capable of doing and he made another comment in a dry voice.

"I'll let you know when we go past one-ninety, which Marriott also achieved in January of 1907 before the car flipped. That run was the penultimate moment for supercritical flash steam."

"Not officially though, Gaby," said Bob Muth in an earnest voice.

"I'm not saying it was, Bob. What I'm saying is that the Stanley car was a hell of a lot faster than *Mallard*, no matter how you slice the baloney."

"But it's so little," said Muth, grinning, "And *Mallard* is so big and green!"

The *Langley* was now accompanied by a considerable fleet of consorts, all flying well ahead of the big plane so as to avoid any problems in the deadly tail-cone of high-level radiation. In addition to the Moosefoot chase helicopter were several other rotary-winged machines from the TV and wire service news groups and the Canadian Air Force, plus two large fourteen-place charter copters filled with periodically-cheering members of the New England Friends of Steam Society. The Commanding General of Northeastern Air Defense Command had scrambled three F-117 supersonic jets as an honor guard for the *Langley*, but these had to be recalled when it was found that they could not, even with wheels and flaps down, go slow enough to stay with the big bomber. Bush pilots, executive flyers, and various light plane enthusiasts in the Maritimes soon joined the parade, so that by the time they were starting over the Straits of Belle Isle, several dozen aircraft of various types were filling the sky ahead of the *Langley*, the whole business moving northeast now at about one hundred and forty miles an hour and accelerating and climbing at almost imperceptible rates.

As the *Langley* made its gradual ascent, Betty Lou Muth found herself watching three different TVs at once and chain-smoking. By the time she heard the fire-service copter coming down in her yard, every ash tray was filled and the place smelled like a pool parlor. She pushed open the windows, dashed about straightening up, then stood at the open door watching her older brother and an extraordinarily rounded young lady in a tight red dress climb down the little ladder and dash under the slowing blades in a ducking posture.

Betty Lou kissed her brother, but he was in a brusque mood and peered about quickly. "Good. The car's here. Listen, Lou, give Emmeline the keys. She's got some errands to do in Moosefoot before this business begins to heat up."

Mrs. Muth looked doubtfully at the round, wide-eyed face of the girl. "Does she have a driver's license, Nate?" she asked.

"Several," said the Congressman. "I have to keep getting her new ones. Look, Lou, it's only a half-mile drive. We've all got plenty to do."

After the station wagon disappeared going slowly down the left side of the road, Mrs. Muth put her hands on her hips and gave her brother a furious look. "Why did you bring your floozie up here, Nate? I've never seen anyone so attracted to big tits! It's terrible! A man your age and you can't even leave her . . ."

Congressman Hazelton had found the scotch bottle and now dropped onto the big couch with several fingers of booze gripped between grateful fingers. "Don't give me any bullshit, Lou," he said. "I've been running since dawn. Miss Pangini also happens to be my personal secretary and I'm damn well going to need her when we get your kids together. Now, where in hell are they?"

"Alice?" called Mrs. Muth, and her daughter, who had been watching the *Langley*'s progress on her own small TV, dashed into the room and planted a solid kiss on her uncle's scotch-sodden lips.

"Uncle Nate!" she screeched. "Boy, your secretary sure has big tits!"

"And how would you like to be found strangled in your own training bra, my pretty?" said her uncle with a snarl. Then he fluttered his hand at her. "Okay Alice. Stand out there and turn around."

Pert Alice Muth looked exactly like every other twelve-year-old girl at Moosefoot Central: faded skin-tight jeans, a ripped tie-dyed T-shirt that said, "Kiss me! I'm Estonian!" front and back, a messy pony tail in an elastic band, and filthy feet with green toenails crammed into split jogging shoes.

The Congressman was already feeling a bit more mellow and he gave his posing niece an actual smile. "Tell me, Alice," he said in an almost avuncular tone, "would you happen to have such things as black patent-leather pumps with button straps? . . ." and when he saw that Alice tilted her head in puzzlement he added, "*Shoes*, my dear. And white stockings that come up to the knee and have a knit design at the top. A dark blue or red velvety dress with lace at the neck and puffy sleeves. Big red silk bows for braids . . ."

"Icky!" said Alice making a monster face. "Who would wear such creepy stuff?"

"I didn't ask you who would wear it," said her uncle in instant impatience. "I asked if you had any such things."

"Nothing like that here, Nate," said Betty Lou, absently snuffing out a butt and pouring a short scotch and water.

"All right, Alice," said Congressman Hazelton. "Let's think if you have a little school friend who might have such an outfit. Someone your size. Someone who goes to church, to confirmation. Someone named Annette, Marie, Jeanne . . ."

"Henriette La Pointe!" said Alice at once. "She lives right down the road and has to go to confirmation classes and all that stuff. And she's got lots of dresses. Her father's a local selectman."

"Ah," said Uncle Nate sitting back and beaming, then pouring himself more scotch. "Henriette and her father a selectman, wonderful! Do you think she would lend you an outfit, my dear?"

"Sure," said Alice. "I'll tell her it's for the Halloween costume dance, you know, Lady Dracula or something. She's super! She wants to be a lesbian nun and teach birth control in Bolivia! I'll go on my bike to get the stuff. Bye, Uncle Nate," and off she dashed.

The Congressman settled back, beaming at his drink and then at his sister. "Well," he said comfortably, "having disposed of the lesbian nuns, but not yet completely departing from the general topic, what about Melissa?"

Betty Lou's gaze turned suddenly icy. "Melissa is *not* a lesbian, Nate. In fact, she happens to be living with a very large and very heterosexual young man in a loft in New York right now."

"I'll alert the Population Watch," said Hazelton cheerfully. "Can lover-boy spare her for a few days?"

"Of course," said Betty Lou Muth. She got up and went to her desk. "She's flying into Bangor this afternoon. Here's the flight number."

The Congressman stuffed the paper into a pocket.

"Okay, I'll call the state police and have them hold her at the airport. Now, where the hell is Junior?"

Betty Lou shook her head frowning. "Well, he's in jail, Nate, over in Vermont. He's been locked up four days. He was in that Clamshell Brotherhood protest over moving the reactor pressure vessel to the Saint Johnsbury nuke site."

"What the hell did he do?"

"I only saw the final part on the TV but there was this very old blind lady who is a very big anti-nuclear person and she had this long, white cane. Bob Junior was with her right up next to the flatbed trailer carrying the thing. It was huge, like the *Langley*, and the trailer had what looked like a hundred wheels. It was moving about two miles an hour. Suddenly, the old lady is shouting, 'Where's it at? Take me to it! Let me touch it!' Well, you know how polite Junior is and how much he likes to help older people, so he leads her right up to one of the big wheels and she instantly sticks her white cane right into the hub. It gets caught there and starts to drag her along the ground by the wrist strap. Of course they have to stop the whole convoy and after they do, some cop grabs at the white cane and pulls the old lady over again. Then Bob Junior . . . you know how much he believes in non-violence, Nate . . . well . . . he urinates on the cop. I suppose it was the only thing he could think of that was peaceful and direct at the same time."

Congressman Hazelton shook his head in disgust and his voice was a thin snarl. "Terrific! The greatest effort in the entire history of steam traction is now underway and Bob Junior is pissing on policemen! Jesus-sweet-Christ, Lou, we've got plenty of problems without needing a whip and gun to control your brood of hell-cats!"

For one dark moment, Betty Lou Muth considered throwing her drink at her brother's head. "You bastard, Nate!" she shouted. "Don't you tell me how to raise my kids, you prick!" She stared at her brother with hot eyes. "What the hell do you know anyway? All that those hookers and floozies of yours think about are pills and diaphragms! I love my kids! They're beautiful, wonderful kids! Melissa has . . . has a beautiful *soul*, Nate. She and I talk a lot . . . oh, *you* wouldn't understand any of that! And Bob Junior is a decent, brave, gallant, lovely person! At least he's got the *guts* to piss on a cop! *You* couldn't get drunk or coked or speedy enough to do anything like that!"

Betty Lou set her empty glass on a coffee table and put her head in her hands while her tears fell steadily onto the oriental rug.

Uncle Nate, pausing only long enough beside the bar to sweeten his drink, went to his sister, sat down beside her, and put an arm around her shoulders. "Bob's going to be okay up there, Lou. Hey, he's the very best there is! Look at that fantastic takeoff! Now listen, Junior's a terrific, spunky kid and you're right. He finally did what every other citizen dreams about doing. Now we're going to have him out in no time, Lou! So, how come he's been in four days? They've got to arraign him?"

Betty Lou Muth snuffled, wiped her eyes, and took a pull on Nate's drink. "He won't give them his name, Nate. The local judge refused to arraign and set bail unless he provided identification. I've called about a dozen times saying I would identify him, even come over and point him out, but they say he has to do it himself. Sometimes I think lawyers and judges and . . ." she looked cold-eyed at her brother, "congressmen are the biggest bunch of shit-brained bastards in the history of the universe!"

Congressman Hazelton smiled modestly. "Now you're just trying to be nice to us, Lou. Well, they can't charge him with too much. Certainly not assault. Maybe insulting a police officer. Maybe indecent exposure. Could you see him do it on the TV?"

"When he began to undo his fly, they cut back up so as to show a part of the vehicle and the big crowd, but you could tell what he was doing since they kept the camera centered on him and the cop. Then they zoomed back down to just show the cop when he took off his boot and poured out the . . ."

Hazelton slapped both knees and grinned. "The boy must have taken on a case of beer to accomplish that! It can't be easy to fill a cop's boot with piss under those conditions. Well . . ." He pulled a small black notebook out of his inside pocket. "Let's see who might be the right person to call in Vermont about . . ." He moved his lips over several names, then gave her a quick grin. "Chief Justice of the Superior Court, Quincy Adams Chisington, the very man!"

Betty Lou expelled a blast of smoke and curled her lip. "What's his specialty, Nate—boots and whips, rubber fetishism, two black girls with big bottoms? . . ."

Congressman Hazelton reached for the telephone. "Nothing too exciting or violent, Lou. Old Quince is basically an enema man. And you can't imagine how few places in Washington properly cater to that special . . ."

"Spare me the crud, Nate. How a world run by you kinks can keep going . . ."

But the congressman was already dialing through to the Superior Court in Montpelier, first talking, next shouting, finally threatening . . .

"Hey, Quince old man! Nate Hazelton here . . . What's that you say? . . . You're on the golf course? Say, that's a wonderful gadget you've got there, Quince. Why I can hear you as clear as a bell! . . . How's the game going? . . . You're only eight over par on the twelfth. Wow! Some of you guys can really play that old game. . . . How's that, Quince? You've got the mobile phone in case the Governor should issue a last-minute stay to the Rutland Bluebeard?"

Congressman Hazelton grinned at his sister and made a monster face even more impressive than Alice's. "Isn't that the fellow who served his wife up in croquettes at the Rotary lunch? . . . Oh, the other one, the chain-saw man who shuffled the players at his wife's bridge party. Look, old man, I've got a little legal problem with you folks myself. Not quite like the Bluebeard, ha, ha. Quince, you remember the Saint Johnsbury nuke demonstration last weekend? . . . Well, there's still this young fellow, Robert Muth Junior, in the can over there. . . . Yeh, he may be the one accused of that, Quince. I've been in Washington . . ."

Hazelton's face hardened and he carefully set his drink down on the glass table. "So if you were the judge, you'd give him ten years, eh? Hell, Your Honor, the Bluebeard will be out on good behavior before then! . . ." Nate Hazelton shot his sister a reassuring glance. "Now, the boy happens to be my nephew, Quince. Speaking as one lawyer to another, let me try this defense on you, ha, ha. The boy is participating in this legal, First-Amendment-protected demonstration on the public ways of the State of Vermont when he innocently becomes involved in a police riot . . . What? Well, how would you describe it? This rogue cop, probably with tape on his numbers, stomps and clubs a one-hundred-and-two-year-old blind woman whom my nephew is trying to assist across the road. He's an Eagle Scout you know? . . . Wha? . . . All right, seventy-two-year-old blind woman. Well, the boy is no fool. He realizes that with these maddened police running completely amuck, his very life is in deadly danger and it literally scares the piss out of him. Any sensible jury would . . . What? You think his unzipping his fly would prejudice that defense? What's he supposed to do, Judge, drench himself, with the possibility of infection after being severely injured by crazed police officers?"

Hazelton caught his sister's eye and waved at the bar to indicate a bit of freshening was needed, and his suddenly-hard expression showed that he was becoming bored with old Quince.

"Look, Your Honor," he said in a very flat voice. "In addition to that defense, the boy's father happens to be the heroic plane commander of the *Langley*, now making aviation history. There's no jury in the country that will let you touch him. And one more point, Quince, to

get to another subject . . . Ahh . . ." Hazelton relaxed
back and gave Betty Lou a thumbs-up sign. "I thought
you'd see the legal problems with it, Quince . . . Well, I
would think to just dismiss the charges, wouldn't you?
You'll have another shot at the boy, no doubt, as long as
you idiots continue to build that stupid plant . . . Yes,
yes, Quince. Have them bring him out to the Saint
Johnsbury airport and my pilot, Stubb Moody, will pick
him up in the chopper . . . Ah, good, Quince! So you'll
be down to old sin town, ha, ha, in a couple of weeks.
Well, call me then, old man. Bye."

Hazelton took a long suck on his scotch and beamed.
"It certainly is stimulating to engage in an intricate bit of
legal philosophy with an old colleague," he said expansively.

Betty Lou peered at her brother and her voice dripped
with contempt. "A brave, idealistic young hero is being
released from gaol because that dirty, sick, old fart likes
to have a cutie shove a . . ."

The Congressman shook his head. "Spare me the
crud, Lou. Nothing is that simple." He rubbed his hands
together. "You've never met Mrs. Chisington, Lou. If
you had . . . well . . . you might get a different sight on
old Quince. I dunno . . ." he said shaking his head again.
"It's always been like this, Lou. Every country, every era,
every political system. Shit, it's not the Quinces that are
something special, Lou. It's kids like Bob Junior." He
suddenly grabbed and squeezed her shoulder. "Lou,
Lou, stop moping! Bob's having the time of his life.
Think, lady, think! Steam's greatest moment's almost
here, and we're conducting the whole damned orches-
tra." He got to his feet. "Well, I'll get Stubb going after
that boy."

Stubb Moody, the copter pilot, was dressed in un-
pressed chino pants and a scruffy uniform shirt with a
Maine Fire Service patch on the left shoulder and a huge
American flag on the right. Alice had thoughtfully left
her two-foot-high collection of *Incredible Hulk* comics
with Stubb before she rode off on her bike, and the pilot

was now seated in a lawn chair in a state of total concentration, his lips moving busily. The thing about the Hulk that so engrossed Stubb Moody was the creature's total inability to relate to beautiful women, even though he seemed to want to most forcefully. How anybody so *large*, *hard*, and with such *stamina* could fail to succeed with any number of women . . . Stubb's imagination populated the comic with different and rather more gaudy scenes.

"Ah, Stubb." The congressman peered pleasantly at his pilot. "Over at the Saint Johnsbury airport is a young man waiting with a police escort, none other than Robert Muth Junior. Go get him and bring him down to Bangor. Miss Pangini and I will drive down direct by car. Now put that creaky copter on full regulator, Stubb! We've got to get those kids into the Bangor department stores before they shut for the night."

Stubb Moody stood up, although this was not especially noticeable since he measured about five feet in all three directions. "Ayeh, Nate." He looked down at his watch. "Should be down thar, mebbe by foah with young Bob. Yew want me to set 'er down on the hospital roof, Nate?"

"No, the airport is fine. Melissa is coming in there. And don't you get that boy all toked up, Stubb! I want everybody straight-arrow in Bangor!"

"Young Bob's a match for 'em, straight or bent, Nate. If I wuz you, I'd worry 'bout that top-heavy Emmeline fallin' over when you ain't around to help her git up." Stubb had a sudden, blinding vision of Emmeline and the Incredible Hulk.

"Comedians galore today!" snarled the congressman, but his face became more crafty. "Stubb," he said sweetly, "there's a gram or so of white nose-candy hereabouts, as fine as any they use at the White House. If you know what's good for you, you'll deliver that boy unstoned to Bangor." Having waved his stick and presented his carrot, Hazelton softened his expression. "The point is, Stubb, I don't want anybody getting ahead of anyone else on this or meeting the press high down there. There'll be time to blow some of your goodie on the way back and then we'll all be together."

The mention of cocaine put Stubb in immediate good spirits and he was able to leave the Hulk behind without regret. "Yew want me ter sign anythin' them cops hand me, Nate?" he asked, pulling on his long-beaked L.A. Dodgers baseball cap.

"Absolutely," said the congressman. "And don't waste any time reading it. Your signature isn't worth a fart in Newark."

After the copter had taken off, Congressman Hazelton returned to the house and thoughtfully finished his drink. "As soon as Emmeline gets back, or a tow truck gets your car here, we're going to zip to Bangor in a police cruiser. Now Lou, my office has this number. If they call before we're back with Stubb, get it all down, then call me either on the cruiser radio or in the chopper coming back. Okay, here's how to do both those things," and he handed her a series of numbers. "And, hey, lay off the scotch, Lou."

Betty Lou grinned at her brother and puffed fiercely. "I wouldn't fall down in front of the President, Nate. You know that." She stared directly at him, shaking her head. "Jesus Nate, this is crazy. Can we pull this off? I mean . . ."

Congressman Hazelton, noting with satisfaction that a large, low, luxurious police cruiser had pulled into the Muth yard and the uniformed driver was now waiting in respectful silence prior to a red-light-flashing chase through the big woods, poured just one more scotch. "Lou," he said thoughtfully, "there's no escaping it. The President has only two viable options . . ."

VII

PRESIDENT O'CONNELL SPOKE WITH IRON CONTROL. "GENeral Zinkowski, I don't want to discuss landing the *Langley* at any particular place or in any particular way until we have first discussed the concept, *landing,* itself. That is . . . and if I'm going too fast, please stop me . . . I know how philosophical digressions bother you practical men . . . can we go over the exact steps needed to put the *Langley* back on solid ground and without nuclear detonations?" The President looked around with thin-eyed mildness. "Unless, of course, you have a place for her . . . up there?" He pointed skyward and his tone was now that of an impatient attendant dealing with a roomful of mental patients.

Zinkowski nodded helpfully. "Absolutely, sir. Glad to help. She comes down to whatever approach altitude the pilot chooses at about one hundred and fifty . . ."

"Miles an hour?"

"Yessir. That's about as slow as the aircraft can go on idle reactor power. We don't want to risk shutting the thing down completely because it might be impossible to restart the plant in the air. Okay, well, in the next step, they drop the wheels to slow her up . . ."

"An aerial brake," said the President.

"Correct," said Zinkowski encouragingly. "But not a very effective one. This gets the *Langley* down to around one hundred miles an hour. Since that is still too fast to touch down, we next go to 'reversal'. You see, Mr. President, the *Langley* is so heavy and has so much momentum that the only way to stop her in any reasonable distance is to reverse the fans. There are separate reverse turbines geared onto the fan shafts, and the propulsion-machinery engineer now has to feed steam to these to stop the windmilling and reverse blade direction, to start blowing air out the front. The thing that's tricky is that at some point the condenser stops working because we're blowing air forward at the same velocity that it's coming in from the front due to the *Langley*'s forward velocity."

O'Connell held up his hand. "Don't tell me, let me guess. The reactor then melts out the bottom, igniting the atmosphere and turning the Earth into a nova?"

"Nossir, but the condenser might blow open. What we have to do is let the steam from the turbines leave the aircraft through valves, run the system 'open cycle' in other words, for the few moments it takes the airflow to really get going the other way."

"And what if there isn't enough water to complete this 'reversal', as you call it?"

Zinkowski drew his brows together. "She carries plenty of extra water, sir. For combat losses and other emergencies. We figure to blow that away during the reversal phase."

"But since none of this has ever been done before there is that small chance . . . vanishingly small perhaps, because we know how wonderfully these gadgets all work, don't we . . . but still a chance, that there won't be enough water?" When Zinkowski made no immediate answer, the President lifted a large finger and pointed. "At Moosefoot, the *Langley* would take out a number of trees in that case, right, General? And if the reactor happened to find a clear path through those trees . . . well, *boom*, as they say. Now, suppose the thing does get reversed?"

"She'd stop in two miles or less, sir. Once they get her fans going in the opposite direction, she'll slow up quick."

"No wheel brakes?"

The general shook his head. "Impractical. The landing gear has enough problems. And reversing the thrust by moveable cowlings, as in most other jets, was impossible from a weight standpoint. The whole wing would have had to have been shrouded."

"Well, we certainly are learning plenty today, Jack," said O'Connell heartily. "And I think what I've learned already is that a landing at Moosefoot AFB is out of the question, so we won't need to waste time on that so-called option! Any questions?"

General Zinkowski grimaced and rubbed his thumb on his forefinger. "I think we could get her down there safe, Mr. President. And it is a remote area."

"Not so remote that a twenty-kiloton blast wouldn't be readily heard, here and in Canada," snarled the President. "We're *not* at war and we're *not* taking wartime risks! And . . ." his voice was acid, "where does one stick the thing in Moosefoot, with no 'hot hangar' in place?"

Zinkowski shrugged. "We could shield her, sir . . ."

"No," said the President in a final tone, "*No* and NO!" He looked around. "Option two . . ." and when no one spoke at once he cocked his head at them. "Well, isn't that Ice Island Number Three, General!" he suddenly shouted.

Zinkowski nodded stiffly. "We can discuss that option now, if you wish, President O'Connell."

"It isn't your first choice then, General?" asked O'Connell sarcastically.

"It happens to be my personal choice, Mr. President. The other men," Zinkowski gestured at the officers around him, "may have other ideas."

"Then I assume the runway on the ice island is long and smooth enough, General?"

"It isn't long enough yet, sir. But we have equipment up there to make it as long as we want, up to the twenty-two mile length of the island in the north-south direction."

"But there is a runway there now, isn't there, General?" The President looked at him through narrow eyes. "For the scientific staff and their support?"

Zinkowski shrugged. "Yes, but it doesn't get much use. Just flying in food and gear now and then."

"It's hardly a little neighborhood grass strip, General Zinkowski! You're flying Hercules and CargoMaster transports in and out regularly!" said the President, snarling again.

"Sir," pleaded Zinkowski, "the whole island is basically flat and hard. It takes very little effort to clear it and keep it swept."

"And that so-called scientific staff," said the President, "it's all young officers and cadets on leave from the service academies, right, General?"

Zinkowski permitted himself a terse smile. "Well, Mr. President, you remember how the First Lady in the previous administration got hot on that business about the service academies not turning out humanity-oriented students and worldly officers. Well, one of the upshots was the 'life experience' junior year, so the young man . . . or woman . . . has a chance to live in another part of the world, see how things are really done outside school."

"Ah," said the President dreamily. "Sort of like a junior year abroad, eh?"

"That's about it, sir."

"So they're all up there with the lacy cathedrals of ice, hanging about the Quonset huts, the cultural opportunities of the PX library, and the scientific insights attendant on following the refueling operations of Russian Badger aircraft on radar! The fact is, General," said O'Connell, his voice rising, "you people have established a cadre of dedicated young officers on the ice island, plus the facilities to move in more buildings, ground-to-air defensive weapons and the rest of it, probably in seventy-two hours, as needed to construct a complete offensive air base and refueling depot!"

The President's Security Advisor swiveled his glasses, shining like tiny twin oil slicks, to focus on his chief. "Zir, lezz zan zat, I zink. More like a day and a half. And Zir, if zat rezearch group vere not on Ize Island Three now, ze Badgerz vould be flying in and out wiz regularity from zat field!"

The President's lips twisted and he snarled at him. "How you people can keep finding these sticks to poke up the fire is simply amazing!" He turned to the other side of the table. "Who's here from State?" he asked sharply.

A small, thin man of advanced age, Undersecretary Wilson Woodford, raised a brown-spotted claw of a hand. "At your service, Mr. President," he said in a dry, crackly voice.

President O'Connell sighed. "Ah, yes, Woodford. What's the status of Ice Island Three in the UN?"

Undersecretary Woodford cocked his small, bald head and pursed his lips, making bird-like noises. He began shuffling large masses of loose papers around in front of him, humming and chirping busily to himself.

O'Connell tried to remember why they had kept this damned old fart on at State. Was his brother a governor? Or a senator? Woodford seemed to have finally sorted his papers into three general piles in front of him and was now pushing these around in a fit of straightening and organization. "Secretary Woodford," said the President in a dry voice, "are we eventually going to get to guess which pile the pea is in?"

In common with other slow-thinking men, Wilson Woodford was relatively imperturbable. He smiled quickly at the President. "Be with you in a moment, sir," he said briskly. "I don't like to start on something like this until I have my documents fully accessible." His hands fluttered like dark sparrows among the papers in a final convulsion of organization. Then he looked up and picked the top paper off the middle pile. He cleared his throat, snapped the paper rather like it was two fifty-dollar bills he was trying to separate, then set his lips and jaws into periodic chewing motions designed to ensure that his dentures didn't loosen during the presentation.

President O'Connell turned his eyes to meet Happy Jack's and the two men stared at each other, outwardly impassive. But what passed between them was elegant in its simplicity: Whomever this idiot was related to didn't matter. OUT!

"So," said Undersecretary Woodford, in his best seminar voice, "Mr. President, we find three different positions on Ice Island Three." He paused and blinked vague, thin eyes at O'Connell.

The President nodded impatiently. "Yes, yes. Well, go on, man!"

"The United Nations' position is that since the island was discovered after 1946, it belongs only to that organization. They interpret the charter as ending the seizure of any territory on the basis of discovery only."

"Mr. Secretary, what in hell does the United Nations want with Ice Island Three? Surely there are enough ice machines in New York City to keep even that bunch of rum-dums happy?"

Secretary Woodford gave a nervous chirp of laughter at this witticism. "They aren't quite sure yet, sir. There has been talk of using it as a storage for excess food."

"A giant deep freezer," breathed the President. "Or they might put their various deceased officials into glass cases for all posterity to come and see. Kind of a chilly Madame Tussaud's, and certainly more terrifying. Now, what is the Russian position?"

Secretary Woodford turned to the pile on his left and snapped the top paper several times, checking his teeth again as he did so. "The Soviets claim that Ice Island Three is not an island at all, but simply part of the arctic pack and that the use of it for bombing planes would be a violation of the UN resolution, of which we are signatories, concerning the banning of nuclear weapons on the arctic and antarctic ice."

President O'Connell held up his hand. "I find that position quite persuasive, Mr. Secretary. It's certainly the one I would adopt if I were working from Moscow. How do we answer such a claim? The island *is* entirely ice, isn't it?"

Professor Bzggnartsky, having prepared a homework assignment on this topic, interjected himself again. "Pleezzz, Mr. Prezident. Ve have wiz us today, Dr. Richard Armztrong, Chairman of ze Nazional Academy Committee on Permanent Ize Ztructurez. He vill explain ze United Ztatez claim, Zir."

That crystal glass with the neat Jack Daniels and the two uncorrupted ice cubes now seemed to President O'Connell as no more than a kind of grail, shimmering distantly in some other and better time and place, a Glastonbury Abbey of the inner heart. No wonder the kids hate school, he thought in a kind of insightful fury, with egocentric, incompetent, insufferable, boring stupids like these freaks preaching absolute shit and nonsense at them.

O'Connell found the sweetheart arrangements between the various scientific academies and the military both politically disturbing and a damn nuisance. They were always egging each other on or else scratching each others' backs. Why, O'Connell wondered in anger, would this good-looking, obviously smart young fellow want to run after death and mayhem with Zinkowski and Bzggnartsky and the rest? The President knew the answer all too well: money, fancy trips, tenure, cunt. . . . He sighed deeply in bitter frustration that there were so many reforms utterly beyond even the most aggressive Chief Executive. I mustn't distract myself, thought the President. We can only take this one day at a time.

Dr. Armstrong, twenty-nine and in a three-piece, single-breasted dark green suit, chain with Phi Bete key, and a shock of blond hair falling attractively across his

large, black-rimmed glasses, sat up to give his lecture. He
had that bright, intent look of an assistant professor at
his final meeting with the university tenure committee.
"Could we dim the lights, please," he said with a
nervous curtness. "Now, sir, in this first slide . . ."

"Oh, shit!" said Happy Jack under his breath. "Stupid
damn slides yet."

But President O'Connell was glad of the chance to rest
his eyes and imagine other, happier scenes in the sooth-
ing gloom.

The first slide showed a cross-sectional diagram of Ice
Island Three. "There are several more or less permanent
ice structures now known in the Arctic Ocean," began
Dr. Armstrong, "but the other three or four islands have
ages of only a few hundred years and will eventually
break up. Number Three is quite different. For one
thing, the sea is quite shallow there and the sea bed on
which the ice rests is solid permafrost down to several
hundred meters. Also, that part of the Arctic Ocean
seems to be a kind of wheel-hub around which the whole
pack slowly rotates. We know that number three is at
least ten thousand years old. It evidently was created in
the last period of glaciation. Slide two shows a satellite
photo of the whole area around the island. You can see
the extent of the permanent ice marked out on the
photo."

President O'Connell came out of his reverie to a state
of sudden alertness. "Just a second here! Let's see that
photo without the lines drawn on it!"

Dr. Armstrong gave the President a tremendously
respectful, yet puzzled, glance. "Well, sir, I don't know if
we have . . ."

"Look," said President O'Connell in a gritty voice.
"The Russians claim this so-called island is part of the
ice pack. Does it *smell* like part of the ice pack? Does it
look like part of the ice pack? Does it *quack* like part of
the ice pack?"

"You mean, how did we determine that boundary,
sir?" said Dr. Armstrong in sudden comprehension.

"Exactly," said O'Connell. "I can't see the slightest visible difference between the inside and outside parts of that line you drew."

"Slide three," said the geophysicist, "shows how we took test borings right across the island. There are two or three good ways of dating ice samples and . . . Slide four, please . . . here you see the age-contour lines of the ice around the island." This slide showed a roughly oval shape surrounded by what looked like concentric contour lines with shapes somewhat different, but generally parallel to, the innermost line.

The screen went immediately dark, but President O'Connell said sharply, "Get that one back!" and the screen was lit again. "Now, Doctor, if I interpret this diagram correctly," said the President slowly, "those various closed contour lines mark out ice of different ages, is that correct?"

Dr. Armstrong nodded. "The numbers give the average age of the ice at that point in tens or hundreds of years; one thousand, one hundred, fifty, ten, so on."

"So," said O'Connell in a silky voice. "Where exactly do we stake our claim? Surely real estate that's lasted a thousand years is a pretty good bet? A hundred . . . well? . . ." The President spread his palms. Everybody stared at him silently.

"Oh, come, gentlemen," he said in his most sarcastic voice. "The point is, simply, that the Soviets have a point! Ice is ice! That supposed island is clearly a contiguous part of the polar ice cap in the exact sense of the UN resolution. The fact that the ice is old in no way alters the legal sense of that document. Turn on the lights!"

As the fluorescents blazed up, President O'Connell found himself blinded by the twin defocused laserbeams off Professor Bzggnartsky's glasses. "Zir! Vatever you may zay . . . or ze UN may zay, ze moment ve abandon Ize Island Three, ze Zovietz vill be zere ze day after."

"And yet," said the President, in the bitterest of

voices, "If you pointy-headed, empire-building, Ph.D.-glutted bastards hadn't found the fool island in the first place, no one would give two shits for that hunk of ice! All right. Let's get on to the other options for landing the *Langley*. I've had a gutful of Ice Island Three!"

The President looked directly at General Zinkowski, who cleared his throat in surprise. "Ah, yes, sir. Well, the other option is to ditch her at sea."

"The *other*? This is the last option, General?"

Zinkowski nodded quickly. "We have analysts examining the whole system again, sir, but at this point it appears that the ditch option is the only other feasible and safe one." He paused and took a breath. "This involves bringing the *Langley* down to a suitably-selected and protected body of water or seacoast region and landing it, essentially as I described earlier, but with the landing gear retracted. In this mode, the pilot would slow the aircraft as rapidly as possible after reversal has been completed . . ."

"If," corrected the President. "If reversal has been completed, General."

Zinkowski shrugged. "Even if it hasn't worked, the pilot can still stall the *Langley* in and kill quite a lot of speed. And of course there's plenty of distance over the ocean in which to make mistakes. Whatever; the aircraft will lose positive lift at about seventy miles an hour. At this point she can be stalled or reversal-braked further as she falls into the drink. Obviously, no matter how carefully we pick the spot and the weather, some damage is probably inevitable. No matter how big the splash, though, we're assuming the *Langley* will stay afloat. The whole condenser structure in the wings is a honeycomb of aluminum and there's no way it can be made non-buoyant by crash damage."

"And General, what chance of 'roll-up' might there be in this sort of landing?"

"We think none, Mr. President. For one thing, we can't see how the plane could ever hit the water hard enough. For another, water would not provide the hard bearing-surface needed for the shielding to crush in the reactor. Of course, there *is* the chance of a positive-pressure implosion if excessive landing shock tears out and drops the reactor into too-deep water."

"Implosion?"

"Sir, it takes a considerable velocity and a hard surface to produce 'roll-up', but much less of a crash to have the reactor and shield fall out of the bottom of the plane. If the water is over eight hundred or a thousand feet deep, the hydrostatic pressure may collapse the reactor sufficiently for a nuclear detonation."

"Lovely!" said the President, shaking his head. "And I thought the takeoff was exciting! What would such a deep-water explosion do, General?"

Zinkowski held up his palms. "Nobody is quite sure about that, sir. Possibly some sort of local tidal wave. But anyway, if we land her in shallow water, say a hundred feet or less, we can avoid that risk."

"And if the *Langley* finally winds up floating around on the ocean, what next? Tow it to Disneyland?" The President rubbed his eyes. "Or perhaps it could be converted to an offshore floating casino?"

"Well, sir, we'd pick a spot to bring her down where we could get her to shore and lift out the reactor and shielding with the RRT, that's the Reactor Recovery Truck, then unbolt the rest of it and carry the pieces back to Moosefoot. The *Langley* is designed to come apart in freight-car-sized chunks."

Shamus O'Connell sat up straight and stretched. "I've made my decision, gentlemen," he said at once. "We will ditch the *Langley* at sea, as you just described, General Zinkowski. As I understand it, the *Langley* will reach the North Pole by tomorrow morning. At that time we will meet again and you can describe, General, just how and where the deed will be done. I assume you can make such a plan by then? Are there any questions?" This was said in a tone that implied there had better be none.

But Happy Jack was not satisfied yet by what he had heard, and he leaned to the President, his hand in front of his mouth, and though he made no sound, his lips said clearly, "What about the crew?"

O'Connell bit his lip in annoyance at himself. Boy, he was really slipping to go ahead without getting into that subject! "And finally, General, what about the *Langley*'s crew in event of a ditch? Can they bail out before she comes in?"

Zinkowski shook his head. "No sir. She *has* to be landed and that takes about half the men anyway. Also, to parachute out of the *Langley* you have to fall through the radiation field astern of her. We think the men should stay right with her, then get out when we bring vessels alongside."

"So, am I correct in interpreting your remarks, General, to the effect that there is essentially no danger in this operation?"

Zinkowski shrugged and his voice was cold. "Nothing involving aircraft and nuclear energy is without danger, sir. It's possible that a rough landing might knock the reactor partially off its mounts and shift its high-field cone toward the forward section of the aircraft. This could irradiate some or all of the crew. In such a case, they would have to leave the aircraft in their own boat at once so as to minimize their exposure time and row to wherever the field was at a minimum."

The President had no trouble detecting a barely-restrained hostility toward him as a result of his rapid and undebated decision, and he felt his own anger growing. He bared his teeth at the whole table. "I know perfectly well," he said in a bitter voice, "that this whole thing is a trick to get us onto Ice Island Three and with both feet. I am *not* going to take such a provocative and destabilizing action, gentlemen! Just get that through your heads at once. I can easily justify bringing the *Langley* into an ocean landing with the public. Never fear that! I will stress the interesting and explosive possibilities of the other choices. And the environmental lobby already thinks this is the maddest madness yet out of you apprentice-sorcerers! I will use them warmly and fully. This meeting is adjourned!"

As the subject of this seminar turned more northerly up the center of Davis Strait, her escorts dwindled away, for she was leaving civilization and its airfields behind. The many small planes and helicopters fell back to be replaced by fewer, larger aircraft carrying the cameramen and the pool reporters.

They were still well south of Melville Bay when the double-century speed mark was passed. This event was greeted with considerable cheering and comment, for they were now without any question traveling faster by steam power than anyone before them.

Captain Jackson had been carefully calculating the *Langley*'s future climbing rate and speed, based on her present behavior, and now he stuck his thumb up again and shook his head beaming. "We probably will get past the triple-century, Bob. Depends on how cold the polar air is up at our service altitude." He looked out at a Reuters-chartered 707 flying above and ahead of the *Langley*'s office. "What do you think they'll have us do, Bob, after we get up near the pole?"

Colonel Muth turned to his copilot and his eyes were bright and sharp. "What they should do, Gaby, is send us on a transpolar flight around the world. Hell, that's the only thing the plane is really good for."

Captain Jackson's large mouth fell right open. "Around the world, Bob? Well, Jesus, why would they ever do that?"

"Because," said Colonel Muth with a thin smile, "when you've done something as spectacularly stupid as building the *Samuel Langley* in the first place, and then letting it fly in the second place, the only way to climb out of the hole is to do something even more spectacular and more stupid when you bring it down! The point is, Gaby, the *Langley* is just too big for anything less. It can land maybe two or three places in the entire world. Just to store the damn things when they get hot uses up a bunch of real estate. I mean, if we lived on a world with maybe three or four times the area of this one, well, then a plane that can cover the whole thing might have some uses." Colonel Muth shook his head and his voice was grim. "The *Langley*'s not the only toy that's much too big for us, Gaby. And it all started with steam. Look at Brunel and that huge damn steamship."

But Captain Jackson's mind was elsewhere. His large mouth caressed the magic words as they might have moved over the lips of a passionate lover. "The transpolar nonstop circumnavigation of the world . . . *by steam!*"

VIII

CONGRESSMAN HAZELTON ARRIVED AT THE BANGOR AIRPORT by police car to find his niece, Melissa, the center of an attentive group of state police officers.

She stepped off two long strides and gave him a cool kiss on the cheek. "Uncle Nate, how have you been, dear?" Her oval grey eyes swept over his shoulder and caught a glimpse of the newly-arrived police car and, in the front seat, Emmeline Pangini's huge front aligned exactly with a policeman's nose, the two of them chatting with much laughter and animation. "Uncle," she whispered fiercely in Hazelton's ear. "Have you ever actually *thought* about *why* you have this thing for big tits?"

The Congressman snarled irritably. "Jesus wept! What in hell is happening in the State of Maine? Sanctimoniousness is coming on like a rabies epidemic! Do the foxes carry it?" He narrowed his eyes and peered at his niece's own lissome bust line, which though by no means in the same league as Emmeline's as to size, was both ample and intriguingly-pointed, and handsomely set off by a wide-patterned Grecian kind of hand-knitted shift whose many open holes showed that Melissa neither had, nor needed, a bra. Below this was a long, narrow skirt cut out and pieced from an ancient set of blue-white dungarees, slit to the right waist and revealing, among other things, stiletto-heeled thigh-high vinyl boots as tight, black and sleek as the highway patrolmen's magnum-revolver holsters.

"Don't talk to me about tits, Melissa," said Hazelton, blinking. He noticed that the police officers had all removed their huge, pitch-black shades, so as not to miss anything, and were now leaning against their cars in a kind of collective daze, obviously waiting for Melissa to either move or speak again. "Hoo boy! We've got to do something about you before the President gets up here!" Hazelton waved futilely at his police car, then attracted Emmeline's attention with a piercing whistle.

Waving her pink fingertips back at her new friend in blue, Emmeline disembarked from the cruiser in a fetching confusion of flying skirts, dimpled knees, and giggles. She made her way pneumatically up to them and, by the time she and Melissa were standing together, the highway patrolmen were in a state of molasses-like paralysis, only their eyes now capable of life.

"All right, boys," said Hazelton, clapping his hands to break the trance, "I need a good shopper. Somebody who knows the town." Everyone immediately stood at attention, four tall erections in blue, but there was never any doubt but that rank would prevail.

"I'm a Bangor boy, Congressman," said the large sergeant in a flat voice, hunching his shoulders to suggest that the escort question was now settled.

"Fine, sergeant," said Hazelton busily rubbing his hands. "Now listen closely, Emmeline. Ready?" Emmeline nodded, smiling brightly. "I want Melissa in flat tie shoes, sensible you understand, and fleshtone, cheap panty hose, the thick kind that itches. Next a neat, decent housedress, short sleeves, skirt hitting her about at the knee . . ." He looked down at Melissa's tremendously long, black-booted, and sinuous calf. "No, longer! As long as you can get it without making her look like an inmate someplace. An oversize, shapeless sweater that she can roll up above flour-begrimed elbows. A full bra built like steel, as flat as you can get her. Nipples, absolutely nix! Jesus . . . the hair?"

Melissa's gorgeous rope of softly-plaited blond hair now hung in shining splendor down her straight back to her waist. The Congressman sighed. "Okay, we won't cut it. Find a parlor that will put a hard-set wave in so it puffs out all over. Or else a beehive? Look, Emmeline, you know the TV ads with the two women?"

Emmeline puzzled prettily over that.

"You *like* those ads, Emmeline," said Hazelton plaintively. "You remember? There's this old woman and this young woman, in a kitchen usually. And either the old one shows the young one some useless, outdated, ancient product or else the young one shows the old one some sleazy, dangerous, new product."

Emmeline's face showed a dawn of remembrance and she nodded busily. "Okay, I want Melissa to look as much like those young women as possible, you understand?" And after everybody gave back another chorus of nods, Congressman Hazelton patted the two young women on their fannies and sent them off into Bangor in the red-lit police cruiser.

Stubb Moody and Bob Junior arrived about a half hour later, and Hazelton walked over to the machine as his nephew unwound out of the cabin and jogged towards him. Bob Junior was well over six feet tall and he wore his hair like Melissa, though not braided but just pulled into a thick, disgusting, tangled horse's tail. His wispy beard was an evident attempt to copy the Ho Chi Minh style, although it seemed to be longer on one side than on the other. His torn jeans appeared to be covered with old blood stains and his shreds of T-shirt could be barely deciphered to read, "Hell no! We won't glow!"

"Hi, Uncle Nate," said Junior giving him a big, crooked grin and a warm wink. Immediately suspicious, Hazelton surprised his nephew by giving him a quick peck on the cheek. But though he sniffed sharply, he

could detect no sign of cannabis residues. "Hey, Uncle."
Junior grinned even wider. "Stubb didn't give me anything, honest. Hey, thanks for getting me out. I never did
have to give them my name."

"Where are your shoes?" asked a bewildered Congressman Hazelton, staring down at huge, filthy feet.

"I gave 'em to an old drunk in the jail. He really
needed them, Uncle Nate. Honest. It didn't matter
anyhow. They ran me around the court house in a
wheelchair most of the time."

"Wheelchair?" The bewildered congressman turned
to Stubb Moody, who had just slouched up to them.
"Junior was in a wheelchair, Stubb?"

"Ayeh. Cops said he refused tuh walk anyplace 'er give
'em his name, either. 'Course when I got thar, Bob was
pushin' this old cop around the airport, 'stead of bein'
pushed."

Hazelton turned a bemused face back to Bob Junior.
"You were pushing the cop?"

Junior shrugged and grinned again. "They assigned
this old fellow they said had a heart condition to push
me around when I refused to walk. So when he was on
duty, I refused to move unless they let me push him.
They kind of had to let me, Uncle Nate, or else tie me in
that chair. And that didn't work because they couldn't
keep my elbows in tight enough to get us through
doorways." Junior paused, his face thoughtful. "I addressed the court about forcing a man to work in this
sort of duty when he had a heart condition."

Hazelton nodded in purest awe. "You addressed the
court? Because the cop had a heart condition?"

"Yeah well, Uncle Nate, the judge called me a commie
and a radical collectivist, you know? So I just pointed to
old Officer Melvin sitting in the wheelchair and said that
the public sector as typified by the Saint Johnsbury
Municipal Government was ten times crueller and more
anti-life than IBM or Exxon could ever be."

Nate Hazelton's voice was filled with wonder. "No

doubt the judge was immensely grateful for your bringing this municipal cruelty promptly to his attention?"

"Yeah, maybe. I actually don't know what the judge thought, Uncle Nate, because when I finished talking, old Mel got up from the wheelchair and came over and began to hug me and cry a little and say I was the only decent man in the room. The court went into immediate adjournment."

"Junior, we're going to get you organized," said Nate Hazelton, although his tone did not have the same firmness as the words themselves. He looked at the remaining cops. "Okay, we're off on another shopping spree. You . . ." he indicated a young officer, "is there a department store or mall open now?"

"Yessir, Your Honor. A couple near here."

"Okay, you drive us to the biggest." He turned to look at his nephew. "I'm going to have you looking like a Marine Drill Instructor on leave. That hair is all going, baby! And thank God! You sure ain't Melissa with that disgusting mop!"

"I'm not on a hair trip," said Bob Junior mildly. "I think a crew cut would be kind of fun."

"Yeah!" said Hazelton suddenly staring at him. "Crew cut . . . no, brush cut. Flat across the top. Say, what about a scout uniform?" He shook his head. "No, you're too big and old. That would be weird. Well, we'll find you something to wear."

And as the shoppers organized their costumes and makeup in Bangor, the *Langley*, now beyond Baffin Bay and approaching huge, ice-covered Ellesmere Island, passed yet another milestone.

"Sergeant Stewart," said Captain Jackson suddenly. "What's the highest steam railway operation in the world?"

Stewart answered promptly. "Central Railway of Peru, Galera section, 15,844 feet, four and a half percent each side of the top."

"We'll soon be up on that, gentlemen," said Jackson.

"Fifteen, eight hundred right now. How many steam locos have they got, Jim?"

"About fifty on that whole section. Did you know, the diesels won't work up there? They even tried special superchargers. Damn things could barely drag themselves around."

The crew considered that satisfying fact for some minutes until Jackson spoke again. "We have now set a new altitude record for steam, and we'll be at an even sixteen thousand in an hour."

Cheers and comments greeted this announcement, and Captain Jackson turned back to a challenging exegesis of steam flow in rotary sleeve valves in *Flash Steam Monthly*, for the *Langley* was now flying on automatic pilot with only Major Fisk, the engineer, needed to constantly adjust the reactor activity to maximize climb and acceleration at each new altitude.

Colonel Muth, back in a gunnery station on an inspection tour when the altitude of Galera section was exceeded, gave the three sergeant-gunners a brief rundown on the problems of setting loco valves at high altitudes, and then walked back through the narrow, featureless, shielded tunnels and passageways inside the forward section of the *Langley*. He went down a ladder into a narrow hole that led, after some more twists and turns, to Jim Stewart's tiny undercarriage office.

Here followed a pleasant chat on the possibility of electronically simulating high-altitude operation on a model mountain railway, and then Colonel Muth partly climbed and partly crawled to reach the much more spacious and active sanctum of Major Fisk and his two engineering assistants, seated side by side in front of a wall-sized control and instrument panel. Fisk was beaming and puffing on a big cigar. "I can't believe it, Bob," he said as the plane commander squeezed in the tiny oval doorway. "I really think we're going to show a power increase all the way to the top. You know, one of the Pratt and Whitney academic consultants claimed the Bird would work that way, but the company's analysis

group ran those zillion computer simulations and said
no way. And damned if that guy with the equations
wasn't right all along. And . . ." Harry Fisk gave Colonel
Muth a big wink, "I don't want to be quoted yet, or to get
anyone's hopes up, but it just looks like we might make
the million! Just when she tops out. So, how about that,
baby?!"

"You guys are making it all happen, Harry," said Bob
Muth, grinning at the three men.

Fisk stuffed his cigar in his mouth, then turned and
grabbed Bob Muth's arm. "Bob, you got us up. I don't
need to tell you how great a moment that was. You've
always been the captain, even when you drove that
switcher right off the layout. Shit, I just wish there were
something interesting we could do with this damned
great auk besides seeing how much she'll put out."

"Don't give up hope, Harry," said Bob Muth in a
level, serious voice. "As the saying goes, we have friends
in high places. Steam Bird isn't extinct yet." He gripped
the shoulders of the two lieutenants assisting Fisk, then
squeezed back out into the crawling tunnel and headed
forward.

He was humming "Flying Down to Rio" under his
breath as he entered the flight office and finally dropped
into his seat. "Hey, feller . . ." he sang in some kind of
tune to Captain Jackson.

"Spin that old propeller!" responded Jackson at once,
and the two men grinned at each other, now sharing
together the possibility of Rio and far, far beyond.

 **IX**

THE REPORTERS AND TV VANS ARRIVED AT THE MUTH HOME in the early afternoon, but Betty Lou and Alice were all ready for them. Mrs. Muth was dressed in an old tweedy skirt, and an ancient chamois shirt washed almost white with sleeves rolled up above flour-begrimed elbows, for she was actually making a cake when they began to arrive.

Alice, in a red velvet skirt, black pumps with white knee stockings, and a fussy, silky blouse, had washed, then brushed her long, straight blond hair so it hung down in a golden shower around her face. Indeed, Alice now looked so much like that other Alice in the Tenniel illustrations that she had spent some minutes in front of the looking-glass practicing saying, "Curiouser and curiouser," and trying to get it exactly the way she thought the other Alice would have said it.

The several cars and trucks randomly parked on the Muth lawn disgorged their cargo of people and cameras, and after some setup time, Mrs. Muth heard a discreet knock on the door. "Ready when you are, Mrs. Muth," said a polite young man.

"All right, Alice," said Betty Lou in a gentle, well-

modulated voice, and when her daughter joined her at
the door, the two of them walked out to face the
cameras, mother's sturdy, bare, floury arm firmly
around her pretty daughter's silken shoulders.

Alice was almost too good to be true, and the cameras
immediately zoomed in on her gamin face and shimmering hair. Ms. Betsy Frankenheimer, anchorperson on the
Nite News at Eleven program, mouthed the silent word,
"Adorable!" to her camera crew and stepped forward
with a wireless mike, dropping on one knee and giving
Alice a blindingly cheerful smile from ten inches away.
"You must be Alice, dear?" she enunciated in a clear but
gushy voice.

Alice Muth nodded gravely.

The TV lady showed even more and even larger teeth.
"I suppose you are *very* proud of your father, Alice?"

Alice thought a moment. "I don't know if Dad would
want us to be *proud* of him," she said in a serious voice.
"I think he would rather have us be . . . well . . . *like*
him. You know, brave, self-reliant, quick-thinking."

Ms. Frankenheimer remembered with sudden and
grievous pain her own father and their last meeting years
before, when he had tried to rape her at age fourteen. It
wasn't that Dad Frankenheimer got any special kick out
of incest, but simply that he was so out of his skull with
booze and downers that he simply didn't recognize his
own daughter. She stared at the beautiful child in front
of her talking about her father as though he were a
family saint, and she felt her throat begin to constrict
and her eyes to mist. "You must love your father very
much, Alice?" she said in a choked but barely under-
standable voice.

Alice smiled, a sudden radiance that enveloped the
cameras and the pool men as well as Ms. Frankenheimer.
"We all love Dad, don't we, Mom?" and she squeezed
her mother fiercely around her middle so that flour
puffed from her apron. "You would too, if you knew
him. There's nobody that knows more things than Dad.
Like . . . well, how Baker valve gears work and what

were the best runs on the *Morning Hi* when she was
steam-driven, and the piston speed on *City of Truro*
when she did the century . . . well, just about everything
like that. You see . . ."

Alice looked out at the cameras with round, serious
eyes and the two wire-service men immediately gave her
wide grins and double, upward thumbs back. ". . . Dad
is tremendously interested in everything and he's always
thinking and asking questions."

The obvious mixture of total love and complete admiration in Alice's every word and gesture when speaking of her father produced a cascade of tears and snuffles
from Ms. Frankenheimer and a brief hiatus in the
interview. Alice, in what the wire-service men agreed
afterwards was the classiest moment in a very classy
performance, instantly produced a sweet, heart-
decorated hankie from her tiny skirt pocket and dutiful-
ly handed it over to the TV lady.

"Of course, Dad and I have a special kind of love,"
said Alice, since it seemed to her that people would get
bored if nobody was talking. "It's the special love
between the father and his youngest daughter. In
seventeenth-century New England they said the youngest daughter was the father's *tortient* and if she were to
die of consumption or one of the million other things
they died of then, the father would be so sad that
sometimes he just gave up and lay down on the ground
next to her green grave . . . I don't mean that Dad loves
me any more than my brother or my sister. Dad would
never do that! It's just, well, *special*, like King Lear and
Cordelia."

Ms. Frankenheimer, herself a youngest daughter, was
now rendered completely unable to continue and Betty
Lou Muth realized they had definitely peaked the interview. She hugged Alice briskly and smiled in a motherly
way at the cameras. "Alice is very good in school and she
has a very active imagination. As you can see, she reads a
great deal." Mrs. Muth looked around. "I think Alice
speaks for us all with regard to my husband. My two

other children are flying in tonight with Congressman Hazelton and some of his staff and I have a large meal to prepare, so if you can excuse me now . . ." She looked questioningly around at the reporters and cameramen but it was evident that no further footage could compete with that already in the cans, and so the Muths were excused.

Once back inside the house Betty Lou Muth peered at her daughter with mingled awe and suspicion. "Where the hell did you pick up that 'tortient' stuff, Alice? Talk about laying it on thick!"

Alice, immensely pleased with herself, shrugged and then grinned at her mother. "We had a unit on colonial New England family life in Contemp History and the book talked about it. And anyway," Alice glanced at herself in the hall mirror, "I think it's true. Dad and I *do* have a special love. I *am* his tortient."

Mrs. Muth lit up a cigarette and puffed furiously. "You're the biggest ham in town, that's what you are! You know how they cut and edit, Alice. They'll have you looking like a cross between Goody Twoshoes and the little match-girl."

Alice was unperturbed. "You know what Uncle Nate says about the public, Mom."

Betty Lou grinned and puffed some more. "Yeh. I know his motto: 'Remember the *Checkers* speech. There is *no* bottom.'"

The meeting with the press held by Congressman Hazelton and his niece and nephew at Bangor airport was also brief, but had no TV cameras. Both Melissa and Bob Junior were now transformed by their disguises into characters from an unlikely Albee play about Middle America. Melissa's great beauty could never be wholly lost in face goop, green eyelid crud, and a buzzy, fluffed-out hairdo that seemed to be held together with shellac or epoxy, but the long brown skirt, sacky blouse, and sensible shoes gave her the unlikely look of a ravishing butterfly trapped half-in and half-out of its dreary cocoon. Bob Junior, tall and keen as any astronaut or young stockbroker, peered alertly at the reporters from behind large, black-rimmed glasses. His single-breasted, conservative, medium-priced suit coat fitted his large shoulders splendidly, but Nate had been careful to get the pants a trifle short so that his huge feet in their brown leather wing-tip oxfords stuck out in undeniable prominence. As Nate explained later to his sister, "I wanted the Maine farmer boy turned Rhodes Scholar ready to boot the ball for Oxford." Junior's hair, now a flat plane across his head and cut so close on top that the scalp showed white beneath, amply fulfilled his uncle's original desire: the Marine DI look.

The local Bangor AP man flashed the congressman a big smile. "Mr. Hazelton," he said briskly, "the wire service says your office will have a statement on the *Langley* this evening. Can you give us a hint on that?"

"I can't, boys and girls," said Hazelton easily, "because we haven't made it up yet. The President and the Pentagon met this morning on the *Langley*'s mission. Obviously, my reaction will depend on that decision."

"Do you think there is any chance the *Langley* might be involved in combat with Soviet fighters?" This from a young female stringer from Boston.

Hazelton grinned at her. "Only through the most grotesque and unlikely series of circumstances. The *Langley* flies far too low and slow to withstand even the most halfhearted attack by jets."

The woman reporter squinted fiercely back at that. "Then you would agree, Congressman, that the launching of the *Langley* has nothing to do with the so-called Russian missile freighters, but is in fact an attempt by the Pentagon to force Ice Island Three down the President's throat? Isn't it true that the Environmental Protection Agency will not permit the aircraft to land at Moosefoot or anywhere else in the US, quoting more recent laws that they say nullify provisions of the Atomic Aircraft Act of 1963?"

Hazelton's eyes glittered and he pulled at his short, foxy-grandpa beard. "That question, I assume, will keep several dozen lawyers busy for months. I doubt the *Langley* has sufficient food aboard to wait out those appeals and reversals. As to what rip-off the Pentagon is presently plotting, my only comment on that is, I am not a student of insect life."

He looked around impatiently at the several reporters. "Ladies and gentlemen, please! Obviously I will not comment now on the various options open to the President. The *Langley* is his responsibility, not mine. What I will say here is that I feel President O'Connell should come up here, to Moosefoot, and sit down with the people, the *only* people, who understand what the *Langley* can actually do."

"You do believe then, Congressman, that the *Langley* has a useful role? That it's not a flying nuclear disaster as the environmentalists are claiming?"

Hazelton nodded vigorously. "The *Langley* can play a large, significant, and positive role in our national life. That will all be made evident after the President has made his own assessments. Now, let me introduce the son and daughter of the aircraft's commander to you, Bob Junior and Melissa Muth."

The young lady from Boston found Bob Junior a little too precious to be true and she spoke directly at him. "Mr. Muth, how do you react to the various charges from the ecologists about the *Langley*'s danger to arctic life, specifically the Friends of Polar Bears?"

Bob Junior rubbed his large jaw with a big hand, the way Jimmy Stewart did in the movie about going to Washington, then cocked his head at her. "If you're talking about Ice Island Three," he said in a slightly twangy, down-Maine voice, "there aren't any polar bears at those high latitudes. There's no food up there, especially around that part of the arctic where there's little or no water left unfrozen."

He looked around at them and his dark eyes flashed scorn. "Any one of you could have looked that up, you know? I learned it for a merit badge in ecology about five years ago." He turned now to drill into the Boston lady at close range. "Of course you press folks would rather make up the stuff to fit whatever sentimental hokum you think will peddle the most garbage . . . with the result that brave and good men, like my Dad, may be driven to give up their lives to prevent some imaginary environmental risks!" This last was delivered with a hard-edged thrust that quite wilted the Boston reporter and she softly retired, blinking at the stern-faced young giant.

Congressman Hazelton put his arm around Junior's large shoulders and smiled frostily at the reporters. "Bob here was an Eagle Scout, you know?" he said coolly.

Nobody else seemed willing to tackle Bob Junior again, so the local AP man smiled tentatively at Melissa and phrased what seemed to be the most innocuous of questions. "Well, Miss Muth, I imagine you're proud of your father up there flying that huge, dangerous machine?"

Melissa nodded curtly. "Of course we're all proud of Dad. It isn't just the first nuclear airplane you know. It's the first steam-driven flying machine as well." She paused thoughtfully. "Well, unless you count Professor Langley's machine that Glenn Curtiss rebuilt and flew a few feet up off the water in 1915." She looked around at them, as if they were white slugs on some bad meat. "None of you knew any of that, did you? You're writing stories on the flight of the *Langley* and you don't know the first thing about it! Why, there are wonders and marvels happening around us every day and you people are all writing about some pro football player or rock freak getting busted for cocaine! Disgusting! And you call what you do a *profession*!"

That pretty well ended the interview, and the reporters shuffled away to consider their worthlessness in the airport bar.

Since Stubb's copter could only handle three passengers, Nate Hazelton sent Emmeline back to Moosefoot with the young trooper who had driven them down. As the car spun away with a predatory-sounding roar, the congressman shook his head with a grin. "I hope that young fellow knows what he's doing with Emmeline. If she talks him off the road and into those woods, he'll find himself mighty busy and that front seat mighty crowded!"

Bob Junior smiled at his uncle. "You'll sure get that cop's vote, Uncle Nate," he said in a practical-sounding voice and with a heavy wink.

Melissa sniffed and curled her long, elegant upper lip at the two men. "You chauvinist sex-pigs are really obsessed by the merest thought of somebody making love. So *what* if Emmeline and that nice policeman find a moment of joy with each other? Emmeline happens to be a very gentle, lovely person, Uncle Nate! And the fact that she needs a forty-two D-cup does *not* mean she's a moron! Look at this great job she did on me at the beauty parlor. She knew *just* what you wanted."

"Don't you lecture me about Emmeline, Melissa," said the congressman in a venomous tone. "There's no reason why a man looking after the nation's vital interests can't share some companionship with a . . ."

"All gassed up, Nate!" shouted Stubb Moody three feet from the congressman's ear, thus ending his lecture.

Bob Junior sat up with the pilot, the congressman behind him, and Melissa behind Stubb. Up chattered the machine into an almost-dark sky with a flutter of hissing sound. Hazelton leaned back in the cramped bucket seat and sighed. "Okay, Stubb. I think we've all earned a puff of that good-old-goodie."

The pilot immediately pulled a dirty-white spit-marked, monster joint from his breast pocket and passed it back. "Jesus, Stubb," said Congressman Hazelton, "where do you get such big rolling paper?" for Stubb's joint was indeed the size of a small cigar.

"Glued a bunch 'o papers tugetha, Nate," replied Stubb in a loud voice. "Then we dun't have tu keep lightin' up all the time."

Hazelton lit up and sucked strongly on the reefer, then exhaled with a slow but complete whoosh. "Ahh, Stubb, this is some of your best shit yet."

"It's the mature stuff, Nate. Young Bob an' me been raisin' it since the end of frost on a south hillside way back up."

"Yeah," said Junior. "I started the plants under lights in the fall, so we had three-footers when the sun began to really get hot. Got the place fenced. Otherwise the deer gobble the damn grass right up."

Hazelton toked appreciatively. "If I get to be President, you boys can have the Department of Agriculture."

Some moments passed in silence as the tiny cabin became more and more filled with the tantalizing smells of burning cannabis. "Uh, Uncle Nate." Junior turned around, "Uh . . . hey, you're kind of Bogarting that joint."

Nate Hazelton took another long toke and let out the smoke in a snarl. "Yes, you would deny an old man a few moments of relaxation snatched from a hectic all-day rush. It's disgusting! What do you young people need with all these stimulants, anyhow? You should be facing the wind, your heads clear, your breath sweet . . ." He crouched back into his corner of the cabin, toking steadily.

Melissa gave her uncle a scornful glance. "*Really*, Uncle Nate! If you're going to get maudlin in your high, at least let us come along for the trip!"

Hazelton took one more deep suck and, holding in, passed the now-ravished joint to his niece. The remaining three now reduced the joint to roach to ash in a round of efficient passing, and Stubb produced a new one.

So the flight went pleasantly forward into the cold Maine sky, the dark continuous forest passing underneath and only an occasional wink of light showing a solitary house. They were still about forty minutes from Moosefoot when Stubb Moody suddenly handed the headset back to the congressman. "Mizz Muth, Nate," he said.

Hazelton reluctantly passed on the reefer and put the set over his head. "Yeah, Lou. What's happening?"

"Nate, your office just hung up. A Mrs. Houghton."

"Right," said Hazelton briskly. "That's Isobel, the best Washington shark in the business. What does she know?"

"The President has tentatively decided to ditch the *Langley* at sea, Nate. They're all meeting tomorrow morning to firm up how and where."

Hazelton smacked one fist into the other palm. "Right! That's what we want, Lou!"

"But Nate, isn't the ditch the riskiest of all for Bob and the rest if we don't get it stopped?"

Hazelton could hear the concern in her voice. "Lou, this has to be the best way for it to go. If Shamus had lost his nerve and just dropped her tomorrow on the ice island, we'd have a problem reversing that. But he's damned if he wants to give in to the hawks. The point is, now all he needs is another suggestion and he'll see the whole thing clearly. Shamus is no fool, Lou. I don't know how he got in. Sometimes the country gets dumb lucky. Believe me, he's down there right now looking for a way out that does it all for him. We're going to give that to Shamus. Okay, what else? What is Isobel doing?"

"She said she called the wire services and the newspapers with a statement. You want me to read it, Nate?"

"What's the gist?"

"That Congressman Hazelton's office has learned from reliable sources . . . she said you'd know who . . . that the President was leaning toward a wanton and dangerous ditch procedure with the *Langley* and that you were attempting to reach the President, and so forth and so on. Here's the part she said you'd want to hear. 'Congressman Hazelton stated that the President had been unaware of the Moosefoot complex and missions until two days ago, and will thus urge the Chief Executive to make no final decision before viewing himself the bombing planes and meeting the trained and dedicated men who are now helping to set records in the northern skies.' "

"Nice," said Hazelton retrieving the joint. "Did she

think the press would call the White House with that stuff?"

"They already have, Nate. Mrs. Houghton has scheduled a press conference at ten tonight, so as to just make the eleven TV news. She's going to give them a briefing on the whole Moosefoot thing and answer questions about your statement. And of course respond to anything the White House might say."

"If they're smart, they'll play dumb," muttered Hazelton. "Isobel is sure doing a bang-up job. I've got to give her a hand with that traction engine she's putting back together. Anything else?"

"Alice and I had a short TV extravaganza, Nate."

"How'd it go?"

"You can decide when you see Sarah Bernhardt on the eleven o'clock news. When do you want to eat?"

"Hold the spaghetti water until after we've landed," said Hazelton. "I'm going to try and call old Shamus as soon as we get down in your yard. Be sure all the outdoor lights are on."

After contact was broken, Congressman Hazelton stared moodily out at the dark carpet of forest passing beneath them.

"What if he won't buy it, Uncle Nate? What if he makes them ditch?" said Bob Junior.

And though he *knew* this would not happen, Nate Hazelton at that moment had a sense of the utter futility that failure would bring. The *Langley*, nothing more than a bad Las Vegas joke for a few days. Bob and the crew . . . what? He stared at his nephew. "If we flop when he comes up here, we've still got my lawyer, Manny Stein, and his injunctions. Manny can keep the *Langley* flying for months. Then there are the weird and wonderful environmental folk. Any dumbo can see that the *Langley* is better off up on permanent ice than underwater in the middle of the Georges Bank fishery, and that position can eventually be forced onto the slack-jaws in the executive branch."

He pointed a sudden finger at his nephew. "If you do your stuff tomorrow, we won't even have to *think* about a ditch! Now listen! The preppy snot was fine with that gang of bleeding-heart ninth-raters in Bangor, but not to the President! Shamus won't stand still for ten seconds for any of that shit. Furthermore, if you start playing fact games with them, Jack Hanrahan will eat you alive!"

Bob Junior ran his hand over the tips of his stiff hair stalks. "I figure I can get on with the President okay, Uncle Nate. After all, I've had plenty of experience facing judges."

"And you think your behavior before judges is a recommendation?" said an astonished Nate Hazelton. "What about that enraged jurist you told should disqualify himself because his sister had a ton of stock in Vermont Traction and Power?"

"It was true, Uncle."

"Of course it was true! And what the hell has that got to do with it anyway? You don't say things like that in an open court when you're under arrest! Jesus!" Congressman Hazelton took a long drag and exhaled with a blast of smoke. But before he could resume his complaints a mellowing Melissa patted his arm.

"Uncle Nate, Junior's going to be great. You know you don't have to worry about him. We want everything to go right with Dad as much as you do." Melissa's eyes were now at an interesting half-mast position and she aimlessly and attractively brushed her hair back. "Hoo-eee, Stubb! We've been doing some pretty good coke down there, but this grass is just *super*!"

"You can thank the boy scouts, Meliss," said Bob Junior earnestly. "When I took my merit badge in agriculture they showed about how you can start plants early and then keep them from flowering too quick by putting them on a protected, south-facing hillside."

"That's what I've always liked about the scouts," said Hazelton in a round voice. "Practical. Stuff you can use in the real world. Don't you think so, Stubb?"

Stubb Moody tried to remember his younger days. "I dunno, Nate. I wuz swampin' logs with mu daddy most o' them early days. Larned to fly in Korea."

"Well," said Hazelton shrugging, "that proves it. You actually lived the life of the scout full time. And look how it's built up your character."

The long silence that followed this announcement was finally punctuated by a giggle from Melissa. "Stubb," she said, "Do you see yourself as *having* character or as *a* character?"

"Stubb is *a* character *with* character," said Bob Junior at once.

But Stubb lost that thread quickly and turned to another topic. "Kin I ask you a question, Melissa," said Stubb in an earnest voice.

"Sure Stubb, anything," she said leaning forward.

"Well," said Stubb in a thoughtful voice, "I wondered if yu had an opinion as tu why the Incredible Hulk can't seem tu git along with wimmen. I mean . . . wouldn't yu figgur the Hulk'd be, well, nice?"

Melissa tried to remember back to those days of such total ennui that she was reduced to rifling Alice's extended and unindexed comics collection. "Maybe he's a faggot, Stubb?" she suggested in the most tentative of tones.

That was a new thought, and Stubb was silent digesting it for some time. Encouraged by this seeming acceptance, and having a huge need to keep talking, Melissa tried to bring forward her woefully small store of chitchat on the comics. "Well, I mean Batman is gay, isn't he? With that nice, handsome boy . . . what's his name?"

"Robin," said Stubb stiffly. The helicopter flew on a while in silence. "Whut'd Miss Alice think 'bout all that?" Stubb asked finally and rather defiantly.

Melissa shrugged. "Oh, you know how she is, little Miss Smarty. She's read all those *books*, about the *comics*, for God's sake, by *psychiatrists*! She says there are no sexual overtones in the comics because comic heroes are essentially children, and that the beautiful thing about comics is that they show a world saved by innocence, by children. Well, you know how Alice can run on," said Melissa, running on herself.

Congressman Hazelton had briefly dozed but now awoke with a comfortable sense of the nearness of food. "I am really looking forward to that spaghetti meal," he said licking his lips.

"Me too! Me too!" said Stubb in immediate echo.

The Moosefoot ground crew were busy making the sauce for spaghetti and preparing the many chunks of garlic bread that Alice was thickly spreading. "You *know* they're going to be hungry, Mom," said Alice, chopping up another gigantic loaf, "coming in with Stubb."

Mrs. Muth looked sternly at her daughter. "Yes, and I don't want you out in the back sneaking any of Stubb's dope with him."

Alice stared at her mother through shocked eyes. "Mom! You wouldn't want me to hurt Stubb's feelings. You know how proud he is of his stuff!" She sat up haughtily. "I almost *never* smoke in school. I think *that* is just disgusting!"

Mrs. Muth sighed and tasted the sauce. "The thing is, Alice, if you grow up smoking and eating you'll turn into a fatty instead of the beautiful woman you can certainly become."

Alice laughed brightly at that. "Melissa smokes her head off and she looks like super-sex-cubed! Only dopes get sloppy from the munchies!"

But that debate was instantly ended by the sound of rotor blades over the house, and they both rushed out shouting haloos as Stubb brought the fire-service copter down into the irregular pools of light created by the patio Japanese lanterns.

Mrs. Muth took one look at her older children as they disembarked and uttered a shocked, "My God, Nate!"

But even more eloquent was Alice's loud, "*Icky-cubed!*"

Melissa turned scornfully from kissing her mother to

stare at her younger sister in the entrance light. "Look who's talking! Who are you supposed to be? Little Nell? Ophelia? Ozma? What did she use to wash her feet before she put on those lovely stockings, Mom? Gasoline?"

Alice, overjoyed at finding her older sister unchanged by several months' absence, stuck out her tongue fiercely. "And *you*," she said with a snarl, "look like the girl in *An American Tragedy* . . . after they pull her out of the water!"

"Food is close ahead, my friends," said the congressman, pressing along with that relentless good will that overrides all contrary discourse.

And from behind Alice came Stubb's "Pssst!" and she saw a cheerfully-glowing spark off in the darkness, so the argument was over before it had really begun.

Once inside Hazelton ordered his sister to start the spaghetti and settled himself at the phone. "Go play with the trains or something," he said to them. "I need about fifteen solid minutes here."

"Yeah," said Bob Junior, "let's go run a turn with the *Dixie Flyer*, Meliss. Dad's got the whole circuit set up to let you run it with nothing else turned on."

Melissa nodded. "Right. And let's triple-head it and try to do the Tidewater-to-Bridgton section at over one hundred average. Then when it's our turn to run the passenger scheduling, we'll know we can do it."

They clattered off to the basement in their new shoes while Hazelton dialed a variety of numbers. At one point it seemed that he might be frozen on hold forever but finally he heard that crisp voice of the last young woman in the innermost office. "Congressman Hazelton? The President will speak with you in a few moments. He's with his family. Please hold on."

President O'Connell was, in fact, sipping a second, or perhaps a fourth, Jack Daniels, when his press aide buzzed his most private line. "Yeh, Dave?" said O'Connell frowning.

"We've got Nate Hazelton on the line, Chief. His office has been grinding out bad press stuff on us ditching the *Langley*. Moosefoot is in his district. You better talk, Chief."

Shamus O'Connell sighed and then grunted, "Put him on."

"Shamus, is that you down there?"

"Ah, Nate. Glad to be here when you called," said O'Connell, making a monster face at Happy Jack. "My people say you're concerned about the *Langley*?"

"Well of course I'm concerned. Those men have been a part of our nuclear deterrent force up here all these years, and now you're going to drop their only mission in the ocean and poison the seas while you're at it."

"Well, Nate," said O'Connell mildly. "I don't anticipate anything like that. They say we'll just fish the thing out and take it apart."

"Look, Shamus, my point is simply this. Your administration has had nothing to do with Moosefoot and I happen to know on good authority that you never heard of the place before last week. So I think you should come up here tomorrow, see the base, talk to General Beardsley, find out what the wing can do for America. You can't consign those brave men to the worst kinds of risks because some weirdos are worried about a few nonexistent polar bears on the pack ice."

"If the plane blows up on landing, the crew will be exposed to considerable risk, Nate."

"The plane won't blow up, for God's sake! Look, Mr. President, that's my brother-in-law, Bob Muth, flying that plane. He's the finest steam engineer and pilot in the world. He'll bring it in on the ice like a baby, Shamus."

Shamus O'Connell covered the receiver and gave his chief aide a piercing look. "Jack, that plane commander, that Muth, he's Hazelton's brother-in-law, for God's sake!"

Jack Hanrahan's wrinkled face was a Noh mask of puzzlement. "I've been in this business forty years,

Shamus, but what these crazy kooks are after escapes me. Put him off until after eleven. We'll see what they're doing on TV."

O'Connell turned back and took his palm off the receiver. "Sorry to leave you there for a second, Nate. Look, I have to see if we can do the Moosefoot thing tomorrow. I appreciate your concern, I really do, Nate. We're not doing anything precipitous. I mean, we really don't have to hurry when the _Langley_ only goes three hundred miles an hour. Ha, ha."

"Your folks will get back to me then, Shamus?"

"_I'll_ get back, Nate," said O'Connell expansively. "Do my people have your number?"

"They do," said Hazelton. "I'm here in Moosefoot with the Muth family. I'll be waiting for your call, Mr. President. Goodbye."

Happy Jack got up from his armchair and peered out at the distant traffic and the lights of Washington. "I don't think we should go up to Moosefoot, Shamus," he said finally. "Hazelton has something going that he understands and we don't. I still don't see his connection with Ice Island Three."

The President shook his head in puzzlement. "What _is_ Hazelton's angle, anyway? He loves the Pentagon just as little as we do. Let's think, Jack. Is it that the flight of the _Langley_ will shut Moosefoot now or soon? Nate must see that, Jack. And maybe Zinkowski has offered to put a SAC wing up there instead?"

Happy Jack tested and then tasted his drink in thoughtful silence. Then he spoke slowly. "That little bribe would suborn most of them, Shamus, but I dunno. Hazelton just doesn't work that way . . ."

"I'll say he doesn't," said the President in a dark voice. "He gets what he wants by pimping, procuring, peddling kinks, and of course he knows everything dirty about everybody."

"Just hope he never writes a book, Shamus. Still, Nate would rather have the generals coming to him looking for a good bondage parlor than him begging them to keep a base open." Jack sat thinking, then said, "Shamus, that General Beardsley, what about him? You say he's a cuckoo?"

O'Connell thought back to the hectic morning. "When I ordered him to start the plane's engines, before you were there, he said something funny."

"Funny?"

"Weird, Jack. He said something like, we will not fail you nor the *world of steam*."

"World of steam?" Happy Jack sat silent for a while. "Shamus," he said finally, "do we have anybody on the staff who keeps track of spare-time recreation among the staff, you know, like softball, bowling, jazz appreciation, chorus, whatever?"

"Let's call Dave," said the President, picking up the phone. "Dave? Listen, do we have any kind of recreation director on the staff who knows what people's hobbies and pastimes might be? . . . Ms. Fran Dugan? Could you try and ring her at home, Dave? Yeh, get right back to us." He hung up and shrugged. "What do we ask her, Jack?"

The phone soon buzzed again and both Jack and the President picked up receivers. "Ms. Dugan?" said the President to a voice that suddenly squeaked in surprise. "This is the President. Sorry to bother you after hours . . . oh, well fine. Mr. Hanrahan is here, Ms. Dugan, and he has a question for you. Jack?"

"Ms. Dugan," came Happy Jack's cool voice. "Is there anyone on the White House staff who might have a hobby related to steam locomotives or steam engines in general? . . . Hmm, a Mr. Fred Purington? And what does he do for us, Ms. Dugan? . . . Hum. Well, we'll get back if we need any more help. Thank you and good night."

Shamus O'Connell grinned at Jack over the phone receiver. "Our single expert in the world of steam happens to be the young fellow who opens the limo doors . . ."

But this did not bother Jack, who waited silently while

Dave tried to reach this particular White House employee. After several tries he was discovered at one of the Washington hobby shops that his mother had suggested to the press aide. In fact, twenty-year-old Fred Purington had been chatting with the proprietor of the Steam?— Yes! hobby shop, the old and legendary steam buff Babe Glanville, when the old fellow handed over the phone with a low, suddenly-respectful, "White House for you, Fred."

"Okay, this is Jack Hanrahan, Mr. Purington. You know me, right?"

"Yessir, Mr. Hanrahan, sir. What can I do?" said Fred in a sudden stutter of confusion.

"You know about steam hobbies, right? Ms. Dugan gave us your name."

Pimply Fred Purington made a puzzled face at the staring proprietor. "Yessir, steam is my hobby, Mr. Hanrahan."

"Okay, Fred. I'm going to give you some names. I want to know what they have to do with steam, okay?"

"Shoot, Mr. Hanrahan."

"Congressman Nathaniel Hazelton."

Purington grinned. "That's easy. He's one of the biggest wheels in the New England Live Steamers, owns a Shay and a small logging railway he's going to get going. Talks at all the northeastern steam meets."

"Great," said Hanrahan interrupting him, "Now, try General Bertram Beardsley?"

Purington thought a moment. "He's on the board of one of the hobby mags . . ." His lips made the name, "Beardsley" to Glanville.

"Consulting Editor, *Modern Steam Power*," responded the hobby shop proprietor at once.

Fred Purington relayed this information, then added, "As I remember, he's building a car . . ."

"Flash steam uniflow racer," said Glanville promptly. "Wants to beat the Stanley record of one-ninety."

"That's it!" said Purington. "He's trying to beat the old steam-car speed record with a racing machine . . ."

"Fine," said Happy Jack. "Now, Colonel Robert Muth."

The young man thought for a moment. "He's a big model-railway man, electronics too, great on simulating the way steam locos work. Also, he and Hazelton work on live steam projects together."

"Okay, now what about Moosefoot, Maine, in the world of steam, Fred?"

Purington pursed his lips. "Listen, that's a big question, Mr. Hanrahan. Mr. Glanville, here, could answer you a lot better."

"Who's this Glanville, Fred?"

"The proprietor of Steam?—Yes! hobby shop. He knows as much about steam as anyone in Washington."

"Put him on."

"Babe Glanville, here," said the old man, giving Fred Purington a wink.

"Mr. Glanville, what does Moosefoot, Maine, mean to steam hobby people?"

Glanville grinned. "Everything, I'll tell you! They got traction-engine people up there, loco people, model steam people, one fellow with a steam roundabout, you know, a merry-go-round. There's several steamboats on the river, a big Corliss some of them are fixing up, and the last I heard a bunch of them were tackling the restoration of one of those godawful Lombard log haulers . . ."

"And this activity is focused around the air base, Mr. Glanville?"

"Pretty well has to be," said Glanville. "Not much else around up there as I understand it. Congressman Hazelton, the fellow you asked Fred about, he's a big leader in the Moosefoot steam thing."

"Do you know Nate, sir?"

"Sure. Nate comes in here all the time. Great steam man, Nate. Lives it and loves it."

"I much appreciate this information, sir," said Jack, "and please thank Fred Purington. You have both been most helpful to us."

President O'Connell had been listening silently on his extension and now he smiled tiredly at his friend. "Who would expect a nest of nuts in the north woods, Jack?"

"It isn't just that, Shamus," said Happy Jack in a grim voice. "A new question is, will the crew of the *Langley* do what they're told? And if they won't, what in hell *will they do?* These people are, to put it as mildly as possible, dancing to a very different drummer!"

"And yet it seems harmless enough. But why the ice island, Jack? What in hell do these nuts care about that?"

"Don't you see, Shamus? There are *two* groups here. The Professor and Zinkowski and the rest of those hard-edged bastards this morning just want to play with Ice Island Three and terrify the Russians. Jesus, the airfield *is* a knife pointed at their throat. But way up there over the rainbow, in Moosefoot, there are different ideas and other imaginations at work."

"And what do they want?"

Jack shrugged. "Evidently they want to get their pinkies black with coal dust. I dunno. I think we ought to stay away from those cuckoos. What they've got up there might be catching."

O'Connell lifted his eyebrows in puzzlement. "He's got us, though, Jack. If we go ahead from here without ever even going up to look at the damn things, and there's some kind of screw-up with the plane or crew, we'll be covered with crud and Nate will never let us forget it. Well, let's see how badly we're being hurt at eleven tonight."

The Muths, Uncle Nate and Stubb sat down to a huge mass of spaghetti, platters of garlic bread, and loads of wine, and soon the dining room was a quiet chorus of smacking lips and muttered requests for this or that.

"Yummy, Mom! Isn't the garlic bread good, Stubb?" said a bright-eyed Alice to the pilot sitting next to her.

"Dun't know when I've had a finer meal, Mizz Muth," said Stubb appreciatively around his sixth piece of bread.

Betty Lou smiled coolly at Stubb and Alice. "When you're stoned out of your minds, my dears, even some three-day-old boiled beef liver can taste pretty good."

Bob Junior shook his head. "That's a fallacy, Mom. Only beginning dopers gorge on junky food. The fact is, grass actually improves your ability to distinguish between tastes. And this sauce is just fine, Mom. Absolutely top rate. Would somebody pass it to me, please?"

Betty Lou looked at her brother in sudden concern. "What if he won't come up, Nate?" she asked.

Hazelton poured himself a large dollop of red wine and licked his lips gratefully. "Oh, in the end he'll come, Lou. You see, they don't know what is liable to happen when the *Langley* comes in for a landing. And when they don't know what will happen about something at the White House, they do back-flips to cover their bets and their butts from every angle. The important thing is not to push them anywhere but to let them discover the answers themselves. The flight of the *Langley* has to be packaged, just like everything else in this wondrous land of ours." The Congressman fingered his billy-goat beard and gave them all a sly wink. "I reckon we Mainiacs can teach them New York City fellers a trick or two. They may peddle off a bridge or a gold brick to us hayseeds now and then, but let them try selling something as big and crazy as the *Langley* to the whole world! Now that's selling!"

X

DEEP IN THE BOWELS OF THE PENTAGON LIES A HIDDEN, CU-bical space, its brass door plaque sternly proclaiming the "Senior Staff Ready Room." Inside, with walls decorated by huge photo murals of the mountain scenery surrounding a Rocky Mountain Air Force aerie, is a cheerful barroom of several tables, all now pushed hastily together for an informal evening meeting of General Zinkowski and his entourage of lesser generals and high-level civilian staff. Zinkowski's craggy face showed a minimum of emotion as he pointed at the Air Force Chief Scientist, a distinguished engineering savant on leave from a distinguished school which, like that of Prof. Bzggnartsky, stretched along a golden mile of Boston's Charles River. "Tell us about the B-3000, Dr. Hardwell," said Zinkowski in a firm and level voice.

Prof. Hardwell pulled at his white beard and cleared his throat. "Certainly," he said, staring owlishly around at them all. "B-3000 is, as you all have been told, a fine and modern bombing plane. It does extremely well what the *Langley* does very badly, notably go fast, faster than three thousand miles an hour. Unfortunately, it does extremely badly what the *Langley* does well; namely, it has a very restricted radius of action." Dr. Hardwell shrugged. "If a B-3000 takeoff occurs from a US airbase, the aircraft can attack targets inside the Soviet Union, but . . ." he shrugged again quite sadly, "it can't get back. A one-way mission, I'm afraid."

Several of the uniformed officers pursed their lips at this and one three-star general shook his head vigorously. "Damn bad for air crew morale," he offered.

"Decidedly," said Zinkowski. "But if the thing were flown from Ice Island Three, the entire northern third of Russia could be attacked and the plane could return to a number of fields, here or in Canada." He stared somberly around at them. "There have already been some overruns and other problems with the B-3000. We need the ice island and we need it badly. I want to stress that to you all."

The cozy room fell silent, except for the clinking of glasses, while a trusted bartending master sergeant busied himself with mixing and refilling. Zinkowski's one bright eye turned to the only woman in his group, a large and formidable one-star general. "What is happening with public relations, General Fishbein?" he asked.

General Hurta Fishbein, the warrior witch and terror of press officers everywhere, swept the small group with iron-cold eyes, her thin and wrinkled mouth set in such an expression of combined distaste and challenge that several of the men instinctively reached down between their legs to make sure everything was still there. "The only place in the world we can land the *Langley* is on the ice island," said General Fishbein in a thin voice that cut through the room like a diamond scratching glass. "We are leaking a study to the press at nine tonight, in just one hour, concerning the expected shifting of the reactor during an ocean ditch and virtual certainty that some of the crew would receive massive radiation doses. The plane cannot legally be landed anywhere in the United States. Even our staunchest allies will not permit the thing in their countries . . ."

"What about Managua?" said a cheerfully-florid lieu-

tenant general, sipping his sixth rum collins. General
Fishbein's frown of disgust instantly reduced his smile
to the grin of a skull and his voice to a croak of apology.

Zinkowski nodded, his face still sombre. "OK," he
said, "this thing has to be landed on the ice island,
sometime or other. We knew that when it went up.
But . . ." and he pointed a sharp finger at frowning
Hurta Fishbein, "does that absolutely guarantee that the
ice island is ours . . . I mean the Air Force's . . . and can
then be used for our bombers?"

Nobody answered and even General Fishbein knitted
her formidable white eyebrows in puzzlement. "I don't
exactly understand, General Zinkowski," she said finally. "Once we land the world's largest bomber there,
doesn't that rather turn the place into a bomber base?"

Zinkowski shook his head. "Only if the *Langley* is
regarded as a bomber on a bomber's mission. I sense
that the crew and the staff at Moosefoot AFB do not
quite see it in such a light."

General Fishbein spoke thoughtfully. "True, and we
always knew that. They see it simply as the largest steam
engine ever built. But we encouraged those nuts, didn't
we? Staff was transferred up there who would fit into the
Moosefoot avocational atmosphere."

Zinkowski knotted his brow. "Colonel Muth, the
plane captain, is a . . . well, I think 'dedicated, professional officer' is the best way to describe him. I doubt
that he shares our exact desires for Ice Island Three."
Zinkowski looked around at the others, then fixed his
gaze on a bald-headed major general, the Air Force Chief
Legal Counsel. "General Forbush, suppose we ordered
the *Langley* to land on the ice island tonight, as soon as
it reaches the pole? We could claim that certain calculations and instrument-reading projections showed a gradual deterioration of the power plant."

The lawyer pursed his lips, then shook his head. "One,
the White House would crucify us. Two, if you suspect
Muth of, let's say, independent ideas, he could probably
claim that the Atomic Aircraft Act required him to

receive such an order directly from the President. Three, since the people flying the *Langley* are clearly the preeminent . . . and proven . . . experts in the field of airborne nuclear fission, I doubt we could convince them that the plane is deteriorating if it really isn't. Four . . ."

Zinkowski held up his hand. "Enough, Henry, enough," he said quickly. "It's clear we are *damnably* at the mercy of events!"

The room fell silent again until Hurta Fishbein spoke, still stern but in a quieter voice. "The White House is in a frenzy of fear about where this thing is headed. Whatever Moosefoot AFB and the crew has in mind for the *Langley*, I can't see the President and his people doing anything but getting it down as fast as possible and as far from the US as possible."

"Then why is Hazelton so desperate to get O'Connell up to Moosefoot?" gritted Zinkowski right back. "His press release stressed that. When he and Muth's kids met the reporters in Bangor, he hit that point again, right?"

Hurta Fishbein nodded. "Oh, he's got something in mind. Our man from the *Globe* said the Muth children were dressed up like a nineteen-sixties episode of the *Brady Bunch* sitcom."

Zinkowski shook his head in total frustration. "Look! General Fishbein . . . ah, Hurta . . . you call the Muths in Moosefoot. Tell them anything, say you're anybody, but see if you can dope it out. If we can get a handle on what's happening, maybe we can step on it before it gets out of control."

General Fishbein imperiously signaled the master sergeant bartender for a cordless phone, then chewed out three different night operators in tones that made even Zinkowski blink nervously. They all heard the phone finally ringing, then a click and a soft, "Hello."

Hurta Fishbein's voice dripped with a honeyed sweetness and warmth that made the others sitting around her stare with astonishment. "Hel-*lo*, Alice," she gushed, "and how are *you* tonight?"

Alice, sitting alone in front of the living room TV,

wrinkled her nose. "Now what?" she muttered to herself.

"My name is Arlene Harrington and I work for the Associated Press, Alice. I know you're terribly busy and excited, but I wondered if I could ask you a couple of questions?"

The tremendous sincerity and good feeling in General Fishbein's voice astounded the Air Force brass. The florid general with the rum collinses turned to his neighbor and whispered very quietly, "Hurta is either the most overpaid phone operator or the most underpaid secret agent in the whole federal establishment."

"Sure," said Alice, flicking her TV remote to shut off the sound. "Go ahead."

The first few questions had to do with Alice's school, grades, and friends, then her father, so that Alice was talking openly and cheerfully when General Fishbein asked, "And what do *you* wish your dad might do with that huge and wonderful airplane, Alice?"

Alice's eyes narrowed and she bit her lip. "Gosh . . . gosh, that's a tough question, Ms. Harrington," she said in as puzzled a voice as she could manage.

"You must have *some* ideas, dear?" urged the syrupy phone voice.

This was the single question that Uncle Nate had told her not to consider. "Don't even try to answer, Alice," he had said in his most serious voice. "If they guess the thing too early, they might stop us, with press releases about dangers, with all sorts of political reasons why we shouldn't do it. It must come to the President like a bolt from the wild blue yonder."

Alice thought hard, and the harder she thought, the more she realized that what Nate and the rest of them planned for the *Langley* was about the only possible thing to be done with it. The gigantic airplane was really only good for one, specific task. Alice felt a chill run up her back. Anyone who thought deeply would have to come up with pretty much the same answer. "Ah . . . ah, well, I guess I wish they'd let the other two planes fly," said Alice as enthusiastically as possible. "Imagine a formation of three of them . . . uh, gosh, Mom's calling. I gotta go," and Alice hung up, then took the receiver off the hook so the woman could not call right back.

General Fishbein shook her head and put the receiver down. "The kid's been coached. She said fly the other two nuclear planes. Even a mewling infant should know that there's no chance of that." Then Hurta Fishbein, who had also been thinking hard, bit her lip and nodded to herself. "Yes, of course," she breathed, "around the world . . . nonstop. They would want to do that, wouldn't they? But . . . but then what?"

General Zinkowski, now thoroughly irritated, was having none of that. "What are you saying? Let it terrify every nation in the United Nations. Come on! O'Connell isn't that stupid!"

The meeting adjourned on this surly note, leaving only the rum collins fan and a younger friend, a brigadier medical officer, behind with their drinks. The older man winked and sang quite jauntily to a familiar tune, "I've been around the world in a plane, I've played the best golf courses in Spain. Still I'm broken hearted, cause I can't get started, with Hurta-a-a-a."

The younger doctor grinned back at this. "You think Hurta would make you squirta, huh?" he said. "I think she'd chew you into little pieces and flush them down her bidet!"

XI

FAR OUT OVER THE POLAR ICE, BEYOND ELLESMERE OR ANY other land, the *Langley* finally achieved her maximum service altitude, twenty-one thousand, two hundred feet, and her maximum speed, a bit over three hundred knots. The cold, dense polar air removed heat effectively from the huge steam condensers and Major Fisk had been able to steadily increase the reactor power during the climb. As they topped twenty thousand feet he spoke quietly. "Bob, she's made it, guy! One million horsepower!"

"Think of that, Gaby," said Bob Muth to Captain Jackson, "a million horses! In *flight*, for God's sake!"

"We can take her anywhere, Bob," said Captain Jackson in a suddenly tight and passionate voice, pulling his mike pads away from his throat. "Even if the President orders us to ditch or go home. We could take her right around, Bob. We could *do* it, baby! They wouldn't dare *touch* us!"

Colonel Muth looked steadily at his copilot, then pulled his mike off as well. "Okay, I've thought about that, good buddy. And they'd touch us plenty after we landed."

"So what, Bob? Then it would be *done*!"

"Gaby," said Bob Muth quietly. "You know Congressman Hazelton is as big a steam freak as any of us, and he's working on this. Nobody's given us any orders yet, so let's see how things seem to be breaking."

Colonel Muth took a deep breath. "Gaby: Gresley, Chapelon, old Riddles, they never spared the regulator, whatever the chances. Hell, we can't do any less at this point. Just pray they get the message across back at Moosefoot."

But Jackson was suddenly seized by a wave of despair. He had been in the Air Force a long time and it suddenly seemed completely impossible that they would sanction such a spectacular junket for a secret bombing plane ostensibly sent aloft to terrify the Russians. He shook his head bitterly. "Bob, they won't do it, baby! It just . . . it just isn't their way of dealing with this mission!"

Colonel Muth put a calming hand on his copilot's arm. "Gaby," he said quietly, turning his head to make sure nobody had wandered into the flight office unannounced, "if we just go and land at the ice island after a few days of prowling around the Arctic, the Washington hawks, who never fly in anything but up-front in a 747 with a decent wine list, will zip all sorts of stuff in to deal with us. Then the Russians can decide where to stab us in return. But . . ." and Bob Muth held up his hand, "think about the *Langley* as the last and greatest act in the history of aeronautics. Now the ice island can be seen as something different. As my son would say, we've got to change this from an Air Force trip to a people's trip."

Captain Jackson grinned and nodded and the two men fitted their mike pads back on and sat quietly thinking their own elevated and sombre thoughts.

Sergeant Stewart had been staring for some moments at the "Great Days in Steam History" calendar hanging over his desk in the undercarriage office and, noting the appropriateness of the entry for that date, he spoke at once to the crew. "Listen to this, Harry and the rest of you. Exactly thirty-two years ago on this day, Engineer

Sam Bouchard, one of the Pennsy's top runners, was scheduled to take the second section of the Broadway Limited out of Thirtieth Street in Philly with a duplex-drive T-1, Number 6110. The engine on the first section failed on start and Engineer Bouchard backed his train down on the first-section varnish, coupled the whole caboodle together . . . over fourteen hundred tons . . . and went tearing out of Thirtieth Street more than an hour late. He'd made back more than twenty minutes by Harrisburg and came into Chicago just about on time. They say that over the last seventy miles, Fort Wayne to Englewood, Bouchard's T-1 *averaged* over one hundred and two miles an hour. Cecil J. Allen considers this performance to be the greatest sustained effort by a single steam locomotive in the entire history of steam traction."

"Wow!" said Colonel Muth. "Stirring stuff, all right! How'd you like to ride the footplate on that one, Gaby? Listen Jim, what about getting a couple of T-1's on the Tidewater Northern? We could speed up the *Dixie*, maybe run her at over one hundred on the Tidewater-to-Bridgton turn?"

"That's a good thought, Bob," said Sergeant Stewart. "Why don't you raise it at the next meeting of the Motive Power Committee? Of course, we'd have to shift the railroad about five years ahead to use T-1's. Getting awfully close to the diesel era."

Colonel Muth frowned strongly at his controls. "Jim, as the Chairman of the Motive Power Committee, I think I can assure you that Tidewater Northern will not enter that later and lesser time. In any case, a properly-maintained T-1 should easily do the century with even an eleven-hundred-ton *Dixie Flyer*."

These hypothetical schedulings were, in fact, being severely put to actual test at about that same time in the Muth basement. Having discovered that the three biggest Pacifics in the loco stud, coupled to a reasonable nine-hundred-scale-ton train, could indeed get from Tidewater to Bridgton at nearly one hundred miles an hour, Bob Junior and Melissa now had to share their experiments with everybody else.

Congressman Hazelton took the *Dixie Flyer* over the route at just about ninety-five, start to pass, and then Betty Lou raised it to a bit under the century. When it was Alice's turn she crammed the regulators hard over and spun her three sets of drivers for a quarter-mile out of Tidewater, saying excitedly, "You slow them up too far ahead of the hill, Uncle Nate!"

Alice, to make her point, came over the top of Sherman Hill doing almost ninety, then hit her brakes and sanders. As might be expected, nothing much happened except that the *Dixie* went on down the hill constantly accelerating, passing the 'Slow-30-MPH' signs doing over ninety-five and coming into the siding and helper-pocket switchwork at over one hundred scale-miles an hour. The big green Pacifics rolled through the curves and points like foundering barques and the varnish jammed through behind with some jerks and a clatter that would have put every coffee cup in a real diner on the ceiling. But the high-wheeled beauties sailed on like the ladies they were and the heavyweight cars stayed on the rails, one way or another, so that Alice came whistling through Bridgton with a start-to-pass average of one hundred and eight scale-miles an hour.

After the power was cut off, Alice sat staring silently out at her engines with a very red face. "Well," said Melissa in an enraged hiss, "what do you think this *is*, Alice? A *Lionel set*, for God's sake!"

Alice stared down at her lap. "I'm very sorry," she said in a little voice. "I forgot the brakes don't work so good over eighty, going down a hill. I really didn't mean to do that, everybody . . . honest." This last word was spoken in a very small and very teary voice.

Congressman Hazelton got up from his position as Tidewater Yardmaster and came over to the engineer's cabs to give Alice a warm hug. "A handsome apology, Alice, and one that we *all*," and he looked pointedly at Melissa, "are happy to accept. And, let me remind you,

Melissa," said the congressman, looking his most foxy and peering over his half-glasses, "that far older and wiser heads than Alice's lovely, golden crown have utterly succumbed to the seductive lure of locomotive speed. For example, when Gresley drove *Silver Fox* to one hundred and thirteen on Stoke bank the whole middle gear blew apart and threw crap back under the train, almost derailing the damn thing. Even worse, old Riddles, Stanier's assistant on the London-Midland-Scottish, got *Coronation Scot* going a hundred and fourteen down the ten-mile bank into Crewe station, trying to break the steam speed record. A mile out of the station they were still doing a hundred and every wooden brake block on the varnish was in flames. They came up on the platform entrance 20-m.p.h. speed restrictions at over seventy and went through three reverse-curves and six entry-points with a slam-bang that put everything in the diner, including the passengers, down on the floor." Nate Hazelton hugged Alice tighter. "So you see, Melissa, Alice is just one more good CME who let her heart run away with her head. My goodness, dear friends, that's the whole point!"

And if Melissa thought that things might have been different if Dad's three best engines had gone onto the ground at speed, she managed not to say it, while the whole crew put the Tidewater Northern back into its operational configuration for the next regular session.

By the time the eleven o'clock news came on, everyone was settled around bowls of popcorn, peering at all three networks and listening to one. The *Langley* was the main topic everywhere and there were several in-flight shots of the plane, all from ahead. "Look!" cried Alice. "There's Dad and Gaby Jackson!" And sure enough, they had taken a massive zoom lens up into the cold, pure air that could bring the *Langley*'s Flight Office up so very close that you could even see the men talking.

Congressman Hazelton gave a bark of laughter. "What'll you bet that Bob is explaining to Gaby why continuous-cam surfaces make the best high-speed valve gear."

The next segment showed a severe-looking older woman lecturing about the *Langley* from behind a big desk. "Ah," said Hazelton, "here's Isobel."

"Ms. Houghton," came a reporter's voice, "can you tell us in a really short statement why Congressman Hazelton is opposed to the ditch option?"

The old lady's eye-glasses glittered. "One, it's the most dangerous for the crew. Two, it's the most dangerous for the environment. Three, it makes the US look like a damn fool. Four, it insults the men of the wing. Five, it casts away opportunities that the *Langley* is uniquely able to fulfill. These, and several other reasons, are why Mr. Hazelton is asking the President to come to Moosefoot before he makes any final decision."

"What about the ice island?"

Ms. Houghton whipped off her glasses to reveal hawk-like eyes. "The ice island is the obvious and inevitable landing place. The position we are taking with the White House is that we believe their needs can be accommodated by that solution. We want to discuss that point."

"Good . . . excellent," said Hazelton as the network on the center screen cut to the next topic: Alice.

Ms. Frankenheimer, looking much more cheerful than in the afternoon, chattered on about the women of the *Langley*'s crew and how she had gone to Moosefoot to see for herself. She turned to her male second-banana assistant and said kittenishly, "Well, Jerry, we went to the Muth's and had a really moving and lovely talk with Colonel Muth's younger daughter, Alice. I was really overcome by it all, Jerry. Here's this beautiful, brave child who loves her father more than anything else in the world waiting to hear . . . well, it was pretty over-whelming . . . as we'll see now."

After some moments' delay, they cut away from the mugging pair to the Moosefoot interview film. They used no shot-and-reverse in this, but held Alice's delicate

face in a full-on or side-angle shot throughout, occasionally cutting and zooming to a quick close-up of Ms.
Frankenheimer during one of her sobbing fits. The Muth
living room became absolutely silent as TV Alice explained with a lovely, slightly sad, yet childishly enthusi-
astic voice about all the wonderful things her father
could do and then how much they all loved him. They
cut to a dripping Ms. Frankenheimer, then back to a
three-quarter of Alice as she solemnly whipped out her
hankie and handed it over.

Congressman Hazelton let his breath slowly out as a
wide smile spread across his sly features. He hunched
along the couch to Alice and put a large arm around her.
"You," he whispered in her ear, "are the biggest,
toughest pro in this whole outfit, me included. Bravo,
baby!"

Alice, utterly unable to deal with so much praise from
her usually irascible uncle, dissolved in tears as the
interview neared its end. TV Alice, now seen from well
back, to show that she really was just a little girl,
explained with a sweetly melancholy earnestness how
her father might lie down by her fresh, green grave when
she died from consumption. Holding Alice, they shifted
the framing to bring Ms. Frankenheimer's teary face in
close-up into the edge of the picture, then cut away back
to the studio.

"So you see, Jerry," said a now-beaming anchor
person, "if Colonel Muth is half as good at atomic
airplane piloting as he is at bringing up kids, well Jerry, I
don't think America has a thing to worry about."

The TVs were shut off but the brief silence in the living
room ended abruptly. "Disgusting!" said Melissa wrin-
kling her perfect nose and turning her upper lip into a ski
jump. "Tortient! It isn't that Dad loves me any more
than the others," simpered Melissa in a devastatingly
good imitation of Alice's special, plaintive quality. "It's
just that he'd *kill* himself if anything happened to
wonderful little *me*."

"You're just jealous that you can't be Dad's tortient!"

shrieked Alice shrinking against her Uncle Nate and
sticking her tongue out. "You couldn't be one anyway,
Miss Bitchy, even if you were the last of a hundred
daughters!"

Bob Junior wrinkled his wide forehead in a frown.
"Well it *was* rather thick, Alice. I mean really . . ."

Alice sneered at her brother and rubbed her hot eyes.
"Well at least I didn't wee-wee on her leg," she said
crossly.

"Cut it out!" said Hazelton angrily to them. "You
can't begin to imagine how good that was! Alice had that
iron-assed dyke broken in half, right in *half,* kids!"

The phone rang and Congressman Hazelton threw his
arm out to sweep in the receiver. "Yes, this is Congressman Hazelton . . . That is correct, *I* am Nate Hazelton
. . . yes . . . yes . . . Hi there, Shamus. Thank you for
getting back, old friend. I appreciate it. . . . You've decided to come up to Moosefoot? . . . Wonderful, about
nine tomorrow morning. . . . We'll be here with bells on,
Mr. President, yes sir . . . What? . . . The Muth girl?
Yes, Alice . . . Ah, you thought she was a beautiful
child . . . ah, a beautiful *soul.* Well, it is seldom that you
see a child who loves and respects her dad like Alice. . . .
Well, *of course* we found it all very touching, Shamus. In
fact, we're all still sitting here trying to recover from
seeing it . . ." Hazelton snapped his fingers impatiently
at his sister who was finally trying some of Stubb's crop,
but Betty Lou shook her head.

"You've had all afternoon and evening sucking this
stuff, you bum," she hissed. "It'll help me to sleep," and
she took another huge toke.

". . . The father-daughter thing, Shamus? . . . Yes,
that *is* quite a beautiful idea. . . . Well, sir, we'll be
looking forward to having you up here. Wonderful thing
for the district. Makes us feel we count with the rest of
America, way up here. . . . Yessir. Good night."

Melissa rubbed her hands together and looked at Alice
from wider and softer eyes. "I'm sorry I said that,
Alice." She spoke in a warm voice. "It was total cornball

what you did, and it worked and that makes it beautiful." She jumped up and ran over to sit down beside her
sister and kiss her cheek. "Just don't get too grown up
too quick, baby. There won't be anything left to do when
you're twenty."

"Alice will turn on the world when she's twenty," said
Nate Hazelton positively. "She's already been made a
Hero of Steam by me and when your dad and I get that
Shay going on my lumbering property, you'll be at her
regulator on the first run, Alice."

Alice, now a focus of approval, admiration, and love,
in addition to being recently named a Hero of Steam,
took a long and thoughtful toke on Stubb's thickest
reefer yet. "Curiouser and curiouser," she said in her
best, Alice-like voice.

# XII

AIR FORCE ONE CAME DOWN ON THE FAR END OF THE LONG Moosefoot runway, and when they had gotten about halfway along to the hangars the chief pilot turned and spoke laconically to his second. "Check the map again, Bill. I think we're on the Pennsy Turnpike."

"That must be Harrisburg in the far distance," said the second pilot. "Boy, they must really like trees up here."

The big jet finally reached the hangar apron and was directed to a circular area by the main gate. The door opened out, the stairs went down, and President O'Connell stepped onto the platform by the door to the spirited strains of massed central-school bands trying "Hail to the Chief," played he noted neither better nor worse than by a similar group of bands in South Chicago or at the L.A. Coliseum. "We govern a melting pot," said O'Connell to Happy Jack thoughtfully as he waved at the crowd, "and the same goop comes out the bottom no matter where you turn the tap."

But the President's philosophical mood was soon ended, for at the bottom of the stairway, in front of the massed, brightly-dressed band-persons stood stern General Beardsley in his dress uniform with sword, Nate Hazelton, and the Muth family.

President O'Connell stared at Congressman Hazelton in purest wonderment. Nate had on a raggedy set of bib overalls, found by Emmeline in a Moosefoot second-hand store, that looked and smelled as though they had been shoveled out of a manure pile, a ripped old L. L. Bean red and black hunting shirt, great green war-surplus parachutist's boots, and a floppy straw hat that President O'Connell was certain must have been the same one used by the model for Norman Rockwell's painting of Tom Sawyer. Nate also seemed to be chewing on a long, thick stalk of hay.

"Sorry not to have gotten myself up better for your visit, Shamus," said Hazelton earnestly, "but we've had some problems with the cows that've been keeping me up nights."

For one arrested moment, the President imagined himself smiling ever-so-sweetly at Nate Hazelton and saying, "What do they need with cows in the discos, brothels, and bondage parlors, Nate?" but he sadly understood that such pleasures had to be given up when one became the President.

"I'd like you to meet Betty Lou Muth, Mr. President, my sister and the wife of the *Langley*'s commander," said Hazelton, pointing his short beard stiffly at the cameras.

The President saw a pretty, sturdy woman in her forties, dressed in spartan, tweedy clothes. She stuck out her hand as a man would, catching the President by surprise. "It's an honor to meet you, President O'Connell," she said in a level, emotionless voice. "And this is my younger daughter, Alice," said Mrs. Muth turning to her right.

The President looked down smiling at pretty, smouldering Alice and realized he was staring into a political grave. He had his hand out and ready this time, but no small, answering hand came up to take it. "I won't shake his hand," said Alice in a dark, intense voice that all the wireless mikes could catch, while her large, hot eyes shot fire at O'Connell.

"Alice," said Mrs. Muth in her most modulated tones, stroking her daughter's lovely hair. "This man is Dad's Commander in Chief. Dad would want you to shake his hand."

Immediately Alice put her hand up and took the President's. "If Dad would want it, I'll do it," she said in a voice that managed to express a silky hatred for the President and unlimited love for Dad.

"Alice," said Shamus O'Connell, deeply panicked, his voice husky as he bent over her, "nobody is going to hurt your father or order him to do anything dangerous . . ." but he got no further, for Mrs. Muth had his arm and was pulling at him and saying loudly,

"Here are my two older children, Mr. President, Melissa and Bob Junior."

The President turned and was confronted by a quite lovely, yet teary face set against a huge buzzed-out hairdo, and next to it a tall young man who, O'Connell noted with a start, looked exactly like a World War II marine.

"I'll shake hands with President O'Connell," said Junior, hooking his left thumb in his belt like Gary Cooper did and sticking out a big paw. "I figure that anybody that gets to be President has to be plenty smart." Bob Junior pursed his lips. "He'll know what to do with the *Langley* . . ." he poked one huge foot into the dust and rubbed it around shyly, the way John Wayne did in *Stagecoach* when he talked to Claire Trevor, "soon as he's learned all there is to know about what she can do."

President O'Connell surrendered his hand to Junior's crushing grip. He felt utterly alone, surrounded by land mines named Alice Muth. He looked Junior in the eye. *Okay, sonny,* he thought, *you people are trying to ruin me up here. What in hell do you want?*

"Bob Junior," said President O'Connell with a steady smile, deciding to take the big risk in front of the cameras, "you seem to have pretty positive ideas about the *Langley*. What do *you* think she should do?"

Bob Junior smiled easily and ran his palm over his brush cut. "Well, Mr. President, the thing is no good as a bombing plane." He grinned at the cameras. "Anybody knows that. But it can fly anywhere and over any distance. Dad always said the best thing it could do was to fly right around the world, nonstop, over the Poles and the oceans. Turn it into a good-will flight, he said, a trip to show everyone how small the world really is and how much we're all tied together. Dad said it would be the last and greatest effort of aeronautics, a transpolar nonstop flight around the Earth."

President O'Connell looked into Bob Junior's earnest young face and suddenly saw what it was they were trying to sell him. The political abyss that had gaped at his feet slid soundlessly shut and, best of all, he thought exultantly, he would beat those damnable hawks and trouble-makers over Ice Island Three! Ideas bloomed in his head. He put his arm around Bob Junior's big shoulders. "General Beardsley," he said sternly to the man still stiffly at attention in front of them.

"Yes, Mr. President," said Beardsley, staring fiercely straight ahead.

"You heard what Bob Junior said. Is it possible? Can the *Langley* fly around the world?"

"Yes sir," said Beardsley. "All the aircraft are stocked for a two-week mission. We can circle the globe twice if you wish, sir."

"Once will be fine," said O'Connell dryly. "Now, I want us hooked into the *Langley* from right here, General. Is that possible? Can we transmit the same picture to them that the public is getting?"

General Beardsley relaxed a bit and gestured to his staff. "We'll have that ready in a minute, sir. And we'll need to get a monitor out here so you people can see them on board the *Langley*."

In a few minutes a big screen had been brought out in front of President O'Connell and the Muths and, after some fussing and adjustment, the *Langley*'s flight office cameras showed a wide-angle view of both Colonel Muth and Captain Jackson, now sitting at attention.

Shamus O'Connell was feeling better, second by second, and when he saw that the *Langley*'s copilot was black, he beamed a vast smile at the cameras pointing at him and saw the two men smile back. "Colonel Muth, Captain . . ." he looked quickly at a note in his hand, "Jackson. Gentlemen, do you recognize me as your Commander in Chief?"

"Yes, Mr. President," they answered in unison. O'Connell shone expansively at the big screen and tossed his white mane to show his enthusiasm. He was filled with ideas.

"I've decided, gentlemen," he said to them, "that my next order to the *Langley* will be given by my appointed deputy . . ." he looked quickly around, "Melissa Muth." President O'Connell put a fatherly arm around Melissa's slim waist. "You haven't said much, my dear," he said to her. "So why don't you be the one to order your father to do what Bob Junior suggested."

Melissa's beautiful grey eyes looked steadily out of the goop and the beehive hair. "Hi, Dad," she said in an easy, cool voice. "Listen, the takeoff was really sensational. Hi Gaby."

"Hi Melissa," said Captain Jackson with a shy grin. "Hey, your idea as to why that spline on the valve gear broke was right. The cam follower was jumping . . ."

President O'Connell cleared his throat and gave Melissa another fatherly squeeze. "Perhaps we should get to the orders dear," he said in her ear. "Then you can go on with your consultations later."

Melissa poked back a long, spring-like strand of hair and grinned a wide, yummy grin at the cameras. "Dad," she said, drawing herself up to a kind of relaxed and sinuous attention, "almost a hundred years ago a young woman reporter for the *New York World* named Nellie Bly went around the world by steam traction and steam shipping in eighty days, to show it was possible after

Jules Verne wrote his novel. Acting on behalf of the President of the United States, I order you, Dad, and the crew of the *Langley*, to attempt a transpolar circumnavigation of the globe, again by steam, but now in *eighty hours!*"

Melissa Muth stood tall, staring out at the cameras, and all over America, other young women stood tall at their sinks in their plastic hairdos and imagined themselves sternly ordering *their* fathers, brothers or husbands to do something exciting and historic.

President O'Connell would have smiled even more widely, if that were still possible. These Muths were making this all so easy, he exulted to himself. They've figured the whole scam out to the final crossing of the T's. Jesus, he thought, Nellie Bly, Jules Verne, eighty days and eighty hours . . . beautiful!

The nation watched handsome Bob Muth turn and grin easily at his dark, serious copilot. "Well, Captain Jackson, what do you think? Can we do that?"

George Abraham Jackson set his jaw the way he imagined Fred Marriott probably did when he climbed into the little racer, then nodded. "I think she'll do it, Colonel. Steam Bird is singing to us now!"

Colonel Muth smiled at his daughter from the screen. "We'll be over the Pole in three hours, Meliss. We acknowledge your orders and will carry them out to the very best of our abilities." He paused, then, "Oh, and you guys help Mom while I'm traveling, okay?"

Much as he would have liked to keep this warm, family scene going, President O'Connell well knew the short attention span of the electorate. "To bring this to a close, ladies and gentlemen," and he bowed slightly right and left, "I think the last word should belong to . . ." and the President went down on one knee, peering and grinning around Betty Lou Muth's legs, "Alice!"

Alice smiled back most warmly at the President and O'Connell hitched forward with knee and foot to put an arm around her shoulders and bask in that sweet glow. The cameras zoomed in.

"Dad," said Alice to the cameras, and now her face had a thoughtful, ethereal cast. "I think Nellie Bly is up there with you now. And all the old aviators . . . and the steam men too. They're all blessing you and the *Langley*. And they'll be riding with you, all the way around the world."

President O'Connell blinked and gave Alice another hug. "What lovely, gentle thoughts you have, Alice," he said in a thick voice. "You really are a remarkable child . . ."

But Alice suddenly decided she had gone on quite far enough with the P. T. Barnum stuff and she gave President O'Connell a smile from the *real* Alice Muth, perky, full of jokes and hokum, eyes sparkling with mischief and she seized the President in a bear hug and planted a big, wet smack on his lips. "I *really* think you're nice," she said grinning. "You're like Uncle Nate!"

And it was strange, but of the many accolades and honors that President Shamus O'Connell received over a long, rich, and active life, there were few, if any, that meant more than that frank acknowledgment of his political competence by twelve-year-old and fellow politician, Alice Muth.

The tour of the Moosefoot facility was pressed along at maximum speed and the President had to admit as he looked at the *Langley*'s sister craft, the *Sir Hiram Maxim*, that things up in Moosefoot had certainly gotten out of hand. "Jack," he said in an awed voice, "that thing wouldn't need to explode. A crash would set off an earthquake." He stood in the middle of the vast array of huge, mushed tires trying to imagine it lifting in flight, but Jack made no response. He spoke not one word at Moosefoot, just walked about shaking his head like a dour undertaker at a cheap funeral.

They were able to climb back into Air Force One just about at noon and retire at once to the President's small, private bar at the aircraft's stern.

President O'Connell, feeling more relaxed than he

could remember, carefully selected two spring-water ice cubes and dropped them in the large crystal glass. Then the Jack Daniels. He carefully studied the brown fluid, noting how the melting ice cubes patterned the brown whiskey next to the cold cubes. "Boy, do I deserve this," he said with a happy sigh, knocking back half the glass in a single gulp.

But Happy Jack still frowned his wrinkled, disgruntled look. "Oh, you were fine after you got the Muth kids on your side, Shamus. How could you help it? Jesus, those little bastards had everything taped. Of course Hazelton coached them. Damn!"

The President grinned at his aide. "Jack, Jack! Don't you see it yet? They worked it all out for us, the *Langley*, the ice island, the works!"

"Yeah," said Happy Jack bitterly. "We're absolutely up shit creek on the ice island, Shamus. How the hell can we deny the thing to the military after it's been made a nine-day wonder by the *Langley*? And the Russians have us by the balls. It is ice!"

It wasn't often that Shamus O'Connell got ahead of Jack and he was in no hurry to end the fun. "So," said the President thoughtfully, "you'd say, suppress publicity on the flight? Keep the press away from the landing with a secrecy order? Keep mum?"

Happy Jack shrugged. "Try and do it after little Miss Nellie Bly and Jules Verne and whatever new bullshit they come up with," he said sourly. "Look at this *Times* head, Shamus. 'Steam Bird Almost Over the Pole.' Steam Bird! Jesus, who would guess that such a hotbed of kooks could be hatching their eggs in Moosefoot, Maine, for God's sake!"

The President poured his aide a drink, identical to his own and put the glass in direct contact with Happy Jack's clenched fist. "Drink that quietly and soberly, Jack," said Shamus O'Connell grinning, "for the sun is over the yardarm and all is right with the world."

He put up a finger. "This isn't an Air Force sabre-rattle any more, Jack. It's a good-will mission and record attempt. You heard the young man. Now, Jack, good-will missions do not end in the annexation of provocative and destabilizing bomber bases. I mean, even the Soviets in their hardest-edged moments would never try and pull that kind of stunt. So we've already chopped a good part of the limb out from under Zinkowski and the missile and aerospace senators."

The President mixed another drink and grinned. "Okay, the landing is a big deal on Ice Island Three, right? Wire service, direct TV link, the works. Now, and stay with me, Jack," said the President, waving his finger again. "After this great thing is ended, what do I announce about the *Langley* and Ice Island Three? Jack, there's only one thing we can do with them. Hell, the *Langley* can't be put in the Smithsonian."

"It's bigger than the Smithsonian, Shamus."

"Right. Also it's hotter than hell. So what to do? Well, the *Langley* can be stored permanently on Ice Island Three at almost no expense. We dig a hole and the ice shields the hot reactor. We know the island is permanent, so the thing can stay up there in the freezer forever. Now, we need our airport there to have access, to caretake this great historic treasure, right? There might even be air tours out of Alaska so some of those steam weirdos can come up and walk inside the shielded part of the *Langley* and look at the damn huge thing. So we have to run the airport since it's our treasure we're looking after, but otherwise we announce that the UN can operate the place. Furthermore, get this Jack, in memory of all the long-distance flyers who have been lost in the Arctic, Langley Ice Field will be open to assist *all* aircraft in trouble at the Pole. How about that, baby? The Russians can't touch it because our big toy is permanently up there and there's no way Professor Busy-Nasty and the cutlass-in-the-teeth crowd can start cramming nuclear bombers into a new shrine to American technology that is open to the world of steam and any other nuttos who get excited over really big things. The place will be neutralized as long as the *Langley* stays hot. Ice Island Three and the *Langley* deserve each other, Jack. We're just going to officiate at the wedding."

And now it was finally possible to see how Happy Jack's name came about, for the lines and wrinkles of his face dissolved and restructured themselves, changing him from a sour, wizened parish priest listening in contempt and shock to the world's duplicity in a confessional, to a sprightly old leprechaun, waking in a bed of shamrocks to find the buttercups swaying over him. "You saw all that with those Muth children, eh Shamus?" said Happy Jack chuckling and shaking his head. "Well, I've always said that the only thing that saves the Republic is that thieves are either unable to combine, or else they eventually fall out. Imagine Zinkowski, Busy-Nasty and those kids in one big package. Why, we'd be attacking Moscow right now!" He sipped his drink, grinning, but his smile was thoughtful. "If the island is open to everyone, what about Russian bombers?"

Shamus O'Connell winked. "Well, Jack, where would you rather have a Russian bomber, sitting on the ice island while we try to find it gas and parts, or attacking Seattle?" The President sighed contentedly. "The great game. Kipling said it. And it's fun to win, Jack!"

Jack Hanrahan slapped his well-tailored knee and broke into a long bright laugh that would not have disgraced the King of the Fairies himself. "Game, Shamus!" he said wiping his eyes, now bubbling over with mirth. "This is no parlor game, sweetie! This is governing a gigantic mental institution using the methods of street theatre! Last month, the defecting Bulgarian ballet troupe at the airport. This month, Alice Muth, Dad, and the *Langley*, your friendly, flying nuclear terror. Next month . . ."

Now President O'Connell chuckled. "Next month, Jack, since they won't get the ice island, we face the so-called racetrack missile system with the big trucks . . ." President O'Connell paused and swished some whiskey around in his mouth to help in catching hold of a random thought. "Jack, those missile trucks. Are there, well, *truck freaks*? You know, people who might want to build the largest trucks or pull the largest loads? . . ."

But Happy Jack was not going to darken a moment that had turned so sunny. "We've got to live this one day at a time, Shamus," he said, relaxing back in his seat. "Let's enjoy Steam Bird's flight along with everyone else."

"Steam Bird," said the President, shaking his head. "I can understand sex, straight and kinky, booze, drugs, cruises to other lands, Miami condos, fast cars, the thousand dollar window at Churchill Downs, roller discos, all that stuff. But Jack . . . steam?"

Congressman Hazelton and the Muths arrived back at the Moosefoot house in a state of noisy elation to find that Stubb, a lifelong if non-voting Republican, had missed the President to smoke and cook up his own special doughnuts in the Muth's deep-fat pot, so that mounds of coarse-sugared, weirdly-shaped doughnuts covered the dining table. It took no time for them to brew up some cocoa and coffee, joining Stubb for a few more tokes, and sit down to a stoned doughnut glut.

Nate Hazelton, who had changed out of his costume, dusted the thick sugar crystals from his silk vest and beamed at the children. "Well, you all know how good you were. I don't need to tell you that," he said heartily. He turned to his sister. "I told you Shamus would work it out. Junior and Melissa made him an offer he simply couldn't refuse."

"But Dad still has to land it, Uncle Nate," said practical Alice. "It's monstrous! It's going to come down fast!"

"Bob will do it, and we'll be there to watch, my friends," said Hazelton. "Shamus has offered to take us up with him on Air Force One when they make the landing on the ice island. He's finally realized that the whole steam and around-the-world thing can be used to deny the Pentagon the ice island. Let's face it. This is fun for us, but it's also going to keep the world from blowing apart for a few months longer."

Bob Junior chewed angrily on his doughnut. "They're always trying to stir things up in Washington, Uncle Nate," he said in a bitter voice.

Hazelton shrugged. "Our hobby happens to be steam. Their hobby is mass murder. Believe me, with friends like the Pentagon and the Joint Chiefs, you don't need enemies!"

But these sombre thoughts were instantly dispersed by the arrival of Emmeline from upstairs, fetchingly, indeed spectacularly dressed in a wonderfully tight set of loco engineer's overalls and a jaunty, blue-striped runner's cap bearing the Tidewater Northern's distinctive logo, a dollar sign rampant on a loco chimney.

"Emmeline?" said Hazelton in astonishment. "It's lovely, but what are you going to do, dear? The corn is all picked up here now."

Melissa peered sternly at her uncle. "Emmeline wants to run an engine on the Tidewater Northern, and I'm going to show her how," she said in a firm, no-nonsense voice. "Emmeline and I can double-head the division peddler freight, then break the train at Bridgton and give it two numbers. Emmeline will drill the Beaver Dam branch while I sort the cars for the Bridgton yard." She looked around. "Anyone who wants to come and be yardmaster and Div. Super is welcome."

Hazelton stared at the two denim pockets on Emmeline's blue-striped bib, which had the size and solidity of large cantaloupes. "Will she be able to see the throttle, Melissa?" said Hazelton in a doubtful voice.

Stubb Moody, who had been staring bug-eyed at Emmeline and licking his lips, now grinned and slapped his knee. "Dang me!" he said. "If they'd had enjine drivers like thet on the Bangor and Aroostook, I'd be workin' on thet railroad tuday!"

Melissa stamped her foot in anger. "She can just sit back a little, Uncle Nate! Now you cut that out! It's really absolutely disgusting how completely and totally sexist this family can get. C'mon Emmeline. We'll go and run the peddler."

Emmeline followed Melissa to the stairs, then turned to give everyone a big smile and to wave the tips of her soft, pink fingers back at them.

Congressman Hazelton smiled fondly after his secretary and sighed. "If Emmeline catches the bug I'll have to take her to the steam meets." He tried to imagine Emmeline chatting about the details of Caprotti valve-gear linkages, but the vision utterly escaped him. "Alice," he said to his niece as he got to his feet, "I will be the Tidewater Yardmaster and you can be the switchman . . . er, switchperson, at Bridgton. And if Emmeline gets her train up to Beaver Dam, I may take everyone out to dinner."

XIII

THE *LANGLEY* CROSSED THE NORTH POLE AND COLONEL
Muth notified General Beardsley that the mission had
begun. The aircraft now ran with port and starboard
watches, like a ship, with Colonel Muth and Captain
Jackson in charge of the respective watchstanders. The
White House had decided to send them south over the
Pacific, so that the ending of the trip would involve the
flight north up between Europe and the east coast of
the US.

They started their long run south, making their closest
approach to Russia as they passed over the Bering Strait,
then the Aleutians and out over the Pacific. They passed
Japan several hundred miles to the east . . . White
House thinkers had worried over the *Langley*, an atomic
airplane, passing close to the only nation ever attacked
by atomic weapons . . . but dozens of planes still went
out to see the gigantic machine go by and the price of
seats on commercial sightseeing charters went to many
thousands of yen. Indeed, the various Japanese chapters
of the Brotherhood of Live Steamers accounted for two
747s full and many more were turned away.

Several aircraft carriers, including the huge *Maxim
Gorky*, managed to get themselves near or under the

Langley when she went by overhead and to fly an honor guard of jets to accompany her for a few hundred miles. The aerobatics team from the *Gorky* went one better and did several spectacular stunts with the *Langley* as a kind of centerpiece. Their final turn consisted of six aircraft in line-astern making a huge, vertical circle well ahead of the *Langley*, then turning on the colored smoke and spiraling in, one at a time, and finally shooting straight out at Mach 2 on their afterburners as they each made a giant roll. The effect put the atomic plane at the center of a gigantic, colored spiral dish or target from which it entered a tunnel of smokes.

"As street theatre goes," said Shamus O'Connell to Jack Hanrahan as they watched the TV shots of all this, "we're packing them in. Let's hope the colonel can land that damn thing."

Happy Jack frowned. "Jesus, Shamus, could he actually blow up in front of his own kids?"

The President shook his head thoughtfully. "Jack, I've been looking through those damn idiot books. You wouldn't believe all that's in there! If the plane should take a dive on the landing and dump out the reactor, *we're* the ones most likely to be crisped or zapped. You see, for the thing to come loose, the *Langley* will be more or less stopped, you know, crashed. They estimate the reactor would have to roll several hundred yards further on before it collapsed enough to detonate, which is likely to be in the middle of Ice Island Three. The crew is probably OK, assuming they weathered the crash, since they're in a heavily protected and shielded cabin. It's the people out on the field that have to stand the gaff."

"Shit," said Happy Jack. "The Secret Service will be pissing in their diapers about that."

"They already have," answered O'Connell, "but they also actually have a plan. We'll watch her come in from an ice trench with that crazy Moosefoot general, that fellow Beardsley. He'll decide if the *Langley* has, or is about to, dump her bloody abortion on the ice. We then have about fifty seconds to go rapidly down into a shelter directly below the trench. Everybody on the island will go into the shelters in an emergency except the men in the two shielded crash-trucks. They'll get the crew out and bring them down. We'll have the press planes and Air Force One circling way back up out of harm's way. They're getting it all dug up now. The problem is that since this isn't a bomb they designed, it could be pretty dirty and keep us in the shelters for a couple of days."

Happy Jack leaned back and ground his teeth. "One thing after another! But you've got to be up there, Shamus. The chances are that they'll get down okay and you can make your proclamation right out there on the ice in your parka, after you decorate that gang of raving cuckoos. Then we can disband Moosefoot AFB and forget about Ice Island Three . . . for twenty thousand years anyway."

"Oh, I think Muth will do it all right, Jack. Good grief, look at that family. If he can deal with all of that, and Nate Hazelton too, hell, the *Langley*'s just one more weird trip."

After another large escort from Australian and New Zealand air fleets, the *Langley* passed over the South Pole and paused to make one huge circle, dropping a hardwood wreath carved with the names of all the explorers who had perished in these regions. This cere- mony was photographed from a long-distance chase copter off the chopper carrier USS *Norton Bank*, flying far below the atomic airplane. The little red, white, and blue chute with the large wooden wreath hanging below popped open in the cold air and, as the memento drifted down on the totally empty ice and the huge, distant *Langley* continued its wide, graceful circle, the black names came slowly down across the TV screen, starting with Sir Robert Scott.

"Ah," said Hazelton unbuttoning his coat and settling back. "This has certainly been a classy flight." He turned to his sister. "Bob thought up the wreath bit. End of the age of exploration, all that stuff."

"Well, it's very easy to play the con man, Nate," said

Betty Lou, frowning and blinking at the screen. She had found the stark image of the vast circle of ice, the distant plane in its gentle arc, and the names marching down the screen, not just knights and Gentlemen of the King, but seamen and dog drivers, sergeant gunners and plain misters, quite moving and appropriate. "You know, Nate," she said, "if our children looked up to those good, brave men instead of the rock freaks, egomaniacs and disco-trippers, we might have one tiny prayer for some kind of decent future."

Nate Hazelton sipped his scotch and pondered. Finally he shook his head. "It's a great idea, Lou, but it didn't really work. All that stiff-upper-lip stuff. Sacrificing to reach the Pole no matter what. It all just delivered a generation of them to the trenches." Hazelton squeezed his sister's arm. "But the *idea* of some interesting and worthwhile goal is good, Lou. That has to be good. We just can't seem to hit on the right combination."

"I think steam is the answer," came a positive voice from a dark corner, for Alice had crept silently in to watch the *Langley* drop the wooden wreath.

"Ah," said the congressman in surprise. "A planner in our midst, I see and hear. Do we have everybody dig coal and pound spikes for the steam locos, Alice? There'd be precious few driver's jobs and a tremendous number of diggers and pounders."

"You have to get everybody *interested* in steam first," said Alice. "Then people would work on the railways as a hobby and eventually they would work enough to let them drive a train, instead of getting wages."

"What do they do for food and shelter, Alice, when they aren't actually driving?" asked Nate.

Alice wrinkled her nose. "Nobody works much any more, Uncle Nate. And running trains does get people places so the government could just give them the food and let them live in some old army camp. There's millions of them around."

"You see, Lou," said Hazelton looking fierce over his glasses, "she admits to being a railfan and steam freak, your honor, but in fact the child is a raving socialist, freebie-commune, barter-society leftwinger."

Betty Lou Muth wiped her eyes over the last name, that of Captain Oates of the Iniskilling Dragoons, who walked away from Scott's party at night to die and not risk their safety. Then she drained her scotch and shrugged. "Well, she's probably right, Nate. Nobody works very much. Nothing works very good. So what's wrong with letting a bunch of harmless neurotics run replica *Flying Scotsman* trains of Gresley teak coaches at one hundred miles an hour and live off surplus food in Quonset huts? Could they possibly do any worse than the fools running the railways now, Nate? And it would *have* to be cheaper!"

 XIV

THEN, NORTH OF THE FALKLANDS AND EAST OF PATAGONIA, Steam Bird began to show teething problems. "Bob," said Gaby in a tight voice, "we're beginning to take some heavy water loss from the condenser."

Bob Muth stared over at the computer display in front of Captain Jackson. "Where? Which wing?"

Gaby was interrogating the various flow meters in the vast steam-flow system. He pointed to the starboard wing. "Out at the end. A condenser seam must have opened up. We're bleeding to death, Bob!"

"Isolate it! Shut the primary valves to that section!" gritted Bob Muth; then, "Harry! We're cutting out a quarter of the starboard condenser. Pay attention!"

"Hang on . . ." A pause from Major Fisk as he consulted his own computer. "Bob, that'll leave us with eighty-two percent of thrust. We should stabilize at thirteen thousand feet and 210 knots. The trouble is, if the condenser is having problems with differential air temperatures, things will get worse in that denser air. The higher we stay above the low-altitude weather, the better."

Muth shook his head in frustration. "What'll we do,

Gaby? Can we isolate that bad section more closely and get some condenser capacity back?"

Jackson shook his head. "No way, Bob. We'd need a zillion more valves to do that. We're lucky to lose only that much capacity."

As the big plane began to slide gradually downward, its reactor running at a lesser power level because the condenser could no longer handle maximum steam flow, Gaby hunted through the specification and in-flight emergency write-ups while Colonel Muth called the Air Force for help.

The off-duty crew, hearing about the emergency on the intercom, drifted into the flight office while Muth talked impatiently to a variety of specialists and communications people at a variety of locations. "Gaby," he said bitterly, "they don't give a damn about this! I'm getting nothing but sympathy from Edwards AFB, the Pentagon, Texas, the Chief Scientist's office, the whole stupid bunch. All they're feeding us is a bunch of the old 'good luck' crap. They want us in the drink . . . or worse! They know if we get to Ice Island Three, they've lost it."

Harry Fisk, who had come forward for a moment to meet with his commander face to face, grinned and shrugged. "Come on, Bob. You knew we'd be pretty much out on our own at this point. What about Moosefoot?"

"Try and *get* Moosefoot!" said Muth in a sudden fury. "We've got twenty-nine different communicators at us now! Gaby, see if you can reach Beardsley on our special frequency."

A moment later Captain Jackson touched Bob Muth's arm and Muth switched channels to hear the distinguished and measured tones of General Bertram Beardsley. "Colonel Muth, good show so far. Sorry to hear about your little problem. Our main computer suggests an application of some SSH, that is, sprayable silicon hardener into the offending condenser entrance passage. Come back to me after you consider that, please."

Bob Muth frowned and shook his head in bewilderment, but Major Fisk snapped his fingers on both hands. "The goop, Bob, the goop!" he shouted.

The several men standing behind the two pilots' chairs all turned as one to look at Harry Fisk, his bald pate shining in the cabin lights.

"Goop?" said Muth in a whisper.

Fisk nodded in excitement. "They gave us some silicon fixit crud. You remember, years ago? To squirt into the bad passages in a leaky condenser and seal off the bum section. If we can find the split seam and flow that stuff into the air channels on each side of it, it'll expand and solidify in the cold air and stop the water loss. The tiny amount of condenser we lose that way won't even be noticeable."

Colonel Muth nodded, half-talking to himself. "Yeh, that would do it, but we'd have to go outside the secondary shield, Harry."

Fisk leaned over Muth's shoulder and put his right hand down over the colonel's own. "You and I could do it, Bob. We've had our families. If we're quick, it won't be too awful a dose. Just remember not to have any chest X-rays afterward."

Muth nodded. "You're volunteering to go out there with me, Harry? Is that correct?"

Major Fisk smiled. "Definitely."

Muth stared at the control panel and sighed, then turned to Captain Jackson. "Gaby, you're the plane commander while we're doing our thing. Call Washington and tell them what's happening." Muth paused, then smiled wanly at his copilot. "Ah . . . you better not call them until we're on our way. They are sure as hell going to order us not to try it."

Gaby Jackson looked at Bob Muth from under drawn, frowning eyebrows. "I wish *I* could order you not to try it, Bob," he said in a tense voice.

Bob Muth gripped the copilot's arm. "You'd give that, your right arm, to drive a Consolidation through snow drifts to Gunnison on the South Park Railway, right? We're not even offering that big a sacrifice."

But Captain Jackson was not satisfied. "Bob, when you two go outside, let us cut the reactor back to minimum activity. For God's sake, do that at least! So what if we lose a couple of thousand feet? We'll get it all back if you stop the leak. Give yourself a chance!"

Bob Muth looked up at his flight engineer and Major Fisk nodded. "We can do that," he said. "Tell my gang to pull back on the throttle just when we get to the wing crawlway. Now, where the hell did they stash the goop and the sprayers?" He seized a mike and spoke with General Beardsley.

A few minutes later, dressed in white radiation suits and bedraped with oxygen systems, Colonel Muth and Major Fisk paused at the entrance to the starboard wing access door and hefted their sprayers. "Cut back, Gaby," said Fisk, and the assistant reactor engineers quickly reduced reactor power to a condition of minimum stable criticality.

"Go, Bob and Harry!" came Gaby's voice on the intercom system and the two men opened the tiny shielded door and began a long crawl through a narrow passageway out into the wing condenser complex. The nuclear reactor of the *Langley* was located deep in the center of the fuselage and was primarily shielded by a massive lead spherical enclosure. The crew area forward had a thick, secondary lead shield wall which Muth and Fisk now left behind, and entered an increased radiation field. They rapidly worked their way out into the wing. The tunnels to the condensers ran along the top of the thick wing and passed over hundreds of panels which could be opened downwards to give the repair crews access to all parts of the aluminum heat exchangers. The problem now was to find the exact section of the condenser that had split apart.

When they reached the outer end of the starboard condenser system, Colonel Muth spoke over the intercom to Captain Jackson. "Open that valve now, Gaby. We've got to see the steam plume if we're going to stop it."

"Washington is screaming to forget it," said Gaby in a hot voice. "They're ordering you back inside the secondary shield now!"

"Washington people live in Washington, Gaby," said Bob Muth patiently. "We live here over the South Atlantic and we're heading down into it. Open the valve, please."

"Done!"

Muth and Fisk began to open inspection panels, one after another, but they could not see the leak. "Gaby, are we leaking still . . . at this lower power level, or did the damn seam go back together?" said Fisk in a tight voice.

"It's definitely leaking," said Captain Jackson. "The starboard gunners can see the steam plume. You're a little far out, I think. They estimate it at between station sixty-five and station seventy."

The two men crawled in toward the fuselage a bit and began opening new access panels. A few moments later they both breathed together, "There it is!" Sure enough, squirting steam was now filling the space beneath them and blowing everywhere; up into the crawl space warming their chilled bodies, out into the cold air behind the plane. Without a word the two men brought the nozzles of their sprayers into position and began to squirt the silicon compound into the air-flow entrance of the leaking condenser section. The steam plume grew less, the air around them cleared, and finally the leak stopped completely. Muth and Fisk clapped each other's back.

"Come back. It's fixed!" cried Captain Jackson, and the two men began a rapid crawl back toward the fuselage. As they hastened along on hands and knees, Bob Muth musingly said to Major Fisk, "You know, Harry, when the British dirigible R-100 went to Canada, he lost the covering on a tail fin and the crew climbed out into the framework and repaired it in flight, sort of like what we were doing."

Major Fisk took a gulp of oxygen and adjusted his throat mike as he crawled. "Not quite the same, Bob," he said somberly. "They didn't need film badges and dosimeters then." He paused, then muttered in a melancholy voice, "I wonder if the rest of my hair will fall out."

Yet as soon as they reached the door into the secondary shield, Major Fisk spoke briskly to his subordinates, "Full power! Goose it! Let's get that altitude back."

When they reached the flight office, Gaby Jackson peered at his commander as though expecting him to glow. "General Fishbein, some crazy old broad from AF public relations, was raving on the radio, Bob. She said you and Harry going out in the wing would wreck the Air Force, destroy our image, all kinds of stuff like that. I said right back you should have the biggest medals ever made . . ."

Bob Muth had been studying his pocket dosimeter and he smiled. "So horrible Hurta cares after all?" he said musingly. "Maybe there's hope for a better world in store. Actually, Gaby, they give people with rectal cancer much bigger radiation jolts than we got."

Gaby bit his lip and frowned. "Yeh, Bob, but yours is a whole-body dose." He suddenly snatched away Bob's dosimeter and studied it. His face brightened. "Well, it's not too bad, you know. I figured you two would be parboiled out in that field, but it'll take more than this to cook two tough old Moosefooters." Gaby was breathing deeply and happily wiping his eyes.

Muth slapped his copilot on the back. "Cutting back on the reactor power was a good thought, old buddy. Maybe we're going to get away with this. Just pray that the rest of the condensers hold together. If we get many more leaks like that one, some of you younger fellows may have to volunteer."

"I think I'd rather wait for a vasectomy," said a grinning Captain Jackson.

XV

THE *LANGLEY* PASSED NORTH OVER THE SOUTH ATLANTIC without further incident, but at the latitude of Washington, D.C. the huge atomic carrier, *Richard M. Nixon*, waited impatiently with its own aerobatics team. They had spent two days looking at the TV tapes of the *Gorky*'s effort and practicing their own goodies, so the show, now involving eight aircraft, was spectacular, with the *Langley* serving as the centerpiece of smoke flower-bunches, pinwheels, and assorted woven, colored-yarn effects. The most impressive stunt was, in fact, one of the simplest. The navy jets, with their flaps partly down, bunched in two groups of four each and flew about a quarter-mile ahead of the *Langley*, so close together that their wings overlapped one above the other. On signal, each group let loose a heavy dose of colored smoke, each plane in the group squirting a different color. The four smoke plumes, staying in four relatively separate vortices, entered the five huge fan entrances on each side of the *Langley*. The position of the smoke from each jet had been figured out so that when the big fans blew the smoke through the condensers and out the entire rear edge of the *Langley*'s wing, two gigantic smoke rainbows were formed, the red smoke being farthest out towards the tips, blending with the yellow to make a smear of orange, then green and violet blending to make blue. For several moments the *Langley*'s two entire wings spun out a complete rainbow of smoke on each side and the two colored ribbons blew backwards and finally united far behind the vast machine.

Watching from Air Force One, President O'Connell slapped Happy Jack on the back and chuckled. "Look at that, Jack. Our boys can outfly, outshoot and outfuck the Russkies anytime!"

"There are damn few political problems that are solved by flying, shooting and fucking," said Jack irritably.

"Professor Busy-Nasty wouldn't agree with that, Jack. His whole idea is to roll your eyes, grit your teeth, then drop your pants."

Jack snorted. "Busy-Nasty! A fuck would turn him into a pumpkin, alright! Shamus, if they had queers on Mars, they'd have to look like the professor."

"Steady, Jack," said O'Connell, looking furtively around the big central cabin. "The gays vote . . . like the eco-weirdos, remember?"

"It's all the same bunch," said Jack. "What this administration needs is a federally-supported public restroom program, warm places where people can make friends unmolested . . . and which uses recycled toilet paper and towels plus soap made from vegetable fats."

"*Sotto voce*, Jack!" said O'Connell again, darting glances around. "They're everywhere, you know. Waiting to catch us using words like fag and fruit . . . Ah, the navy boys are all done and off we go to Moosefoot."

"Dinner with the Muths," said Happy Jack with a twisted smile. "Dinner with the PLO and the IRA Provos would make more sense, and probably be safer."

President O'Connell gave Jack a grin. "Jack, the Muths are international celebrities, as well as being the most down-home folks since Harry and Bess Truman.

Colonel Muth has already been awarded more decorations from countries he's gone past than anyone else, including three from Iron Curtain air forces."

"You going to let him take those?"

"You bet we are, Jack. This is a good-will flight to knit us all together, remember? And I understand that we'll have a chance to see and even operate Colonel Muth's remarkable railroad, one of the most electronically-advanced in the country, anyway, according to Alice Muth, who talked to Dave this morning."

"Railroad?" said Happy Jack incredulously, "The son-of-a-bitch owns a . . . oh, you mean the hobby toys?"

"No, no, Jack," said Shamus O'Connell. "A model. It works exactly like the real thing. The electronics make the little engines run exactly like the real ones, at least that's what the child told Dave."

"Well, if you try something like that, you'll just make a damn fool of yourself in front of the press."

O'Connell shrugged. "If a twelve-year-old can do it, and Nate Hazelton can do it, I sure as hell can do it too."

The press was excluded from the actual spaghetti dinner at the Muths, so that the President could speak frankly with these typical citizens without fear of instant quoting. Extra leaves had been put in the dining room table and extra tables put in the closed-off living room for the press and Secret Service people. In spite of some White House press output, very little, in fact nothing at all, was said at dinner about the debt, abortion, Washington's insensitivity, or praying in the schools. Instead, things seemed to center about what General Beardsley had, earlier, called the world of steam.

After a brief grace and prayer for the *Langley* by Betty Lou, the President lifted his head and blinked, for he was seated across from Nate and Emmeline, once again resplendent in her Tidewater Northern driver's uniform. He cleared his throat. "Well, Nate, it certainly looks like Miss Pangini is ready to drive a train."

Congressman Hazelton shot out his most genial smile. "Emmeline is a recent convert to railways, Shamus. Melissa showed her how to run the peddler and drill the Beaver Dam branch and she's been at it ever since. A rail nut if I ever saw one."

"Ah," said Shamus O'Connell radiating cheerfulness in every direction and focusing his gaze on Emmeline's bursting pockets. "Well, I can see there's much more to this steam business than I imagined."

"Drill the Beaver branch?" said Happy Jack absently, his eyes also riveted on Emmeline.

Nate Hazelton chuckled. "Emmeline drove a freight train up the branch line to the Beaver Dam end, Mr. Hanrahan. In fact, that would be a good way for you to start, Mr. President."

"You've *got* to do it," said Alice positively to O'Connell. "The man on the phone said you would."

But Shamus O'Connell had no intention of *not* running the Muth's toy trains. "Can I wear a hat like that, Alice?" asked O'Connell, pointing at Emmeline's head, "and can Miss Pangini . . . May I call you Emmeline, dear, since we're going to be engineers together? . . . run the other train with me?"

"We'll get you dressed up right, Shamus," said Nate at once. "You're big. You can get into Bob's outfit. How about it, Emmeline? Want to double-head the peddler with the President?"

Emmeline colored prettily and nodded, smiling sweetly and tilting her head. Shamus O'Connell beamed some more and helped himself to spaghetti. When the conversation shifted briefly away from him, he leaned over to whisper in Jack's ear. "Jack, is our photo man here with the wire service people?"

Happy Jack nodded. "Right. There's Fogarty and the two pool men. We're limited by the Muths to three photo people down cellar, what with the Secret Service and the rest."

"Okay," said O'Connell, "see if Fogarty can possibly get me and Emmeline playing trains together, from at least the waist up, Emmeline in front, my profile just behind. You see it, Jack?"

Happy Jack's wrinkles transmuted into his best leprechaun grin. "Four by six feet I see it, on the walls of the labor precincts I see it . . . you bet I see it, Shamus!"

O'Connell beamed and beamed as he let his eyes linger on Emmeline. "It won't matter what we write underneath. They can cut that off. But I'll be right up there next to Emmeline. Be sure we both have those hats on. And Jack, tell Fogarty that the picture has to clearly show *Emmeline instructing me* in running the thing, right? Young railroad enthusiast shows the President how to run her advanced electronic train set is the message. We don't want any flat-chested, and possibly militant, ladies to think we're exploiting any particular physical portion of Emmeline for some nefarious male purpose." O'Connell chuckled quietly.

The operating session was a great success, even though the narrow-gauge roundhouse did get scrunched by a clambering photographer. Emmeline guided the President with her pink, gentle fingertips through his first drilling of the Beaver Dam branch and the resulting pictures became, two years later, a sensation in the reelection campaign.

It wasn't long before President O'Connell was driving the *Dixie Flyer* at over ninety and he and Alice were only deterred from having a final try with one of the big coal drags up Sherman Hill by an aide whispering in the President's ear, "Sir, if we're going to get to the Pole with the *Langley*, we've got to go at once."

O'Connell sighed. "Ladies and Gentlemen," he said loudly. "We must adjourn to Air Force One. The *Langley* will be reaching the Pole in the morning."

The layout was shut down and everybody went clumping up the wide stairs, Alice and the President chatting amiably as they climbed.

"And you say the *Morning Hi* went between Chicago and the Twin Cities at over eighty, Alice?" asked the recent convert to steam, Shamus O'Connell.

"The fastest steam-hauled services in the world," answered Alice positively. "President O'Connell, why can't the railroads do things like that now?"

The President turned his head and saw Jack coming up behind them. "Why is it we can't build and run decent railroads any more, Jack?" he said in a plaintive voice.

"Why should the railroads be any exception?" answered Jack, shrugging in surprise.

"If we went back to steamers," said Alice excitedly, "we could use American coal and everybody who wanted could learn to drive or fire, and . . ."

The President sadly shook his head, then took Alice's hand and squeezed it. "They'd *never* let us do it, Alice; EPA, NOAH, NIOSH, NIH, Commerce, Labor, the clean air societies, the UAW, the noise pollution people, the Teamsters, the Railway Brotherhoods, Exxon, the . . ."

"But, you're the *President*?" said a bewildered Alice. "If *you* can't do anything . . ."

The child and the man stared at each other for an instant in a kind of complete and shared comprehension and Alice shivered.

"Alice," said Shamus O'Connell, warmly putting a hand to her cheek, "you see, dear, we have to get through each day . . ." but then he stopped and gave her a large smile. "It isn't a compartment on the Broadway Limited, Alice, but you can sleep in a berth on Air Force One and then, tomorrow, your Dad will be back on the ground. Think of that!"

Alice cheered up at once. "And then after you boot Dad and the rest out of the Air Force, we'll get Uncle Nate's Shay fixed up and in steam." She clapped her hands. "And it has the loveliest whistle!"

The *Langley* crossed over the North Pole for the second time just a few minutes less than eighty hours after the first crossing, to the accolades of the world, then headed south again to her landing at the ice island. Air Force One left the Pole and scooted on ahead to the island so as to disembark her passengers and get back into the air before the *Langley* showed up.

Halfway down the runway were a series of slit trenches, set well back, and leading down to rapidly-assembled blast and fallout shelters in case the landing turned sour.

In fact, the only things visible on the gigantic platter of ice were the few, now-empty Quonset huts for the permanent staff, a small, prefab control tower, and the two shielded crash trucks that had been flown up from Moosefoot in two straining Hercules cargo jets.

The Muths and President O'Connell's party were all bundled up in army-issue fur parkas and OD wool mittens, but the day was calm and bright, a modest north wind blowing almost along the runway and the temperature only at about zero. They all stood, stamping and beating their hands and peeking nervously over the edge of the ice, when a cry went up from the adjacent TV and reporter trench, "She's coming!"

Sure enough, way out to the south they could see the gigantic and distant *Langley* making a wide turn to start her downwind leg. She flew parallel to them, then banked and turned again, still miles away, lining up for her final landing run. As she came ever closer her black shape grew, but the day was still quiet. The *Langley*'s engine noise was no more than that of a steady gale flowing through a forest of hissing trees.

The wire service and pool men watched with growing apprehension as the gigantic wings thickened and spread. "Damn! It looks like the Hindenburg," said the AP stringer, an older man, "but going sideways!"

The young fellow from Reuters turned and grinned. "Have you by any chance heard of the phenomenon of 'roll-up'?" he asked innocently.

"Very funny," grumbled the older man. "You don't have a wife and kids to worry about."

"At least you've *got* kids, my friend," said the other. "If this things blows up dirty . . . hey, look at that!"

Everyone stared through their binoculars as Sergeant

Stewart began to lower the acres of undercarriage spiders, wheel-tier by wheel-tier.

Colonel Muth, now carefully watching both the flight and reactor instruments, began to break his glide. "Okay, Harry," he said to Major Fisk. "Stage Two. Reverse the fans, now!" Fisk pressed the transfer switches to send steam through the ten alternate turbine runners, set to drive the fans in the opposite direction. At first these machines fought the steam, for they had to dissipate the huge rotary momentum of the big fan blades. Fisk watched the condenser temperatures rising like a rocket but he continued to cram steam through the reactor.

"Blades are coming up to stop, Bob," said Major Fisk. The long, white runway now stretched ahead and they were still doing well over a hundred m.p.h. Colonel Muth watched the condenser steam pressure indications shooting up, for now the air to cool the steam came entirely from the *Langley*'s forward motion.

"We've got to start the bleed, Bob. She's gonna pop!" said Fisk in a tense voice.

"Do it now!" said Muth and the *Langley* went into open cycle, the steam blowing back out of the aircraft in spectacular giant plumes that deflected off the nearby runway and produced instant pools of water wherever they touched the ground.

"Bob, we're not getting enough reverse fan acceleration! We're going to run out of water!" hissed Gaby Jackson, whose landing responsibilities included projecting condenser activity, fan reversal, and water-loss, moment to moment.

"Major Fisk," said a grim Bob Muth at once, "windmill turbines one, three, five, six, eight and ten! Give the other four absolute full reverse! Let's see if we can use parts of the condensers to feed them!"

"Right!" said Fisk, busily cross-connecting condenser and turbine systems. Now four of the turbines received plenty of steam and spun more rapidly towards full reverse.

President O'Connell, suddenly gaping and growing cold at the huge cloud appearing magically below the *Langley*, now saw this diminish. Yet the plane did not seem to be going much slower. "Well, General," he said in a hard, tense voice, "Now what?"

General Beardsley peered through a set of huge binoculars and licked his dry lips. "He's apparently decided to perform the reversal in groups, instead of all at once. That way, part of the condenser system can serve part of the turbine group."

The air rushing past the windmilling fans condensed the steam for those now running in reverse. Bob Muth held his glide, as long as he dared, then finally began to flare the *Langley*. He spoke grimly to Sergeant Stewart. "We've got to start touching here, Jim, fans or no. Talk me in, baby!"

In his undercarriage office, Sergeant Stewart watched the hydraulic gauges for the first sign of contact. "Hold her level, Bob. Steady . . . okay, first touch aft. We're taking about two percent now. She's rocking a bit, Bob, watch it! Port wing is heavy."

While they gradually dropped each set of wheels down on the ice, Major Fisk, his undershirt sopping wet under his coveralls, finally got the first four reverse turbines fully up to speed. "Bob, they're in full reverse. Shall I try four more?"

"No time for that," said Muth quickly. "Put the rest on line, now! If we pop a condenser seam or two at this point, it won't matter!"

"Second tier bearing," said Stewart. "Drop her nose a degree, Bob. The back wheels are a bit over one hundred percent. Steady, down slow, Bob . . ."

"Condenser is over twice its design pressure now," said a tense Major Fisk. "Spin, you bastards!" he gritted.

And spin they did. The more rapidly the other six fans went into reverse, the more steam the condensers could handle. The condenser pressure-excursion peaked terrifyingly at over three times the maximum design pressure, but when Bob Muth saw that it *was* the peak and that all the condenser parts had begun to fully function in reverse, he knew they had finally mastered the beast and could stop her.

"Over sixty percent of load on the wheels now, Bob," said Stewart. "She's settling nice. One more degree now. Watch that starboard tilt . . . steady. . . ."

Major Fisk ran the reactor back up to full power and they could feel the reverse thrust now acting to slow the *Langley.*

"You want to park her anyplace special?" said Major Fisk, wiping his face and grinning at his assistants.

Colonel Muth looked out at the ice island ahead. "I think we should run her abreast of the hole they're making, Harry," he said. "No point in making them tow Steam Bird four miles."

As the *Langley* gradually decelerated, she was accompanied by the two shielded crash trucks, one on each side, rumbling along with the people behind the thick, lead glass excitedly waving and shoving their thumbs up.

They finally rolled quietly to a stop and Colonel Muth took a deep breath. "Gentlemen, mission complete. Cold shut-down, if you please." He felt suddenly drained and drawn out, and he knew that if he were to take his hands off the wheel, they would shake. "Gaby," he said with a great sigh. "If I don't have to do that again, I won't miss it."

Steam Bird had landed.

The crash trucks soon delivered the crew to the slit trenches, where a heartfelt reunion took place between Bob and Betty Lou. Bob Muth next kissed his older children and swept his younger daughter into the air.

"And here," he said with a mighty grin, "is Cordelia herself, my very own tortient!"

Alice planted a heavy, wet smack on her father's lips, then hugged him to whisper in his ear, "I didn't really mean all that, Dad. It was just part of the whole scam that I thought up."

Her father set her back down on the ice and waggled a finger. "Oh, no, you don't get off that easy. You just fall down with consumption into that green grave and see what *I* do!"

Everybody laughed at that and then the President let Alice pin the Distinguished Flying Cross on her father. Next, he pinned one on all the others, spending some time chatting with Captain Jackson to make sure the TV footage of that would be good.

By now Air Force One had landed again and Shamus O'Connell was about to make his statement about the canonization of the *Langley* and the neutralization of Ice Island Three, when a protocol person urgently whispered in his ear.

"Wha . . . *more* medals?"

The aide continued to whisper, thrusting a pile of medal boxes at the President.

O'Connell sighed and turned with a half-smile to Colonel Muth. "Colonel," he said, "it seems that when the Congress wrote the establishing legislation for the NASA astronaut medal intended for anyone who completes one or more orbits around the Earth in a spacecraft, they inadvertently used the term 'circle' instead of 'orbit.'" The President paused and shot a grin at Happy Jack, completely lost in a furry parka. "Hell, Jack, they just didn't know there was any difference between circle and orbit. Going around is going around, right? The education of congressmen in this country is a scandal!"

He turned back to Colonel Muth and took the medal out of the top box, looking around at the Muth family. "Anyway, Colonel, within the present meaning of the act, you and your crew are entitled to one of these. Let's see, Alice did one. Who wants to pin this on their father?"

Bob Junior looked over at Melissa, then grinned and stepped forward. "Mr. President," he said, "I think medals that are given by mistake are the best ones of all. I'll be proud to pin that one on you, Dad."

XVI

A FEW WEEKS AFTER THE PRESIDENT ANNOUNCED THE UN
stewardship of Ice Island Three and the frozen apotheo-
sis of the *Langley*, the Moosefoot base was shut tight, the
other two planes dismantled, and the men reassigned or,
in the case of most of the officers, retired at the conve-
nience of the government.

So that next summer the Muth family went off on
holiday to Wales where various small steam railways still
chuffed tourists around the Welsh scenery. What started
as a mere jaunt turned into an extraordinary summer of
engine driving. They were recognized at once on the
Ffestiniog and spent a full week driving and firing. Riots
and punch-ups soon developed around Portmadoc when
every tourist in the West Country wanted to be on the
trains driven by the famous Colonel Muth and spouse,
or one of his talented children, undisputedly the 'first
family of steam' in the world.

The family decided to split up so that other lines
might benefit. Bob and his wife went off to the Tallylyn,
Bob Junior to the Dart Valley, while Melissa and Alice
decided to stay a few days more at the Ffestiniog. Alice
especially loved the double-Fairlies, which had two

independent engines back-to-back so that you could really get them driving up the bank by juggling the two regulators, keeping everything just below wheel-slip. Best of all, Melissa fired from the other side of the boiler and couldn't keep screaming about how Alice had the cut-off set too high.

Eventually all the railways were visited and all the engines driven and the end of a cloudless, bright English summer came at Bressingham when British Rail brought *Mallard* briefly out of her museum berth and Colonel Muth and Lord Brackenburse, Minister for Transport, alternated driving and firing the big green engine. As Bob Muth said later to Captain Jackson, "We didn't get her much over sixty, Gaby, but they can have my right arm anyhow!"

So the perfect summer passed on to a cool fall. The little railways shut down for the year. The last steam boats ran on Lake Windermere and the coda of that wonderful summer of steam came in October at the annual banquet meeting of the Stephenson Society. For Colonel Robert Muth, USAF (ret.) was to be made the president of the society and to receive a special gold medal bearing the bust of George Stephenson and the simple legend, *Locomotion No. 1—Samuel Langley*, and the dates.

The affair turned out to be one that everyone wanted to attend, so that the society was finally faced with hiring a huge old guildhall in the Westminster section of London and having the thing catered by three different food services.

The hall was old and shabby, but they decorated it up with Union Jacks, rail posters, and bunting. The head table stretched along one entire long wall, up on a temporary platform, while out in the gloomy, huge barn-like room were dozens of other tables and hundreds of members of the society, their friends, and guests.

The men at the head table were mostly in black ties and boiled shirts, the women in long dresses, although Congressman Hazelton decided that Emmeline's now-famous engineer's outfit, Tidewater Northern logo and all, would be entirely appropriate. Everyone who was anybody in steam was strung along the head table with Nate, Emmeline and the Muths: Lord and Lady Brackenburse; Lord Rothmare, Chairman of the Main Line Steam Trust, and Lady Rothmare; General and Mrs. Beardsley; the crew of the *Langley*; a gaggle of high-level British civil servants and young, titled wastrels whose hobby happened to be steam; and several other distinguished, ancient, nodding CMEs from other days.

This was all far too stuffy and highbrow for Melissa, so she dashed down on the main floor, dragging Alice with her, and found seats in the midst of the old top-link drivers in their shiny pressed blue suits and thin ties. These old men were run in from the nursing homes and retirement cottages once a year to have supper and tell each other, or better the young clerks and hobby nuts, lies about engine driving.

When a friendly nursing sister asked one of the old gaffers the next day just what Melissa Muth really looked like to so impress him, the old gentleman could only smile and repeat the single word, "Splendid!" over and over again.

In fact, Melissa had on a neck-to-toe flesh-colored semitransparent body stocking tantalizingly decorated here and there with pastel butterflies. Over this she wore a single, long sheath of pure-white macramé panels, slit to both sides of her waist, and with far more open holes than there ever was rope. This extraordinary dress, dug out of a Bond Street boutique after days of search, fitted so cunningly that as Melissa shifted her hands, head, or torso, one had the impression of an amazing moving moiré pattern of interacting breasts, butterflies, braided string, and downy, delicious arms.

Many of the retired drivers simply sat paralyzed and grinning, but though they were all old, they were by no means all feeble. Driver Farrington of Doncaster Shed, who had driven the queen several times and who was still called out to drive on steam-loco fan trips, realized it was largely up to him to keep this remarkable young woman interested and talking. He looked in dismay about the big table at the open, toothless mouths, the riveted, if rheumy eyes.

"Aye, lassie," he said in his best last-driver-in-steam voice, "but I've driven plenty of Gresley A-4's in my day, and never had one over thirty percent cut-off, even doing a hundred."

"That's not the point, Driver Farrington," said a serious Melissa. "The Gresley derived gear simply has to go sloppy at high speed. Don't you see? It's driving at that steep angle from the forward axle, while the outside Walshaerts are coming off the middle drivers . . ." This explanation was all accompanied by a kinematics demonstration using both her hands and arms and, almost at once, the several tables around the one holding the old drivers also fell into transfixed silence.

The oldest driver at the table was wrinkled, silent Billy Bayne, so ancient that no one knew really how old he was, although some claimed he had fired a Stirling Single in the London-Scottish train races of the late nineties. The men always debated whether to bring old Billy, for nobody was sure whether he took much of anything in, but in the end they always shook their heads and took him along.

Now he suddenly sat up and his eyes came fully open. "Miss Muth," he said slowly but very clearly, "when I drove on the Highland Railway, the summer butterflies would fly up from those fields of heather like a carpet of living flowers hanging over the purple sedge."

The other men turned, astounded, to stare at old Billy, but Melissa clapped her hands in delight, then sighed and smiled warmly at Driver Bayne. "How lovely to drive on the Highland!" she said at once. "And the engines were so handsome."

"Aye, my dear," said Billy Bayne alertly. "And the hills steep. I was Drummond's test driver on the big, new engines then."

Driver Arthur Mock, well over eighty but usually the one who accompanied Billy Bayne to these affairs, turned in astonishment.

"You knew Dugald Drummond, Billy?" he said. "Lord, I never knew that!"

"Aye, and his brother too," said Billy. "As to three-cylinder gears, Miss Muth, the problem was always keeping them working at the same cut-off."

"Exactly," said Melissa. "But they partly solved that problem on the American Hudsons . . ." and again the explanation went forward with much gesture and movement.

Old Driver Mock sat with the others in a daze of wonder, and always after that time he told everyone that the Stephenson dinner that year was the most exciting night of his life. This was an assertion of some note, since in 1944 Mock's train on the Southern main line took a direct hit from a V-1 flying bomb and the engine rolled over three times coming down the bank.

But Alice, who in her heart of hearts thought valve gears 'Boring, boring, *boring*!' was deep into a far more contentious discussion with young master Freddie Farrington, grandson of Driver Farrington and attending his first society dinner. This slender youth was a year or so older than Alice and had a long, gentle face with a shock of straight blond hair falling over wide blue eyes. These eyes now glittered in anger at pretty Alice, as master Farrington delivered an opinion. "Well, it's completely *stupid*," he said with dripping contempt, "to say that the *Hiawatha* service was better than *Flying Scotsman* just because it was a little *faster*!"

"It was a *lot* faster!" snarled Alice right back. "And the trains were bigger, and the service was better! So there, Mr. Stupid!" And unable to contain her anger, Alice stuck out her tongue at Freddie Farrington and made a monster face at the same time.

Master Freddy was unimpressed. He stared at her with a lofty expression. "I don't see how you think you can win an argument by making yourself completely ugly," he said in a sarcastic voice.

The perfectly evident logic of this remark only enraged Alice all the further and her eyes grew thin, her lips set. "If you say one more stupid, wrong thing, I'll bounce this hard roll off your stupid head!" and she hefted a very hard roll out of the bread basket.

Young Farrington sniffed, unafraid. "Right! Well, you Yanks think you can make anybody do anything by threatening to throw things at them, don't you? And if the *Morning Hi* was so bloody wonderful, where is it now, Miss Muth?" He glared at her and curled his lip. "The fact is, the *Scotsman* is still running. Our trains are now tremendously faster and better than yours are. And the French trains are better. The Swiss trains are better. The Danish, Norwegian, Swedish, Russian, trains are all better. The . . ."

Cutting, hurtful, bitter words, and Alice clenched her teeth in unbridled rage, thinking what a fine target master Farrington's large, high, white forehead actually made.

But before British-American relations, or the world of steam, had to suffer such a set-back, Driver Farrington managed to wrench his attention momentarily away from Melissa, who was now sinuously explaining why continuous-contour cam gearing was best for one hundred mile an hour running, and lean down to his grandson.

"'Ere, 'Ere, Freddy. Don't say such hard things to the young lady, boy! Miss Muth is a real driver. Why, they say she took that double-Fairlie up the bank out of Portmadoc as slick and tidy as any man on the line, plenty of times."

Something hard and prickly melted instantly inside Freddie Farrington. His eyes grew large and soft and his high forehead wrinkled in astonishment. "You . . . drove the Fairlie . . . on the Ffestiniog?" And as he looked at Alice, Freddie realized at once that she was not only tremendously pretty and bright and lively, but that she loved the very same things that he loved, no matter where they ran. He smiled tentatively; and dimples appeared in his now-pink cheeks.

"Miss Muth . . . Alice," he said in a small voice. "I'm going train-spotting down at Euston tomorrow. *Evening Star* is taking the *Scotsman* out. Would you . . . well, like to come down with me?"

For a brief moment, Alice, who had instantly realized that her triumph was total, contemplated driving a knife of words into his gentle heart. But as she looked at Freddie Farrington she suddenly wondered why she would ever want to hurt somebody who really loved the same things she loved, when there were so many hurtful people around who didn't love anything at all. Her heart melted then and she dropped the roll back on her plate and nodded. "I'd love to see *Evening Star*, Freddie," she said in a suddenly-shy voice. Then she smiled like a burst of sunshine. "If we can get Dad to come, they'll probably let us drive her up the line a ways."

Freddie's mouth fell open and his heart turned over in a giant, sudden thump. "*Drive* her? You mean on the footplate?"

"Sure," said Alice. "Well, actually Dad would drive, but he always lets me have a go at it, even on the big ones."

Freddie could not immediately answer but his shining face and sparkling eyes said all that Alice needed or wanted to know about Freddie Farrington.

But the banquet finally moved on to the dessert, coffee, and then the speeches. Colonel Muth was to be introduced by Lord Rothmare but it soon became evident that this old and distinguished worthy intended to treat the society to a considerable history of steam before bringing on Colonel Muth.

Lady Rothmare, a white-haired old lady of distinguished bearing, leaned over to Betty Lou Muth and her eyes crinkled as she smiled. "Well, dear, they really are just like little boys with it," she whispered, then winked.

Betty Lou smiled back. "Oh yes, that's true. But it does give them so *much* pleasure, Lady Rothmare!"

The old woman thought a moment, then nodded. "Like that other thing!" she said positively. "Well, I guess we just have to learn to enjoy it along with them."

Betty Lou nodded. "Like that other thing, Lady Rothmare," she said and the two women chuckled heartily together.

But Lord Rothmare was finally approaching the time of the *Langley* in his remarks and Bob Muth prepared himself to rise and give his speech. He looked out over the huge throng, sipping their coffee and staring up at him. All of a sudden, it seemed that there were others, many others, standing in the shadows at the back of the great hall. He narrowed his eyes and knew in a moment who they were.

First were the Chief Mechanical Engineers standing together: Gresley, his moustache bristling, elegant André Chapelon of the Paris-Orleans and the Nord, George Jackson Churchward in his cutaway and high collar, old Bill Buchanan of the New York Central in a derby, chewing on a dead cigar. And more and more, Patrick Stirling, Dugald Drummond, all the others. But now, standing in amongst them were the top-link men, the runners; and shadowy behind them were their engines. Duddington with *Mallard*, Bill Sparshott with *Scotsman*, stubby Charlie Hogan and his high-wheeled lady 999, Driver Ruddock with handsome *Tregenna Castle*, and always more and more, stretching out into the gloom at the back. It wasn't just the loco men either, they had *all* come back. The tiny bearded Stanley twins and Abner Doble stood with keen-eyed Fred Marriott. There was squatty, ugly Brunel in his high plug hat, John Fowler the farmer and traction-engine genius, distinguished George Stephenson himself on the footplate of *Locomotion* that ran like a horse. The shadows spilled everywhere. There were so many! The brakie with his hand gone, the hogger lost and frozen in a three-day blizzard on Cumbres Pass, the moustachioed fireman with one leg who rode a runaway down off Shap Summit, all come back together. And finally, far behind them all, huge, hunched, his eyes glowing like the coals under one of his iron-plate boilers stood Vulcan himself, old Watt, his lined, hard face a mask of resolve, and standing around him the keen young men of the Soho works, their sleeveguards and fingers black with ink, their rules and pens clutched in eager hands; and if he listened, for a single moment, Bob Muth thought he caught the slow, steady chuff of the gigantic lifting, pumping, and blowing engines that had built a rich, dangerous, exciting world of steam.

Lord Rothmare finally reached the end of his remarks and introduced Colonel Muth in a flattering series of biographical references, and Bob stood to thunderous applause.

He grinned out at his two daughters down in front who were clapping with wild enthusiasm, then reached down and squeezed his son's shoulder on one side and his wife's on the other, and when she looked up he gave her a loving wink. He cleared his throat as they finally quieted "Lord Rothmare, distinguished guests," he turned to look both ways along the head table, "and all friends of steam everywhere . . ." he paused, remembering the shadows at the back, ". . . and everywhen! My crew and I bring you greeting from the *skies*!"

Hurricane
Claude

Sept. 5, 1400 hrs.—Sept. 7, 1700 hrs.

AT ITS MOMENT OF CONCEPTION, THE STORM WAS NO MORE than an unnoticed, swirling tube of air, its father a rising current off the northern edge of the largest island in the Caicos group, its mother a thin barometric-depression wave lying east and west across the southern limits of the Bahama Banks. The upward-moving thrust of buoyant air, penetrating the mild depression and gaining energy from it, set a kink in the pressure wave, a bend that eventually closed itself and created a turning cylinder, an atmospheric swirl. The tiny product of this gentle meeting, driven by that ponderous force derived from the rotation of the planet itself, began to rotate in a counterclockwise direction, and this spin rapidly drew in more energy and moisture from the hot, surrounding sea. Its mild and almost-indetectable parents were consumed and destroyed during its first few hours of life as the baby storm drifted on an erratic northeast track out over the deep but unusually warm waters. By chance, no reporting vessel passed through the blustery but unfocused center of its babyhood, so the storm grew unnoticed for almost a day.

Then, that next afternoon, a large American sailing

yacht, *Passage-Master*, Norfolk to Puerto Rico, ran
through the western sector of the tiny, diffuse storm.
Winds were moderate, no more than twenty knots, but
there was a heavy sense of tropical disturbance and
moisture, and the sky was very dark. The barometer
dipped two-tenths of an inch of mercury over a three-
hour traverse, and *Passage-Master's* professional skipper
spoke over the ship-to-shore with Miami around supper-
time. The next morning, Miami Hurricane Center dis-
patched a hunter aircraft, and it located the storm out in
the Gulf Stream, where the hot surface water fed the
young hurricane-to-be its continuous, ever-increasing,
energy requirements. The storm was still invisible from
the synchronous weather satellite, *Nimbus IV*, masked
by a larger fan of high altitude cloud, but the aircraft
made a run through the storm center at about 10 A.M.
and found a well-defined circulation, almost half an inch
of gradient across the storm cross-section, and winds
now over forty knots.

At noon that day, four men in shirtsleeves met in the
Miami Center and studied the records and maps. The
storm was now growing in area rapidly and also extending itself vertically upward into the atmospheric column, so that the *Nimbus* cameras were beginning to
show a typical spiral cloud pattern, imposed on the
older, more passive cloud structures overhanging a vast
middle Atlantic low-pressure region. They named the
growing baby Claude, since it was the third rotating
storm of the season, and its predecessor, which had
fizzled south of Cuba, had been called a lady's name,
Barbara. At 1300, Miami issued its first bulletin on
Claude.

"Tropical storm Claude is now located at approximately 25°1′ north latitude and 71°5′ west
longitude, or approximately 400 miles east of
Miami. The storm is strengthening in both baro-
metric gradient and size and its movements are

erratic. Maximum wind velocities of 40 miles
per hour are now concentrated within 50 miles
of the storm center, but further strengthening is
to be expected. All marine interests are urged to
remain informed about Claude, which has the
potential of becoming a large and dangerous
storm."

By 1500, Claude had begun to move sluggishly almost
due north at about five miles an hour, and Miami
established a tropical storm watch along the Atlantic
coastline north of Wilmington.

The board of directors' meeting at Techoceanics had
not been hastily called until around noon that day, but
by 3 P.M. the men from Boston and Hartford had arrived
by car or charter plane and over a dozen people were
assembled in Techoceanic's spartan conference room.
The company owned a series of Butler-type metal-sided
buildings located mostly on barges moored next to the
swing bridge connecting New Bedford to Fairhaven to
the west. When not used for meetings, the room doubled
as a meteorological work space and one end was filled
with electronic racks.

Ray Alexander, chief of research at Techoceanics, was
a small, very thin man, almost sixty, his hair a stiff,
white, crewcut brush, his eyes hooded and cold, his
mouth no more than the dark cut of a sharp knife. "Let's
get going," he said in a loud, hard voice. "We've got a
storm and it's growing. Come on, you people, shut up!"

The two business-suited men from the Hartford underwriters looked up, startled from their private discussion, then lapsed into sullen silence. "Okay, Bettina,"
said Ray Alexander in almost a snarl, "work your
magic," but his tone was completely sarcastic, with no
sense of joking or kidding.

Dr. Bettina Holbrook, for two years the forecasting
meteorologist for Techoceanics, was a plain-faced,
thirty-year-old woman in tailored slacks and a severe,

simple blouse, entirely trim and businesslike. She stood
up to fire a look of pure hatred at her boss, then flipped
off the lights and turned on the slide projector. "Okay,
here's Claude twenty minutes ago . . ."

But Ray Alexander let out a snort of disgust and
muttered loudly, "Claude! Those raving faggots in
Miami sure do like the fruity names!"

Bettina stopped speaking at once and turned an angry
white face to peer at Ray Alexander. "Do you really
want to shoot yourself in the foot, Ray?" she said in an
icy, distressed voice. "What sense is there in making that
kind of sick, stupid crack, anyway?"

"You going to give a weather briefing or a gay rights
lecture, Bettina?" snarled Ray right back.

Tall and angular Dr. Cora Alexander, chairman and
chief executive officer of Techoceanics, spoke even more
coldly than her husband. "Ray, if you make one more
comment about fags, fruits, queers, or whatever, you're
out of this thing on your ass! I mean that, you bastard!
We don't need your nasty cussedness, Ray. Moke can
pilot the *Telsa*, and probably better than you!" Where
her husband's face was simply thin and spare, Cora
Alexander's face was thin and extravagantly ugly. Her
downward-hooked nose and her upward-hooked chin
almost met in front of a huge, wide mouth that often
snapped open to show large, tobacco-yellowed teeth.

Ray aimed a sharp finger-point at his wife, sitting at
the other end of the long table. "You'd like to cut me out
of it, wouldn't you, you old bag! After four years of
shoveling shit against a tide of stupid incompetence, I
get tossed into the street . . ."

The man from State Street Trust turned to the Boston
lawyer sitting next to him and raised his eyebrows in
pointed astonishment. The old attorney, Arthur
Goodspeed, whispered. "Things here are worse than we
heard. They must be going to shout the storm to death,"
but the banker just shook his head ominously. Techoceanics was into them for over $2 million.

Cora paid no further attention to Ray, but turned to nod impatiently at Bettina Holbrook, who reset her face in as pleasant an expression as possible and indicated the projected satellite photo with her pointer light. "Miami is forecasting hurricane strength by six tonight, and I agree," she said, indicating the spiral form of the storm that now showed clearly. "There's a low trough of wet air lying flaccid just off the coast between Hatteras and Montauk. It then runs northeast near Nantucket and it's going to suck Claude inshore. Miami isn't quite ready to predict that, but I think it's likely. I think we should proceed on the basis of that assumed storm track."

"Rate of advance?" asked Cora Alexander in an expressionless tone.

Bettina gave a thoughtful shake of her head. "At least 20 knots by the time it's beyond Hatteras—I mean past latitude 35°—but I don't like the look of the whole map. The depression up over Long Island is deep and narrow. Things look a whole lot like the '38 storm. Claude might work up to 50 or 60, but I just don't know how to forecast that kind of acceleration from what we have now."

The Techoceanics attorney, Arthur Goodspeed, raised a finger. "Then you predict the storm will come ashore on this coast, Dr. Holbrook?"

The meteorologist nodded. "Somewhere it will hit land, Arthur; perhaps Long Island, perhaps Cape Cod."

The lawyer turned to Cora Alexander. "Cora, I thought we agreed not to attempt this if the hurricane was certain to do damage ashore?"

Ray answered him bluntly. "Don't be stupid, Arthur! We're busted, broke, out of cash! This may be the last storm this year."

One of the Hartford men cleared his throat and spoke in a low, well-modulated tone. "My instructions are to urge you to attempt to modify the storm. My principals are not willing to continue this sort of funding level for a full additional year. But if you should destroy or divert the storm, you will have repaid our underwriter's group handsomely. Obviously, further funding in that case would be an easy matter."

The man from the Boston bank shook his head ruefully at his lawyer friend. "I understand your problems, Arthur," he said, "but we also hope to see the method tried now."

"After all, Arthur," said Cora Alexander in a dry, cold voice, "if we get sued for making the storm worse, instead of breaking it apart, they'll just be going after a bankrupt wreck with no assets or prospects. Also, there's no physical reason why we should make it worse. The worst we can do is to do nothing at all."

"Well, let's hope so," said the old lawyer, shrugging in doubt.

"Can we vote on this?" said Cora suddenly. "All in favor of attempting modification of tropical storm Claude, raise your hands." They all put up their hands except the lawyer, and Cora stared at him. "Are you abstaining or voting no, Arthur?" she said icily, but he suddenly put his hand up.

"Try it," he said in a cracked, excited voice. "Try it, Cora. To hell with the lawsuits!"

Sept. 7, 1700—2400 hrs.

IN DOUBLING ITS LENGTH AND WIDTH, THE STORM
Claude increased its energy uptake from the Gulf Stream
by a factor of four. This added impetus for growth and
activity was manifested in two ways, in addition to the
further linear expansion of the storm's perimeter, mostly
north and west. Claude's rotary energy increased so that
in its 1800 advisory, Miami declared Claude a hurricane. The weather buoys dropped by a late-afternoon
overflight were showing gusts near the center to seventy
knots. But Claude could also expend its overabundance
of energy in another way, by moving its entire system
north at increasing velocity.

So the ocean energy resource was tapped too rapidly
for the storm to eat it by simply spreading. In addition, it
spun ever more fiercely and moved ever more rapidly.

Coming across Claude's big, ragged funnel just at
dusk, the Miami hunter pilot saw that Claude had grown
from a childish, petulant disorder towards a fearsome,
mature beauty. From over 30,000 feet up, he could look
down into the sloping, roughly circular maw, indistinct
with the sun setting, and see the stark white funnel of

cloud that led down and down out of sight into a well of
gathering violence. Claude was maturing, gaining in
self-integration, forcing its way further and higher to
involve ever-larger air masses. And everywhere it moved
and spread, it ate moisture and thermal energy with a
frenzied voracity.

Yet, in Indianapolis and Pittsburgh, people shivered
under thin blankets and pulled summer jackets tighter
around themselves. A gigantic thick finger of Arctic high
had poked down from Canada over the middle eastern
states. Though Claude was mighty, and would become
mightier still, it had neither the resources of energy nor
momentum to seriously challenge this vast, stolid mass
of dense and quiet air.

To the east another, far smaller and weaker, high-
pressure ridge of cold air stretched south, tentatively
poking its weak leading edge towards Bermuda. Claude
might have challenged this air mass, and probably broken through to the northeast, but the modest Greenland
high had its control over Claude, not through sheer
strength but by a more subtle yet more certain influence,
the steering currents of thin air above 30,000 feet. The
Greenland air mass had diverted these ordinarily
easterly-flowing winds to the north, and huge, powerful
Claude followed with the blind obedience of sheep after
a Judas goat. Claude, driven by inexorable need to spend
its energy, yet in so doing obtaining ever more, began to
stride north into a deep valley of low barometer pointing
at the New England coast.

The late-evening New Bedford weather felt damp and
heavy. Though the storm still lay over a thousand miles
south, there was an oppressive sense of tropic air and the
greasy, sheet-metal sidings of the barge cabins dripped
and ran rivulets of water. In the center of Techoceanics'
biggest barge sat a huge SeaCrane twin-rotor freight
helicopter, but instead of the usual modular pods, this
machine had been modified to sling an entire, whale-
shaped boat, fat and double-ended, with two big screws
showing under the stern. The boat stretched fifty feet

under the rotary-wing freighter and seemed to be constructed entirely of welded aluminum sheets.

The air was dead still and the barge was brightly lit by many searchlights and TV light-columns. Four persons stood in front of the thirty-odd press people: Ray Alexander and his tall wife in padded jumpsuits, and two other short, squatty men in bulky flying clothes. Around behind these four clustered some of the Techoceanics engineers and financial people in business suits.

Cora Alexander held up her hand for quiet and shouted, "I'm going to make a statement and give you the tech briefing. Okay, here's the way the system is supposed to work. I've sketched the storm in a vertical cross-section on this blackboard. Now what we found some years back is that the top of the storm, about 25,000 feet in the case of Claude, has a very high negative potential—tens, hundreds of thousands of volts —with a similiar high positive at the base." She indicated the two locations on the diagram. "Now in a thunderhead or line squall, or similar type of nonrotating storm with high atmospheric electrical potentials, the electron excess in a cloud is mainly produced by the movement of rain and hail. The water particles carry charges around in the cloud, or between clouds and the earth. This electrical phenomenon in revolving or hurricane types of storms is based on a different principle. It's produced by the motion in the earth's magnetic field. If you remember your electrical physics, you know that if you revolve or move charges through a magnetic field, you develop potential."

"So the storm is acting like a huge generator, Dr. Alexander?" asked a reporter up at the front.

"Correct," said Cora, showing a mouth full of large, startling teeth, "but a generator with an open circuit. There's all that voltage potential, but no external wire. We're going to provide the wire. We're going to short-circuit the storm by creating an electrically conducting path between its foot and its top. Our computer simulations suggest convincingly that the core of the mature hurricane will not be able to sustain its order and identity when this energy drain begins. The storm will fragment from the eye outwards, break into a series of small storms which will eat energy from each other. Most important, we hope to break the grip of the stratospheric winds, the steering currents, on Claude's upper levels, to cut the storm loose so it takes its natural northeasterly direction that the Coriolis force would dictate. That is, away from this coast."

Several of the reporters stared at each other in scorn and disbelief. The man who had spoken before said, "You claim you can string a wire up through the eye of a hurricane?"

Cora patted her tight bun of gray hair and gave a sudden hee-haw sort of laugh. "Not even my husband would try something that dumb," she said gruffly, hooking a thumb at frowning Ray. "We're going to create an ionized column of air for the current to follow. The material of the core itself, air and water vapor, will be our wire, but we have to get things started."

She turned to point at the huge, silent helicopter and its oddly shaped load. "That boat, the *Nikola Tesla*, will be the lower terminal in the atmospheric circuit. It has two very powerful diesel engines and these have two uses: first, to drive propellers to let us move around at Claude's center, and second, to drive a generator and power a large induction coil inside the boat. Once the *Tesla* arrives at the proper location at the center of the storm, we will extend a high mastlike structure above the *Tesla* with a large openwork electrode, and the high voltage will be maintained between the top of the mast and the aluminum hull of the boat. This will create a high-density cloud of ions around the *Tesla*. At the top of the storm, our aircraft will be doing essentially the same thing. That is, it will maintain a potential between its own metal skin and a large electrode towed some distance below it. In this way, we will create two large ion pools, of proper sign, at the top and bottom of the storm, and our calculations indicate that a self-sustaining current flow will be set up over the five-mile vertical air column."

"But the boat and the plane must remain there if the electron flow is to be maintained?" said a man at the back.

Cora gave a single nod. "We think we must maintain the ion generation for a few minutes. Our computer models suggest that as the eye rotation falters, and the structure begins to collapse, there will be leakage and short-circuiting all along the vortex face. At that point, the storm will not need us any longer. It will destroy itself, blow out its own heart."

A young woman who had worked her way forward along the edge of the barge now held up her hand. "Dr. Alexander, isn't it correct that three ecological groups have gone to Judge Goldfarb of the Federal District Court in Boston to gain an order to stop this experiment? I wonder if you'd care to comment on that?"

Cora Alexander gave the cameras a fearsomely witchlike frown, her wide mouth turning down in disgust. "Our attorney, Mr. Goodspeed, and our friends from the insurance underwriters group were forced to fly back to Boston to meet with Judge Goldfarb because of that. In my opinion, this action is a damnable outrage!"

"Then," said the reporter, "the ecologists' claims that you may create several dangerous storms out of one have no merit? Is that your position?"

Dr. Alexander stared at the young woman with an undisguised mixture of pity and contempt. "The storm, my dear, gains its energy primarily from the ocean's surface. Its power and its danger derive from its singleness, its integrated nature. Once we take that same energy total, and break it into a dozen or a hundred smaller parts, we draw the thing's teeth."

The woman pressed forward and persisted. "But that's just more theory. What if it's wrong? Haven't we meddled enough with nature? How do you know what essential part hurricanes may play in the ecology?"

Cora's yellow fangs snapped terrifyingly together.

"Did you major in home ec, dearest?" she said with a
sarcasm so fierce that even Ray grinned at her. "And
does your uncle own the paper where you work? What in
hell do you think hurricanes do for the ecology? I'll tell
you what they do. They decimated the terns south of
Cape Cod. The wild oysters went and never came back.
Scallop and cohaug beds that had lasted since Indian
times, hundreds of years, were blown away. The salt
marshes were wrecked, the Great Ponds infiltrated, the
aquifers turned brackish. The ducks were gone, the
shellfish small and thin, everything ruined, destruction
and death, not to mention a billion dollars in human
property losses plus some dozens of human lives gone if
sweetie-pie Claude comes ashore on Long Island or
Rhode Island at the wrong time of the tide. And those
damned fools are up with a damned federal judge to tell
us we can't try and stop that bloody mayhem! Go to hell,
you dumb, bleeding-hearted broad! I've got my men in
that SeaCrane office right now, and if that fat-assed
judge tries to . . ."

But Bobby Winthrop, thirty-one-year-old project
manager of the hurricane modification attempt at
Techoceanics, saw how badly it was going and stepped
quickly forward to seize his president by her elbow with
a sharp squeeze of warning and to send off to the young,
flinty-eyed environmental reporter a warm and apolo-
getic smile. Bobby would soon vector them into the
storm center, then decide on the proper moment for the
ion fields to be energized. It was his combination of
even-tempered urbanity with a careful use of understate-
ment that had mainly kept Techoceanics afloat in trou-
bled seas for four years. Bobby wore a conservative
three-piece suit, dark blue with pinstripes, and since he
was as tall as Cora, and broad-shouldered as well, he lent
a sudden air of corporate stability to the ranting, ugly old
woman in her outer-space-look jumpsuit.

"I remind you, ladies and gentlemen," said Bobby,
and his voice became progressively warmer and more
engaged in the matter, "that Ray and Cora Alexander

will be risking their lives in our attempt to destroy the storm. Risking their lives to save others. I hope you'll forgive Dr. Alexander's excited and inaccurate comments. I think we'd all be happier if we could simply go ahead with the job instead of having to justify ourselves at the last moment to a federal judge who knows nothing of the matter."

The young woman was not placated and she dearly wanted to get at Cora again. "Look," she persisted, "Dr. Alexander implied that she would fly off this barge at once if she learned of a federal restraint order. Do you deny you meant that?" she said, pointing fiercely at Cora.

"We deny it absolutely," said Bobby Winthrop in a smooth, breathy voice. "However, our simulations and weather predictions suggest that we must be airborne with the *Tesla* within the hour. Since issuing such a restraint order on the basis of emotional and scientifically implausible speculations would effectively end the experiment, and also this corporation, we feel certain that Judge Goldfarb will not make such a precipitous and economically disastrous decision."

"Oh, save that stupid crap for the Hebe judge," said Ray Alexander in a soft, disgusted snarl, but not quite softly enough.

"Did you have a comment, Mr. Alexander?" said the young woman in an alert, hard voice.

While Cora whispered fiercely at her husband and shot him an enraged glance of warning, Bobby Winthrop stepped toward the reporters, so that they would not get any closer to Ray and Cora. "All right," he said, and his voice was full and hearty, "we're engineers. If we can break this storm at sea, people, perhaps plenty of people, will be alive tomorrow instead of dead. If you had a beach house at Montauk, or a fishing vessel in Mystic Harbor, I wonder whom you'd rather have looking out for your life and property: the judges and lawyers, of which this country has more than anyplace else in the known universe, or Ray and Cora," and he tossed his head backwards to indicate the Alexanders. "Words are great, my friends, but when Claude comes ashore like a million express trains over the shelf, those sixty-foot breakers won't recognize any restraint orders."

A tall, older man in the center of the group waved a notebook and several others turned respectfully toward him, for this was the science editor of the _Times_ itself, the dean of American science writers. "I agree, Mr. Winthrop, let's drop the legal monkeyshines," he said cheerfully. "Can I ask the Alexanders about the terminal phase of this? Specifically, will the boat and aircraft be able to maintain the field and then escape? What about conditions at the eye when the storm disintegrates?"

Bobby half-turned and said in a hopeful, almost plaintive voice, "Cora?"

Cora Alexander nodded brusquely at the reporter. "The simulations we've run on the collapse phase are very sensitive to the assumed initiating conditions. The _Tesla_, as you can see, is sealed and can be inverted without injury or danger. If the storm bifurcates at a low altitude, well, there may be a problem with the aircraft."

"By problem," said the _Times_ man at once, "do you mean the plane might be torn apart in the upward-moving turbulence?"

"That can't be ruled out," said Cora at once.

"Mr. Alexander," said the reporter, "Techoceanics lost a plane and two men in a big thunderhead two years ago. Do you have any comments on that accident as it relates to this project?"

Before Bobby Winthrop could intervene, Ray had lifted his head and pointed an angry finger directly at the reporter. "We were forced into that idiotic stunt by our financial people. The goddamned upper cloud had a reversed polarity. When the induction machine ran into that electron excess, the stroke blew off a wing. We lost the finest geophysical pilot, the best and smartest man we ever had in this whole freak show. . . ."

"That was an entirely different experiment," said

Bobby hastily, "an attempt to electrically seed a thunderhead, you know, make rain. . . ."

But the man from the *Times* had pivoted and was now peering at the two short, portly, middle-aged men in bulky flying suits standing close together, but somewhat apart from the rest of the group. "Captain Stein, what are your ideas regarding Dr. Alexander's doubts about your aircraft?"

Milton Stein was a pudgy, forty-year-old avowed homosexual. He was Techoceanics' pilot and was usually cheerful and quiet, becoming more and more cheerful as a situation grew tighter. Now, the wet and humid dark pressing around him, the hostility of the reporters only thinly held back, the mission about to start, his flat, open face seemed almost a mask of bland cheerfulness.

"*Gay Enola* is a strong airplane," he said in a clear voice. "Smitty and I have stiffened her up, and those old Grummans were made tough." He turned and patted the shoulder of his long-time friend and associate, Bertram Smith, another short, pudgy man with another cheerful moonface. Stein and Smith had roomed together during graduate school, received doctorates in atmospheric physics, and together had started a geophysical contracting service. When Techoceanics had lost their chief pilot two years before, the two men agreed to join the hurricane modification project as full-time consultants. The young engineers around the shop called them Tweedledum and Tweedledee, but with respect and affection.

The *Times* man blinked at Stein. "*Gay Enola*? That's the name of your aircraft?"

Ray Alexander gave a snort of disgust, but it was partly covered by his wife's response, a warning snarl. The short pilot beamed at the press. "We're trying to do the opposite of what *Enola Gay* did, so Smitty thought it would be nice to reverse the name."

Bobby Winthrop gave a hearty but slightly nervous laugh. "What Captain Stein means, ha ha, is that our big bang will save lives, not end them."

The tall reporter gave a bemused shrug. "And don't you feel the name implies anything more?" he said almost slyly.

The pilot retained his benign expression, but he turned to directly face the *Times* man. "You imply, but we fly," Stein emphasized with a nod, "and so we will name it what we choose." Bertram Smith gave a chuckle and smiled shyly at his friend.

"Those weirdos'll fly without the Grumman," muttered Ray in a sour whisper, but this time too quietly for even his wife to catch it.

The *Times* man spoke once more. "Forget the name, Captain, what about the risk? What if *Gay Enola* isn't strong enough?"

"We people built close to the ground are hard to kill," said the pilot with a smile. "And our bonus, if we succeed, will buy a fleet of *Gay Enolas*. The world, I mean the remote-sensing geophysical world, will be ours."

Bobby Winthrop saw with relief that this was creating a sympathetic impression with the reporters, but then his stomach tightened as he felt Bettina Holbrook's hand suddenly grip his elbow. "Arthur called," she whispered close to his ear. "Judge Goldfarb is still taking arguments from the underwriters' lawyer, but Arthur thinks he's going to issue the restraint order. He put Arthur and the Hartford people under oath not to call us until the presentations were over."

Bobby blinked several times and reached at once into his inner, left-breast pocket. His hand moved swiftly from the pill bottle to his mouth. "Arthur broke his oath to the judge and they haven't even restrained us yet?" he whispered back. "Okay, you know the drill, Bettina sweetie. Get the Gold Dust Twins"—he made the smallest motion toward the pilot and his air crew—"over to the airport when the SeaCrane lifts off."

Bettina put her arm around Bobby's waist and hugged. "Promise me, when this is done, we'll walk away for a while. Promise, Bobby! Why should your gut hurt all the time because these crazies haven't got the self-discipline of a disturbed rattlesnake? Why, dammit?"

"We're in too deep. My God, Bettina, you know how bloody gigantic this thing is! Bettina, it's a whole hurricane! And we're going to rip out its gut from the *inside*, baby!"

Bobby Winthrop affectionately patted Bettina in a familiar place, then stepped sturdily forward again. "Dr. Holbrook, our project meteorologist, just notified me that Claude has accelerated and our rendezvous time has moved ahead." He strode through the reporters half-shouting these words and, as he strode, he pointed his two arms straight upward from each, and began to whirl them in rapid, tight circles. Instantly, the four big jet engines of the SeaCrane began to puff and rumble. With its two broad rotor-blade assemblies sagged limp and lifeless down around the fat machine and its fatter load, the idea of flight seemed ludicrous, but now the blades began to move. As they stiffened up and out, forming two great, hissing circles of air, the SeaCrane took on a far more businesslike aspect.

Bobby beckoned for Ray, then gave him a good-natured slap on the shoulder and wished him well. He seized Cora and to her astonishment, put his lips to her cheek. "They think the judge is going against us," he whispered. "Tell the pilot to stay offshore and as low as he can. Come around Montauk and scoot in from the south. Good luck, Cora."

She gave him a huge and fearful grin and scuttled after her small husband, under the safety ropes and into the small, open hull port on the otherwise smooth side of the *Tesla*. The door shut flush into the side of the boat, and Bobby now had his thumbs both vertical and he was throwing his fists upward, over and over again.

The SeaCrane whined and roared in answer and the chatter of the blades increased in both loudness and frequency. Flashbulbs popped, the cameras panned upward, and the SeaCrane lifted straight up, accelerating as it went, and was lost from sight in a moment, even its flashing navigation lights winking out at once behind the heavy mist. Bobby was pleased to note that _Gay Enola_'s crew, plus Bettina, was also gone. The noise of the SeaCrane was so great, he hadn't even heard her start her car.

"Thank you for coming," called out Bobby, waving his hands in a bye-bye gesture to the reporters. "Good night, wish us luck." He turned and walked into the after deckhouse and shut the door, then sat down at his messy desk in a straight chair and swallowed spit for a while. But he didn't quite throw up this time, and soon the nausea faded away and he swallowed some more pills and shakily wiped his forehead with a large, mono-grammed handkerchief.

As he sat, blinking and cold, waiting for Bettina to come back, the door opened and the young woman who had asked the environmental questions stepped in. Bobby stared at her from half-shut eyes. "Sorry," he said, "the press conference is over."

"Not quite," said the woman. "You people didn't finish the briefing. For example, the SeaCrane can't possibly reach that storm from here and return to land, so it has to be refueling someplace. Where? Long Island? New Jersey? And where did those pilots go? There isn't any Grumman Goose aircraft at the New Bedford air-port. Are they working off the water, out of a cove someplace?"

She looked around. "And you're going to vector the thing, but where? Where are the antennas and the satellite dish and all that stuff—on any of Techoceanics' properties around New Bedford?"

She took several steps towards him. "The fact is, you people knew there were going to be court and legal problems, and you planned for them. Your whole team is just going to disappear, and no federal marshal will know where in the hell you're at, until after you try your dangerous little trick!"

Bobby took some deep breaths, then managed a cold smile. "Tomorrow or the next day, dear, you're going to feel like the biggest damn fool in the whole world, because those two mad, infuriating geniuses in that nutty boat, and those two gentle queens—who incidentally have ten times the guts of any of you standing on our filthy barge in your double-knit suits—and a few other not-especially-nice people here and there, are going to blast Claude's guts into little pieces and save the world. You got onto an interesting story, dear, but you got it from the wrong end. You grabbed the wrong handle."

The woman took another step, and angrily lifted her finger to point at Bobby, but behind her came a sharp "Hold it!" The woman turned to see Bettina in the door behind her, hands on her hips, her face a mask of resolve. "Get off this property," she said icily. "The press conference is over!" and when the woman hesitated, she called, "Mike?" and a large and greasy workman appeared instantly at her elbow.

"I'm going," said the reporter stiffly, picking her way across the littered barge deck, "but not far. The bridge and the road aren't owned by Techoceanics!"

As soon as she climbed the ladder up to the roadway, Bobby got slowly to his feet and lifted a slicker off a hook. He grinned tiredly at Bettina, and they walked rapidly across the barge deck to climb down into the big Whaler resting at the bottom of the ladder. Mike grinned down at them. "Ya bust that storm, ya hear! Blast her ta pieces!"

He threw down their lines, and Bettina backed the boat out of its narrow space, the ninety-horse engine barely grumbling. Neither of them bothered to look back at the bridge, where the reporter stood peering after them, for within a hundred yards they had disappeared into the heavy mist, and the engine sound faded soon after.

Bobby pulled on his slicker and looked over at Bettina. "I love you," he said tenderly. "I'm going to be better . . . we're going to be better, after this is over."

Bettina smiled and nodded at him. "If it works,

everything will be better. Poor Arthur, what will he say when the judge asks where we've gone?"

Bobby shrugged. "The truth, I suppose. He really doesn't know where any of our refueling or rendezvous points are, or where the project management will locate."

Bettina shook her head. "They won't believe it. Dear old Arthur, in jail at last—and at his age, too."

Bobby sighed, then gently patted Bettina's slightly rounded slacks. "I'm going to be better, sweetie. Afterward. After it's done. I promise."

Sept. 8, midnight—0300 hrs.

HURRICANE CLAUDE REACHED ITS FULL MATURITY IN THE early morning of its fourth day of life. It now occupied many thousands of square miles of ocean, had extended its circulation pattern to over 30,000 feet, and had begun to move north at a steady 12 knots. Yet the Gulf Stream had swung close to land that fall and so the fuel that drove Claude's vast engine was plentiful as the storm neared the latitude of Hatteras. Ashore, along the barrier beaches, there was dark wet weather, gusts and freshets of warm tropic rain, and fitful swirls of heavy fog, but the dangerous eastern semicircle still lay 200 miles offshore.

But as Bettina Holbrook and the other meteorologists in Miami and Hartford and Boston had all feared, the storm was starting to hook west and run like a bowling ball right up the New Jersey gutter of low barometer. With the midnight advisory, Miami hoisted hurricane warnings as far north as Long Island, and hurricane watches north and east of that. Claude's energy flow was continuously out of balance, and that lack of equilibrium drove the great cyclonic winds around Claude's center at ever-greater rates.

At a little after midnight, the Panamanian container

ship *Commercial Queen*, struggling east and south to
escape the dangerous eastern side of the storm, was
caught by Claude's rapid acceleration and broken in two
by a wave, described by crewmembers later as over 100
feet high. Most of the men stayed with the stern of
the vessel and were saved by Coast Guard aircraft two
days later, but five men on the bow section were blown
out of sight to the west and never seen again. The
western fringe of Claude had already disabled several
yachts, but this was its first major kill. As it hooked
toward the distant Long Island shore, boatmen from
Washington, D.C. to Calais, Maine, began to think
about their anchors and their tackle. And suddenly, everybody wondered about the tide and when and
where the storm might come ashore. The old men
who had seen the harbors after the '38 storm just
shook their heads. If it came again like that, they said,
you just run for high ground. Forget the boats and
houses.

Bettina skillfully brought the Whaler alongside the
Michael Faraday, Techoceanics' forty-foot workboat,
where it lay off the Fairhaven docks hidden in the mist,
waiting for them. Bobby was feeling a bit more pep and
he jumped over the side with the Whaler's painter and
then helped Bettina climb up.

"Go, man," he said to Walter Nunes, the young
communications engineer running the *Faraday*. "Let's
get out of this harbor before they shut that crazy barrier."

"They're aiming for 10 A.M. or noon for that," said the
young man at once. "They called us, the Corps of
Engineers I mean, and asked for Bettina. When we said
she was at a press conference, they asked if she could
give them a call and her thoughts later, as they put
it."

"Screw that," said Bobby briskly. "Listen, they'll see
the boat going through the hurricane barrier, but there's
no point in their seeing me or Bettina. Where's Mr.

Equal Opportunity?"

"Sacked out below," said a grinning Nunes. "He's going to take her the last half of the run."

Bobby motioned for Bettina and they went down into the dark forward cabin. On one of the bunks, snoring strongly, was a large, rather scruffy young black man. His stained T-shirt had a mushroom cloud motif set next to a circular hurricane cloud, the two united by a lightning bolt. Above and underneath was printed a still deathless quote from Ray Alexander at a still-regretted Techoceanics environmental debate one year earlier: "Nuke 'em, shock 'em, who cares? I hate hurricanes!"

Bobby sat down next to Bettina on the other bunk and sighed, staring at this emblem of stupidity and needless defiance. "If we do it, Bettina," he said, as though trying to convince himself, "it will all be worth it."

"Don't despair, dear Bobby," she said softly, now hugging him to her. "You got us this far. But, oh, what if those two sweet little men . . .?" She did not finish, but hugged him silently and tightly. The *Michael Faraday* chugged along through the narrow gap of the New Bedford hurricane barrier, and the man in charge saw only one of the bearded Techoceanics engineers waving cheerily up at him. Well, they came and they went, he thought, and turned to talk to a reporter from CableNews about exactly when the barrier gate might be shut that next day.

The conspiracy to burst Claude's mighty heart had three final points of focus. On the south shore of Long Island, just west of Moriches Inlet, a major stockholder in Techoceanics and thus a much-interested bystander, had made a protected inlet and beach area available, plus his summer home. In the tiny shallow harbor sat a small fuel boat, filled chockablock with JP-2, ready to replenish the SeaCrane with its needed fuel for its final dash offshore to meet Claude and dump the *Nicola Tesla*.

* * *

On a tiny grass airport in central New Jersey, the old but sturdy Grumman Goose known as *Gay Enola* hid demurely under canvas coverings in a quiet corner of the field. When the sun set that day, the wraps came off, and now the local crew tensely awaited the arrival of the small executive plane Stein and Smith had used to leave the New Bedford Airport after midnight, leased under the name of one of their earlier, and now defunct, companies. Somehow, the flight plan had listed Albany Municipal Airport as destination instead of the Jersey strip.

To bring these giant-killers to the right point in time and proper location in space required a third and very complicated participant. Fortunately, a director of Techoceanics happened to be a trustee administering the almost deserted island of Wasque located south and west of Cape Cod. He had arranged for Geodata, a wholly owned but independent part of Techoceanics, to establish a satellite-communications testing lab at the low center of the island. In the small building there was the weather-access and communications gear that brought in all the ordinary channels, but most important, two big white, slow shifting dishes on top that gave this remote place direct and interference-free communications access to both *Gay Enola* and the *Nicola Tesla*.

Techoceanics had leased two channels for open use, and they were now locked on a high, Bell System transpolar satellite that would be up over them for several days, until long after the matter of Claude would be decided, one way or the other.

The early-morning fog thickened as they ran south and east of New Bedford. Bobby tried to sleep, with Bettina's arms around him, but a sudden foghorn hoot woke him up with a start and a shudder and they went back up to the wheelhouse. Walter Nunes lay on a cabin bench on his back, seemingly fast asleep, his beard pointing stiffly upward. Moke Mogamo, the black youth with the inflammatory T-shirt, now urged the *Faraday* at a quiet pace through the murk, the big engines only muttering. Every now and then he pushed the hooter button.

"Jesus, Moke," said Bobby Winthrop, "where in hell are we?"

Moke peered out with every appearance of confidence. "About a quarter mile northwest of the entrance buoy," he said with a careless wave of his hand.

"Why can't we hear the bell, then?" said Bobby, and he felt that familiar fist begin to close inside his gut again.

Moke gave him a relaxed grin. "Not enough swell to rock the big mother, Bobby. Damn thing is sitting there trying to fart out a big bonger and it can't even poop out a little ping."

"Think we could hire some ghetto folks to come and bong those bongers and poop those pings, Moke?" said Nunes without opening his eyes. "On the calm days, I mean."

"You been bongin' your bonger too much, old buddy. That's your whole problem. You gotta get your old lady away from that meditation stuff," said Moke in a cheerful and practical voice. "I got in three suggestions to the Screening Committee for ways to bong that buoy bell in a dead calm." He shrugged at Bobby. "Well, they said all the time at Harvard Business School you got to diversify, get into new, publicly visible projects. I don't mean busting hurricanes isn't visible, but you need homier stuff, too."

"Boy," said Nunes in a yawning voice, "nasty old Ray sure said it for once. There's nothing worse than a smart nigger. It isn't so much he stuffs the Haaavaaad B. School in your ear night and day, but then he's got all these public-spirited ideas about bongin' the bongers. Makes a man feel small."

But Moke was lost in thought. "It's really something to imagine that wonderful little ship is going to be driven to death or fame by the spiritual head of the Ku Klux Klans of the World. I mean Ray hates *everybody*. Nobody is discriminated against."

"Including Ray," said Bettina sourly.

Moke shook his head. "If he can do that, Bettina, drive that chariot to glory out there where old Claude's balls are hanging wild and loose, shit, the rest doesn't matter, right? I mean old Ray can crap on me for the rest of his mean old life and I'll still kiss the fucker's feet!"

"Where's that damn bell?" said Bobby, his whole body tensed, leaning forward.

Moke blinked and focused his thoughts. He turned his head slightly one way, then the other, and let his eyelids droop. "There," he said, "it oofed out a ding." He paused, then pointed. "Again!" he said.

"I hear it," said Bobby, blinking at Bettina and suddenly sitting down on the bench opposite Nunes.

"Our bow wave set the mother rocking," said Moke with an even more elaborate casualness. Like many shoal pilots, he had learned that the slower you went, the more confidence you showed. "There she is," he said, peering and pointing to starboard. "Fog's not so bad close to the island."

But Bobby once again crouched in the corner and tried to conceal his intense efforts at swallowing. He had easily imagined them lost, running circles or on a bar aground as the storm came north over them. Only Bettina noticed, and she sat next to him, stroking his forehead and whispering encouragement. They seemed like a unlikely bunch, to be challenging a giant like Claude.

Moke brought the *Faraday* alongside the main dock in the small protected harbor of Wasque, and they were assisted in tying up by Professor Wilson Worth, a retired expert in electrical engineering and friend of the trustees of Wasque Island. He served Techoceanics as an unpaid consultant and caretaker on the remote Wasque, and, like the others, awaited the attempt to dismember

Claude with complete anticipation.

Professor Worth was a tall and vigorous old man with a bushy white moustache. "Moke and Walt," he shouted down, "better get the *Faraday* on that one-ton storm mooring, the black one to the left, and be sure to put chafing gear on those lines. You can huff the Whaler up the rollers with the sixfold tackle. Run her way up, I think."

Moke shook his head sadly at Professor Worth. "Doc, that storm's not coming ashore. Ray and Cora are too mean to let it come in. Man, you gotta have faith."

Worth grinned and shrugged. "True, and I've got faith, but there may still be, uh, a slight elevation in water level." He helped Bettina, then Bobby, climb onto the wharf and threw the lines back on the *Faraday* as Moke backed her out and turned to make a circle out to the mooring.

"C'mon," said Worth to Bettina and Bobby, "I'll run you guys to the shack while they do their stuff with the boats." They climbed into an open jeep and began a brief, slow, bumpy trip over an old sheeping meadow down to the bowl of a tiny hidden pond where the small concrete-block communications building squatted at its edge. Two big white dish antennas sat pointing at the same section of sky, and a thin 200-foot guyed mast poked high over Wasque, another microwave dish at its top.

"Anything come in?" said Bobby in a dispirited voice as they walked into the fluorescent-lighted space, filled along three walls with consoles and instrument racks.

Professor Worth lifted his thick eyebrows. "Nothing from Long Island or Jersey yet, but they won't be arriving for a little while. Miss Philips, Arthur's Girl Friday, sent us a message through the answering service. Judge Goldfarb issued the restraint, and when he found there were no corporate officers, or even a project manager, to serve, he ordered Arthur to tell him where everyone had gone. Arthur said he didn't know, and

Goldfarb charged Arthur with contempt."

Bobby sighed tiredly. "Goldfarb and Arthur were classmates at Yale Law School," he said.

Bettina shook her head. "Yeh, but Goldfarb was president of the Jewish law fraternity and didn't even get on the Law Review Board until his last year, even though he was No. 1 in his class. Arthur was editor. Hateful Ray knows all those nasty kinds of things."

Professor Worth stroked his moustache and cleared his throat. "I'm afraid Judge Goldfarb is subjecting Arthur to torture," he said somberly.

"Come on, Willie," said Bobby in an even more tired voice. "In Boston, they're going to torture a seventy-year-old former president of the Bar Association?"

"Judge Goldfarb decided that Arthur should be held in custody, until he purges his contempt and tells where we are, but he didn't want to toss classmate Arthur in with the drug-pushers and hookers. So instead, he's had two cots set up in his chambers, and he and Arthur are going to live there until Goldfarb has convinced Arthur to obey the law and purge himself. He's going to talk to him, to lecture him, man to man, judge to attorney, Jew to Gentile."

"So it *is* torture," said Bettina, simultaneously grinning and squeezing out a tear. "Dear old Arthur," she said fondly. "Everybody is fighting so hard for us, Bobby. Oh, we must win! How's Claude doing, Willie?"

Professor Worth led them over to the weather consoles and the large visual display showing the eastern seaboard and the western North Atlantic region. "Seems to be coming along nicely, Bettina. I ran your combined statistical projection and map-analysis program on it about a half hour ago and got that output there for First Touch."

Bettina peered down at the printer-drawn map, the concentric ovals of pressure gradient showing the eye with the first oval just meeting the Long Island shore at about Montauk Point at the eastern tip. "About eighteen hours to that point, huh?" She shook her head in thought. "Bobby, we'd better make a full vector projection right now. Ray and Cora won't have much time to hang around on that Long Island beach."

Bobby nodded, grimacing, then shucked his suit coat and dark silk vest. "Okay, let's do it. Willie, keep an eye on the com channels so we know when our wandering friends reach their destinations." He sat down heavily in front of the main computation racks and shook his head. "The closer we get to this, the more impossible it becomes," he said almost to himself. "But maybe that's for the best. If it doesn't work, *Gay Enola* might make it back out of the eye."

Professor Worth patted Bobby's shoulder and his voice was thoughtful. "I don't know as I wouldn't rather be in that Goose with Uncle Milt and Aunt Bertie flying me through the exploding eye of a hurricane, than in those chambers being lectured by Judge Goldfarb on law and order."

Sept. 8, 0300—0800 hrs.

HURRICANE CLAUDE WAS NOW A GIGANTIC, FULLY MATURED, rotating storm, extending over thousands of square miles and influencing the entire circulation over the North Atlantic Ocean west of the Azores. To the east, in its dangerous sector, the winds blew from the south and east with gusts of over 100 miles an hour. To the west of the storm center, where the mammoth Canadian high had dipped deeply into the continental heartland to challenge Claude for the American coast, thunderstorms and drenching rains ran along the ridge of increasing barometer, and buffeting northwest winds rattled windows as far west as Cleveland.

Yet when it came abreast of Hatteras, Claude's life-to-be was well established by the heavy, supine Canadian and Greenland cold-air masses. The long low-pressure trough, lying like a great snake up the Jersey coast to cross Long Island and bisect Cape Cod, drew Claude north and helped it to run. Low attracted low, and each system fed the other's needs.

Most of the predictions agreed that the three-quarter-moon tide would be high one to three hours after Claude came ashore at Montauk, then struck Rhode Island and Cape Cod. Everywhere, boats were desperately lifted and hauled, moorings checked and worried over, plywood sheets nailed up over the big picture windows at Quogue and Matunuck, Menemsha and Madaket. And when people peered, in those summer towns and fishing villages, at the old marks painted after the '38 and '54 storms to show the water rise, then turned to look out at the close, foggy, sullen water, they knew that nothing would save the boats and houses, if it came like that again.

The huge bloated SeaCrane drifted in, hissing and roaring, from the south over the foggy Long Island shore. A transponder, set in the center of the small beach, brought the big machine down next to the fuel boat, itself barely floating in the tiny inlet. Cora had the hatch open and was unwinding out of it before the big blades drooped down to a lifeless sag. As she jogged towards the big angular modern house, embellished with its own white microwave dish pointing upward, she met the Techoceanics communications man-in-charge running to meet her.

"We've got Wasque on the beam and they give us two hours, twenty minutes to lift, Cora," he said in a tense voice.

"Where does that put the final moment, in relation to Long Island?" said Cora, turning in impatient annoyance to see Ray finally tumble out of the small hatch and sleepily begin a walk to the beach house. He had snoozed during the entire trip from New Bedford.

"You better talk to Bettina on that, Cora," said the young man as they stalked briskly through big double doors and into a book-lined study, now turned into a wire-laced and sophisticated communications link.

Cora put on a headset. "Who's there? Moke?"

"Hi, Cora. They fueling the chopper? You got to move out soon, lady."

"Where's Bettina?"

"Here, Cora. Listen, we're sending the vector-final

map-fax. Stand by," said Bettina, and the SatFax machine began to create a North American operations map, complete with the tracks of Claude, the SeaCrane-*Tesla* mission, and *Gay Enola*'s course to the final meeting at the eye of the storm, all with times and headings.

Cora and a still-sleepy Ray watched the map develop, and Cora shook her head. "But that puts breakup at less than 300 miles south of land, Bettina. And you've got us going into Claude head-on, or at least almost."

"Claude may be hitting over fifty knots up there, Cora. Do you want to miss the eye? If you try to enter from the northwest quadrant, you might be driven too far south. The oval-of-confusion-of-intercept has a bag to the south of the center with that kind of approach." Bettina spoke in an intent and professional tone.

Ray stared sleepily down at the map. "Better 300 miles than zero, stupid!" he said in a slurred, insulting voice, and Cora nodded without expression.

"Okay," she said, "that's our baseline plan. What's the ninety-five percent lower-limit on lift-off here? They said we should go in two hours and twenty minutes?"

"Be ready in the *Tesla* by one hour and thirty minutes from now," said Bettina. "Start your engines by two hours, if we haven't given you the go by then. You'll definitely lift on or before two hours and twenty minutes from now."

"Okay, and I'll be back to you again in one hour, if something hasn't come up before then. What about Arthur?"

"Cora, look," said Bettina, "I want to get back to the storm. Willie got the whole thing direct from Arthur's sec. Here he is . . ."

And as the story of Arthur's incarceration and inquisition flew out to near the moon and back again, Cora turned and snarled at Ray. "Get some water boiling for the damn lobsters, dummy! We've only got an hour and a half."

"Jesus, lobsters!" said Ray in disgust, speaking to the communications engineer. "We'll be setting up a five-million-volt field in a pool of stinking lobster upchuck.

Wait'll that boat takes a couple of 180-degree rolls. That lobster won't stay in her gut, sonny!"

But the young engineer had dealt with Ray before and he gave him a slap on the back. "Ray, forget the five million volts. You just piss on that storm and it'll crawl right back to the Caribbean. Come on. Let's go have a drink."

A short time later, in the thin dawn over a murky New Jersey landing field, the small plane from New Bedford came in to land and then taxied directly to where *Gay Enola* waited.

As he bounced over the grass, Stein saw his tall and rangy crew chief, Stew Johnson, waving them in from under *Gay Enola*'s right wing. The big man had on flight coveralls, and over his shoulder was a parachute pack, and they could see that his face was grim. "Smitty," said Milton Stein in a tight voice. "We got trouble! Is your stuff together?"

"Just my kit bag, dear," said Smith in a squeaky voice. "Everything else is on *Gay Enola*."

"Then let's get going," said Stein, cutting his engine and popping open the hatch over the side-by-side seats.

As they climbed quickly down over the wing, the big crew chief strode over. "The weather lady at Wasque called about ten minutes ago and said that the Boston judge sent marshals into the New Bedford offices to seize all of Techoceanics' records. She thinks this place will be compromised. She said we should get off the ground and go over the lake to wait. There's still about six hours until you go out, she said."

Stein looked over across the field to the tiny control tower and the small complex of hangars and parking lot. "Any marshals show up yet, Stew?"

"Not as far as we can tell . . . Wait, isn't that a car coming up the access road, way over there, Milt?"

"Let's go!" said Stein. "You come to the lake with us, Stew."

"Oh dear, *two* cars!" said Bertram Smith in a small, dismayed voice. He turned and jumped up into *Gay Enola*'s open cabin door.

Stein and Johnson followed him and pressed rapidly forward between the large electrical machines in the main cabin area of the Goose, up to the pilot's office. "She's ready, Milt," said Stew Johnson, settling into the copilot's seat and hitting both engine starters. The two big radials began to swing their props and in an instant they were banging and grumbling.

"Get the door, Smitty," shouted the pilot over the engine noise. "Here we go!"

Gay Enola trundled out onto the main east-west strip and started her takeoff run. There was almost no wind, and the pilot shoved both throttles ahead to full-emergency power. *Gay Enola* had new, supercharged double-radials, to give her the altitude capability needed to reach the upper parts of storms, and she bounded ahead on her small wheels with an almost rabbitlike motion.

"They're coming after us!" said Johnson as the two cars swung rapidly through the small parking lot next to the control tower and dashed out onto a taxi strip. "They're trying to cut us off!"

"Techoceanics Goose, this is control tower. You are not cleared for takeoff. Repeat, you are not—"

Stew Johnson turned off the radio with a curse, closely watching the two approaching cars. "They're going to get ahead of us, Milt. They can go faster," he said in a low voice, and moments later the first car dashed onto the runway ahead and slewed in a skidding, half-circle as the driver slammed on his brakes.

Bertram Smith, who stood behind them at the rear of the pilot's cabin, sighed and shook his head. "Oh my," he said, "eight hours still to go and we're already in a game of chicken with some nasty police. It really is one thing after another, isn't it, Miltie?"

Milton Stein made no comment. His expression was completely, blandly cheerful and he seemed to be hardly watching as the second car swerved to a stop beside the first one, while four men rapidly jumped out waving their arms. They soon stopped this as they realized that the big amphibian was getting both larger and noisier at a rapid rate. As one, they all fell down flat on the ground in front of their cars, and at that moment Stein pulled the wheel sharply back and *Gay Enola* gave a big hop, passing over the cars at an altitude of about ten feet. The amphibian staggered and sagged a bit lower, but did not touch the runway again, and they felt the ground effect cushion her until full flying speed was achieved and they began to climb steadily.

Stew Johnson let out a great gasp of breath and wiped his forehead. "You did it again, Milt. At least the bastards didn't shoot at us."

"Isn't he wonderful!" said Bertram Smith, who leaned to kiss the pilot warmly on his right cheek. "Everything is just so *exciting* with Milton!"

Stew Johnson shook his head and gave them both a huge grin. "Boy, you guys are really something else! By God, I wish I could go all the way in with you!"

Stein turned to smile at the crew chief. "So do we, Stew, but we might not get back with an extra man aboard to worry about."

The crew chief nodded, staring at his boots. "I know that. Still, I'd sure like to see you do it."

Gay Enola flew south and west for twenty more minutes, then came down to land on a small and private lake on a large and private estate in northeastern Pennsylvania. Sitting on a pier, his expression bored and pouting, a thin twelve-year-old boy was idly throwing stones at some ducks, which eventually flew off, quacking angrily. He turned in surprise as the big amphibian settled onto the water and rapidly taxied over to the float. His sneering, spoiled expression faded as he noticed the name of the plane, then its logo of a hurricane vortex pierced by a lightning bolt. The hull gently bumped the float as the engines died away, and Stew Johnson jumped out of the door onto the dock and grabbed a rope.

"Your dad around, son?" asked the crew chief, but then, hearing a distant shout, he looked up to see a short, fat, bald man walking rapidly down to the lake from a sprawling house. "Ah, here he comes," said Johnson.

The boy's eyes had grown large and round. As the pilot and Bertram Smith stepped out of *Gay Enola* onto the dock, he blinked. "Are you guys the hurricane busters?" he said in a high, astonished voice. "What are you doing *here*?"

Milton Stein pointed at the big house. "Smitty and I are going to sack out until the mission, but Stew can show you around the aircraft." He indicated the crew chief, then stepped across the dock to shake hands with a small, excited fat man who had hurried up, puffing and sweating in the tropical-feeling, damp morning. "How are you, Mr. Heartshorn? Nice to see you again."

"It's certainly a relief to see you people," said the overweight little banker. "One of your gang called up to tell us you were on the way."

"Any of them get caught?" said Stein, beaming cheerfully at the fat, agitated man.

Heartshorn shook his head angrily, his jowls vibrating. "Your bunch left in a van while those cuckoos were playing car games on the runway with you. By God, I'm going to see those federal bastards in jail when this is over, believe me." The banker shook his head. "The trouble is, with the Techoceanics management and PR staff essentially out of the picture, our adversaries are having a field day in the press. They're beginning to sound as though we really were going to use a hydrogen bomb on the damn storm! And that loud, public flap drives the federal cops into playing James Bond. Well, they got their tit in the wringer this time, Captain, believe me!"

The small boy stared, his mouth an O, at his fat, ugly little father. "Hey, Dad, wow! Are you in this, *too*?" His usually scowling or sneering expression was replaced by a combination of hero worship and complete astonishment.

The banker stared at his son, and his small, angry eyes

became softer and his expression was one of sudden, surprised pleasure. "I'm in like Flynn, Peter," he said with a grin. "One million bucks worth I'm in, and if we do it, even that plane won't be big enough to carry the hundred-dollar bills to the bank. Come on, boys, breakfast is waiting, and then you can take a nap until we get the go from Wasque." He walked back up the dock between the pilot and Bertram Smith, talking animatedly to both.

The small boy watched his father walk away, and shook his head. "I thought he just went to a bank and yelled at people. Wow, and he owns some of *this*!" He made a worshipful gesture at *Gay Enola*.

Stew Johnson gave the boy a wide smile. "Big ideas, like hurricane busting, take all kinds of people, Peter, and you're one of them. Come on, we want to get old *Enola* here alongside that inner float and well back under the tree leaves. You never know who might come snooping by overhead."

As the boy and the man pulled the Grumman deeper under the tall, spreading trees at the edge of the lake, the boy shook his head. "How come they're trying to stop us, saying all that dumb stuff on TV, Mr. Johnson?"

"Oh," said Stew Johnson, scratching his ear, "we just happen to be living at a time when most people like talking better than doing. But it'll all turn around, Peter. It always does."

"Well," said the boy, staring at *Gay Enola* now rocking gently deep in her shady bower, "when I grow up, that's what I'm going to be, a hurricane buster!"

The tall man put his arm around the boy's shoulders. "Peter, you remember, once you get started on something like this, it's just awfully hard to stop."

Bettina stared bitterly and almost unseeing at the operations map displayed on the biggest computer scope. They had saved *Gay Enola*, just barely, but they had paid a price. While the technician in the ops shack on the New Jersey field excitedly described the near-disaster of the takeoff and escape, Bobby had suddenly doubled over in his chair and vomited down between his legs. After five minutes of mostly dry retching, Moke had poked him with a big syringe of morphine from the medical kit, and Bobby had gone off to sleep in the corner of the room on a mattress. Bettina had been careful not to mention Bobby when Cora's one-hour call-back came, and *Gay Enola*'s narrow escape in New Jersey had swept everything else from Cora's head. Bettina's eyes were pinched and red and her face was gray, but she had managed the first phase of it, including warning the New Jersey crew, and now the final part was close, and with Bobby rested, they might get through it.

"Moke," said Bettina quietly, "you give them the lift-off final, and any other stuff they need. And send them now. There's no point waiting for another five minutes if they're ready."

Moke leaned forward and spoke. "Cora, Bettina says go when you're ready, okay? Your update vector-final is still looking good."

"Engines are on," came back Cora's deep voice. "We're light. Mark! We're airborne," and Professor Worth set the time against the digital display line, SEACRANE LAUNCH AT MORICHES, FINAL.

"We're going up," said Cora; then, more sharply, "Ray, you blew a fart! I told you to go and shit . . ."

But riding over that was Ray's retort, "It's just your own sweet breath blowing back into your kisser, my dear," and behind this came a roar of laughter from the SeaCrane pilots.

Bettina sat back and looked over at Professor Worth with a tired smile. "Imagine trying to run this zoo without a whip and a gun," she said. "Willy, I've got to get some sleep. Moke and Walt can run the system for a couple of hours. We really don't have to sweat until they drop the *Tesla*."

Professor Worth, whose moustache now drooped

somewhat in the humid morning air, sighed deeply. "Even if we lose Moriches to the feds now, it won't matter," he said, "but what if the marshals come here?" Bettina didn't answer. She had gone over to lie down close to Bobby, pull up a blanket, and throw a protective arm over his large, quiet form.

Sept. 8, 0800—1600 hrs.

CLAUDE, THOUGH STILL EXTENDING ITSELF TO THE EAST, WAS now running straight north at over forty knots. Ahead of the eye's violently steep gradient, terminating at 28.6 inches in the core of the storm, a series of great waves ran as consorts, preparing to lead the storm ashore. In the deep water, out beyond the thousand-meter line, these wind- and pressure-driven waves were only a few feet high and would pass a beleaguered vessel unnoticed in the terrible slash and confusion of the storm. But they were very long and they were driven at speeds far higher than such waves normally exhibited. As the storm accelerated, so would these leader waves gain velocity, and when they came over the Long Island and New England extensions of the Continental Shelf, their enormous energy of forward motion would be transformed in a few moments by the bottom friction into vast, tumbling breakers, forty to sixty feet high. When four such barometrically driven water waves struck the southern Rhode Island resort town of Misquamicut during the '38 storm, every house was broken into small pieces, the rubble driven a mile or more inland across a salt pond, and dozens of householders killed in an instant of smashing destruction and unimaginable violence.

The warnings increased on TV and radio, and people began to draw back from the coasts. Small towns and beach-house rows on the south Long Island coast emptied out, and in some places only the water people —charter skippers, scallopers, and cohaugers—gathered to assist each other. It's the rise in the water you've got to watch, they said to each other, that and the wind shift after the eye passes.

A big steel dragger, *Judith Ann*, with twelve aboard, lost her engines at just the wrong moment, north and east of Claude's center, the most dangerous quadrant, and was soon rolled upside down and sunk in a few moments as two huge seas came together in *Judith Ann*'s sea-space. "Killer Claude" the Globe named the storm then, and soon all the papers headlined more or less the same thing: KILLER STORM WILL STRIKE BEFORE MIDNIGHT!

Bettina and Bobby set zero hour for the attack on Claude at 1520, midafternoon, at which time they estimated Claude's eye would have reached a location 290 miles south of Montauk Point.

The mission profile for the SeaCrane phase was for the helicopter to penetrate from the north to within the storm system as close to this attack point as possible, then ditch the *Tesla*. Though the boat had over a thousand horsepower that could be delivered to two big propellors, the *Tesla*'s sea surface mobility was intended mainly to correct or improve local position and to maneuver once it was inside the eye. The idea was that Claude would come to where the *Tesla* waited. The trick was to deliver the boat as close to the final moment as possible, to minimize wave pounding and damage, but not so close that the SeaCrane could not penetrate the storm's northern edge.

At about 250 miles south of Long Island, the SeaCrane's first pilot was shaking his head and fighting his buffeted machine. "Bobby," he said, "I don't think this should be pushed. This damn storm is getting wild, even this far north."

The SeaCrane staggered along at about 1,000 feet above the churning ocean, struck by vicious side-gusts and whipped by wild sprays of salt spume and rain, blown in every direction by the increasing wind. Even at this altitude, the roar of the storm wind was overwhelming, masking any other engine and airframe noises.

An acrimonious argument then started among the SeaCrane pilots, Cora and Ray; Cora wanting to press further, Ray wanting to try hooking a bit west to see if they could sneak in closer to the eye that way, and the pilots wanting to ditch the *Tesla* then and there.

Bettina now had the *Tesla*'s position established on the big system's map. "They're almost 260 miles south now, Bobby, and Ray can run south and gain some more miles. Do it! Get the thing into the water!"

"It isn't that bad yet, damn it," said Cora, starting to argue again.

"Shut up, Cora!" said Bobby sharply, and she stopped talking at once. "I'm the system's manager and I order you to ditch *now*. Commence your descent." He wiped his forehead unsteadily. "The *Nimbus* interferometer is showing mean wave height of only five or six feet under you. Ray can run at least some of the way south if you start now, Cora." He said this more quietly and slowly.

"We're at 500," came the pilot's voice. "Very stiff, turbulence bad and visibility is zilch . . . 300 . . . two . . . whup, almost caught us that time . . . Okay, 50 feet, we're staggering, 20 . . . prepare to drop, Ray."

"Safety locks off," said Ray.

"Disconnect," said the pilot, "you're free, Ray," and the *Tesla* fell ten feet to hit the choppy ocean surface with a giant splash as the SeaCrane, free of its huge burden, darted up and off to the west like a dragonfly caught in a sudden upward wind gust.

The pilot cabin of *Tesla* contained two side-by-side foam-padded seats that could be reclined for sleeping. Ray, in the left-hand (or pilot's) position, navigated the

Tesla with his wheel and throttles, and he now engaged the propellers and started off through the white, breaking chop at a good eight knots. The boat took some bad thumps and hammering from the steep waves, and Cora looked over at her small, intent husband with a sneer. "Slow up, dummy. We exceeded our allowed shock limits twice in thirty seconds."

"I thought you wanted to go south," said Ray, making a lip fart, but he eased back on the throttles and the *Tesla* went more easily, now only snap-rolling occasionally when an especially large sea swept over her whale-shaped upper body. But the day was dark, and it grew darker as they struggled slowly south.

At a little before 1300, *Gay Enola* lifted off the small private lake into a wet, now-blustery, rain-filled sky and made a graceful circle to the east. Only three people saw the start of the mission: the short banker, his son, and the crew chief, and they all waved from the float as *Gay Enola* lifted off the water in a spatter of white foam. Stew Johnson soberly watched them rise and finally fly out of sight, then thoughtfully bit his lip. "Mr. Heartshorn, I don't know whom rich bankers pray to in a tight corner, but maybe you ought to try it now for those two men."

But Peter Heartshorn's eyes were like stars, and he hugged his father. "I'd give anything to be there with them. *Anything!*"

Gay Enola climbed and climbed as she sped east, and there was darkness and turmoil at every level. Thunderstorms were dodged near the coast, with Bettina's help, and finally the Grumman broke into clearer air at 20,000 feet, and turned on the final-vector run into the eye. The turbulence and updrafts were fierce and continuous, but *Gay Enola* was approaching Claude's great heart from the west, where the headlong, forward run of the storm subtracted part of the force of the rotary storm winds. Higher and higher they went until, a little after 1500, *Gay Enola* burst through some high scudding cloud and entered the vast and open oval eye of Hurricane Claude.

Below, everywhere, were sloping, steaming banks of cloud, ranged in a mounting, ridged vortex of unimaginable proportions. Along that rough yet shockingly organized confusion ran thinner sheets and daggers of ripped, slashed cloud, torn out of the face by the howling circular winds.

Bertram Smith had started the big generator which comprised _Gay Enola_'s main payload, and now he looked down from a hull blister and talked to Bobby Winthrop.

"It's quite lovely, Bobby," he said in his high, calm voice, "but, oh my, so big!"

As they flew further east, the whole shape of the eye became apparent, opening out beneath them, and in the slanting afternoon sun that burned brightly above they caught a glimpse of the white froth and dark confusion of water surface through the smother of cloud far, far below. And as Smith peered intently, he saw, suddenly and faintly, a tiny wink, an intense speck of light against the dirty gray-white of racing clouds and raging sea.

"Bobby," he said, "I see Ray and Cora's flasher. They're north of us, maybe six miles."

"We have them near you," said Bobby. "Ray, keep that xenon beacon going. _Gay Enola_ can see you now."

Ray grunted in assent. The last half hour had been the worst for the _Tesla_, as everyone had expected, and even the partial lowering of an antiroll keel had not prevented two or three near-total upsets. Through all this, Ray had maintained a running fire of remarks about yorking and Dramamine, especially annoying since Cora had never been seasick in her life, but she had her revenge when it took Ray ten minutes to urinate into his little seat container, a process Cora did not help by making pointed suggestions and coarse insults about Ray's inadequacies.

The waves were gigantic on the northern edge of the eye, and impossible to anticipate since visibility was down to ten feet in a continual, horizontal blast of torn wave tops. The _Tesla_ rolled halfway over in a wild cross-sea, caught an especially vicious blast of dense rain, and then, an improbable miracle, came out into sunshine. In a few minutes, Cora could see partway up the huge funnel of cloud sweeping around them, an endless, complex, wildly moving structure, beyond imagination and beyond hope. For an instant, Cora's heart turned to water and her breath caught in her throat. It was impossible. There was too much of it.

"Losing your nerve, Cora?" said mean, sharp-eyed Ray, for he had seen that moment of weakness, that flicker of dissolution in his wife's face. "Kind of like pissing on the sun to put it out, eh?" he snarled.

"Connect up the generators, put the keel all the way down, and cut the bullshit, Ray," said Cora in a steady voice. "Bobby, I'm erecting the electrode mast."

"Do it!" came the words right back. "I'm bringing *Gay Enola* north over you along the storm track. Bettina thinks the northern edge of the storm is in a near state of instability now, because of this wild forward velocity, so I'm going to plug you both in as soon as we get vertical alignment with *Gay Enola*. How's the sea state?"

"Bad. We're rolling twenty degrees, but it's getting less and the keel helps. The mast is up and we're getting some stability as the wind drops. Bobby, we're sitting in warm sunshine."

"Steady," said Bobby to both his distant charges. "You set, Bertie?"

"Our electrode is down and the generator is running. Just give the word, Bobby. How big it all is. Oh my!"

"Hold it, we're coming up on alignment," said Bobby in his tightest voice, and clustered around his chair in front of the systems map display were the four other members of the Wasque vectoring team. Five pairs of eyes watched the tiny light point that identified *Gay Enola* move up the screen to finally cover the steady point that showed where the *Tesla* pitched and waited.

"Now," breathed four voices.

"We've got alignment!" shouted Bobby. "Hit it!" Over the speakers came simultaneous confirmation from Cora and Bertram Smith in identical words "Field is on! Full power!"

In the strange, sun-drenched, seemingly benign eye, the *Tesla*'s 5-million-volt field immediately produced a huge cloud of ionized air and water vapor. This immense field immediately drew solid strikes from low clouds to the north, and these flashing, ionizing trails crossed and drew more strikes, so that in less than ten seconds the entire sky over the *Tesla* was filled with continual, massive ripples of lightning. But there was no thunder to these displays. The bolts did not discharge a static cloud and then stop, allowing the colder, surrounding air to roar back in. They were replenished by the giant, rotational motion of Claude itself. The ripple of fire now rode rapidly up the air column, strikes and bolts opening up new current paths everywhere.

To Ray and Cora, it seemed almost like an explosion of electrical fire around them, harder and brighter than the sun, but a slow explosion taking almost a full minute to reach its peak, and when the sky was totally filled with rippling, wavering, expanding bolts, they dropped sunshade lenses over their goggles and saw only that they were bathed in the brightest, most intense, yet coldest light they had ever seen.

At the top of the storm, when *Gay Enola*'s field was switched on, the path was longer, about a thousand feet down to the towed electrode, and so the glowing field was both longer and thinner, but within a few moments the field had drawn strikes and the whirl of electrical discharges had disappeared down into the maw, where a white, intense glow was flowing upward. A moment later, the gigantic circuit was completed and sustained from top to bottom. Later, Techoceanics' atmospheric physics group estimated the maximum current flow at peak activity was over a billion amperes. Claude's entire eye was filled with electrical fire, and its fearsome integration, its wonderful, deadly balance was destroyed in an instant.

Only four persons actually observed that climactic

moment, and to them it was simply a sense of light so intense and increasing so rapidly in intensity that the world became entirely light. And though the *Nimbus IV* cameras surely caught that vast, sudden glow of Claude's death, the vision passed unseen by all the world because when the final circuit was complete, the explosive production of electromagnetic, longwave radiation, blasting and bouncing around the earth, interrupted every channel of nonwire communication of the globe with a static disturbance so strong that absolutely no signal transfer was completed for several minutes. So bank balances were upset, phone connections lost, and TV programs interrupted, and the greatest electromagnetic signal to be generated in the history of the planet was sent out in all directions to tell even the stars of Claude's sudden end.

In the Wasque operations center, they heard the static scream begin, and saw the TV pictures dissolve to shards of jagged confusion, and they stared at each other in elated disbelief. Of all the communications specialists, everywhere in the world, attempting to retrieve some signal or bit of information at that moment, they, most of all, understood the meaning of that blast of wild electromagnetic confusion. The speakers buzzed and screeched, but no one touched a volume knob.

"That's old Claude dying, good buddy," said Moke, throwing his arm around Walter Nunes's shoulders, "and you know what he's screaming over those speakers while mean old Ray and tough old Cora shove a lightning bolt up his ass? 'Why me?' that's what he's saying, *'Why me?'*"

"Look at that electromagnetic disruption!" said exultant Professor Worth. "My God, think of that energy release! This is unbelievable!"

"I wonder how our friends are doing in this?" said Bettina soberly, and they watched and waited, for what seemed like hours but was no more than two and a half minutes, until the screens began to clear and the wavery images to strengthen. And when the pictures came back from *Nimbus*, at Wasque, and in Boston, and Miami, and many other places, several dozen sharp intakes of breath occured simultaneously, for in that smallest interval, Claude was irrevocably changed. The eye was collapsing. They could see the deep instability ripples on the northern edge begin to smear and overrun the eye. The sharp, crisp look of the hurricane vortex was being ruined and the eye was disappearing, losing its form and identity.

As that final collapse accelerated, Claude's agony intensified, and the storm finally bifurcated, broke apart at about 8,000 feet, and the downward-moving pressure wave hit the *Tesla*, cushioned by the sea, with no more than a tremendous thump of overpressure.

What happened in the next five minutes at the sea surface was far worse. The winds, which had been no more than 90 miles an hour along Claude's northern sector, now began to switch direction and to accelerate to brief, sudden gusts of more than 300 miles an hour. Since this brief, wild reversal of direction occurred in a vertical sense as well, these sudden, huge gusts caught hailstones and sent them at immense speeds through the wet clouds until they were as large as lemons or baseballs, then drove these hard and deadly missiles around inside the storm interior like a million random cannon shots.

The *Tesla*, her mast torn and battered away, was suddenly beset by a massive hailstorm that penetrated the hull in several places with thunderous crashes, the entire bombardment producing a deafening roar of damage as the ice balls broke apart on impact with shuddering force and rocketed off to continue their screaming courses downwind.

Ray instantly curled up in a tight ball in his seat, his arms over his head, but Cora turned and snarled, "We're holed, stupid! Come on, get off your ass! We're sinking! We'll get back to you later, Bobby . . ."

Yet that message of alarm and danger was not the worst to come. The people at Wasque, and in the *Tesla*, listened mutely, their stomachs constricted in fear and anguish as Milton Stein spoke steadily from a background of wild noises and obvious transmission problems. "We lost an engine, Bobby. Turbulence just ripped it out of the wing. Never seen this sort of air movement before. Very wild, very strong. We're in a flat spin and the tail controls seem to be severed."

"Milt, Bertie, get in the capsule! Get out, Milt!"

"We're trying, Bobby. Listen, I'm going to try an inflight prop reversal with the other engine, to break the spin. Maybe we can get clear then."

"You'll tear off a wing!" shrieked Bobby, but the signal from *Gay Enola* went suddenly and completely dead, and Bobby's flushed, intense expression instantly vanished. He half-rose and turned to Bettina with a vague, puzzled expression on his face. "Bettina, help me, plea—" and he fell forward on his knees and then onto his face, and his right foot made a terrifying little tattoo of three or four thumps on the floor.

"Moke! Willy! He's dying!" screamed Bettina, and in an instant Moke had Bobby turned on his back and was listening intently at his chest. "Oh man, his ticker's stopped!" said Moke at once. "Come on, old buddy," he pointed a finger at Nunes, "you took the course, too. You pump and I'll puff. I don't smoke that wheezy old reefer your woman grows in those window boxes."

"Bettina," said Professor Worth in a low, worried voice, "Quick! Give him a shot of heart stimulant!" He pulled the big medical kit off its shelf and opened it on the floor next to Bobby. While Bettina desperately stripped wrappings from the disposable syringe and then drove the needle into Bobby's right arm and Walter Nunes pushed downward in rhythm to give the heart massage through Bobby's chest, Moke expertly cleared Bobby's tongue with a forward finger sweep and began to puff air into his mouth while watching Bobby's chest rise and fall. On the fourth puff, Moke saw Bobby's eyes fly open and look directly into his, and he lifted his mouth and sent him back a grin and a wink. Bobby gave several rattling coughs, but his color was coming back a bit and he finally returned a weak wink. "Moke, dear, I didn't know you cared," he said in a faint voice. "How come you didn't mention it?"

Bettina knelt by Bobby's head and the tears streamed down her face. "Baby, don't leave me again! Oh, Bobby, my sweet, don't go away!"

Bobby took, then squeezed her hand. "I'm not going anyplace, Bettina. I got where I'm going."

But Bettina was now down acoss him, her lips against his pale cheek, and she was speaking with a passionate intensity. "Bobby, listen, we'll do all those things you want. We'll go to Club Med, for weeks, _months_, Bobby! And I'll get a bikini, _ten_ bikinis! Oh, I promise. I love you, my darling Bobby!"

Bobby reached a large arm up and over and hugged Bettina closer. "You'll wear a bikini, really, on those beaches, Bettina?"

"Only until you take it off me, baby," said Bettina in a new, sultry voice, snuggling closer and softly catching his lower lip in both of hers.

Moke looked up from his watch and released Bobby's right wrist so he could now encircle Bettina with both arms. "That's the kind of talk that gets that old mother pumping again," he said in a formal, consulting-room voice.

But now Professor Worth gave a shout of amazement and joy. "Hey! We've got _two_ signals now! They must have gotten down in the escape capsule. Bobby, we're getting a message from the _Tesla_ emergency transponder —'Leak's fixed. Vessel totally disabled. Awaiting rescue' —but now there's a second radio beacon signal showing on the plot, six miles to the east!"

Everyone stared at the professor, and Bobby made a motion to sit up, but Bettina restrained him with chidings and kisses. "Are they modulating it?" said Bobby in a low voice.

"Not yet," said the professor in a tense and expectant voice. "It's sending the automatic recognition signal for the *Gay Enola* capsule . . . Wait . . . wait, here comes some modulation . . . Wait . . . wait . . . message is, 'Tell the underwriters we want a Blackbird and a drone the next time.' Message repeating . . ."

"What's a Blackbird?" said Bettina.

Moke shook his head in admiration. "One of those big spy planes, 90,000 feet, Mach 3," he said. "Old Milt will be king of the sky in one of those mothers. He can pop ten Claudes and never lift a wing."

But at this moment the door to the communication building flew open, and five large federal marshals crowded in, two with rifles pointed at the floor, all with brown tie shoes and new yellow, yachting slickers over their suit coats. "Everybody line up against the . . ." said the leader, but his voice trailed away as he saw the open medical kit, the grouping around prone Bobby, and Bettina passionately kissing his face and whispering in his ear.

Professor Wilson Worth's face turned to stone and his expression to one of total contempt. "Who the hell gave you people permission to land here? This is private property. Get back to your damned boat!"

But Moke was up on his feet, a huge smile across his face, his hand extended in friendly greeting as he strode across the room. "Where're your manners, Willy?" he said briskly. "Can't you see who these folks are?" He seized the bewildered marshal's hand. "Why, it's the Brownshoe Hurricane Protection Society. Put me down for ten bucks, boys," he said expansively, "I haven't given at the office."

Sept. 8, 1600 hrs.—Sept. 9, 0930 hrs.

THE DESTRUCTION OF CLAUDE'S CORE SPREAD DISORGANIZATION outward in all directions. The polar air mass to the west, sensing weakness and disorder, now flowed inexorably eastward throughout the evening, and most of Claude's western energy excesses disappeared in a heavy series of offshore rains and thundersqualls. To the east, the dying storm set several small and feeble children in motion, truncated, circumscribed pools of low barometer that were mostly eaten by the Greenland air mass or that spun themselves to death while moving and feeding from the same depleted patch of cooler ocean as their neighbors.

The great leader waves, no longer driven by a fifty-knot barometer hammer, turned into tremendously long swell, low humps of water losing speed to friction and identity to the natural process of separation by period. As they came onto the south Long Island coast, they mounted the shallows close to shore, and suddenly, almost from nowhere, a series of steep, sharp, far-separated breakers hammered the Moriches, Shinnecock, and other inlets with high, regular surf, completely blocking the entrances for several hours. But no one was out facing Claude, and when the breakers dropped and were replaced by a steady hiss of sullen, hot rain, the boat and water people looked at each other and shook their heads in wonder at the miracle of their deliverance. At least a hundred old, wrinkled men turned to another hundred, identically leathery friends and they all said more or less the same thing, "What in Tophet won't they think of next!"

The deluge of 300-mile-an-hour hail had turned the high-tech interior of the *Tesla* into a wrecked shambles. Cora and Ray had managed to plug the holes near the waterline with expanding putty, so the *Tesla* could roll and wallow without shipping more water, but the switch-gear for the engines, the communications equipment, and most of everything else was in ruin. For a while they amused themselves with the hand pump, getting water out of the *Tesla*, each berating the other for any slow or partial strokes during turns at the pump handle.

The rolling and pitching slowly abated, though the rain came down steadily, drumming on the aluminum hull. Cora lay tiredly back in her seat and her thoughts turned hard and bitter. They had won, but they had paid too high a price. She remembered Milton Stein's calm, professional voice as he spoke of death and ruin in a flat spin, just before the *Tesla*'s radio gear was smashed by a grapefruit-sized lump of ice. Their hard-fought triumph seemed spoiled and stupid.

At that moment Ray, who was peering at his bare feet and his socks hanging on the control wheel to dry, said in a thoughtful voice, "I wonder if fags get to go to heaven?"

The comment seemed entirely too much for Cora, and she bared her large teeth in rage, then turned to Ray. "Listen," she said in her most acid tone, "do you realize why you've got this stupid thing about hating homosexuals, Ray? I'm going to tell you. You had something going with Van Stevens, either in your head or for real, and when he died piloting in that crazy thunderhead project you organized, you just flipped right over the edge on that subject. You should go to a shrink, Ray. You're sick in the head!"

But for once, Ray made no answer or change of expression, and Cora, replaying those cruel words in her own head, realized she had gone over the edge herself. She reached and put her hand on Ray's arm. "Ray, I'm sorry. I didn't mean that. We're both upset over this, over Milt and Bertie." But even this dropping of her defenses had no effect on thoughtful Ray, and he said nothing more while the clouds cleared away and a big yellow sun popped up over the rim. Fifty yards away, Techoceanics' substantial recovery vessel, *Alessandro Volta*, stopped to put down her power launch to take off Cora and Ray, then fasten the falls from a stern-mounted A-frame to bring the battered *Tesla* aboard. Nearby, two big offshore cutters, *Dauntless* and *Intrepid*, carried the overflow of important guests who had come to see the heroes be rescued amid the ruins of the storm they broke in half. Elected officials, important persons in the federal meteorological establishment, and high-level bureaucrats including a secretary or two from several departments, watched from the cutters, but not, as the *Times* sarcastically noted in a waspish editorial about federal meddling, anyone from Justice or the federal judiciary.

While the launch brought still-silent Ray and introspective Cora across to the *Volta*, a big Coast Guard machine descended onto the after platform of the *Dauntless*, and still more dignitaries climbed rapidly out of the helicopter cabin to peer across at them.

The chop was still two or three feet high, but Cora, then Ray, made the jump to the lowered, slanting ladder and clambered up to the main deck of the *Volta*. All the hurricane modification team and its friends had been brought out by a triumphant Techoceanics Corporation. Bobby, white and grinning and allowed to come only because the doctors knew his not being there would be even more harmful, was held tightly around the waist by a slim, now happy and thus pretty, Bettina in a bright and shapely dress. Arthur Goodspeed looked exhausted, a thousand years old, and completely at peace, and beside him stood Professor Worth, Moke Mogamo, and Walter Nunes. Nearby was a completely dazzled Peter Heartshorn, clutching his father's hand. Mr. Heartshorn's pouched and puffed cheeks gave him the aspect of an overweight squirrel finally, happily, ready for the winter. Stew Johnson held Peter's other hand and now and then explained some technical point to the gaping boy in a stern, professional whisper.

Clustered together near the front were the Hartford people, many more now and including the great man himself, B. B. Broadhurst, president of gigantic Hartford Fire and Casualty and chairman of the Underwriters Weather Modification Group. Taller than his lieutenants, his silver mane of hair was a shine of power in the TV lights.

But as Cora and Ray stepped from the ladder to the deck, to loud cheers and applause from everyone and hoots from the cutters' sirens, the first people they saw were Stein and Smith, for the small escape capsule and its large parachute had been taken from the water only a half hour before by the *Volta*, and the two men stood in their mussed coveralls, their bulky flying suits still over their arms, beaming at everybody.

At that moment, the most extraordinary thing of all happened. Ray, his eyes suddenly blinded by tears, dashed unsteadily forward with a cry of "Oh, thank God!" and flung himself on the astonished pilot, sweeping up an owlishly blinking Bertram Smith with his other arm, and then kissing and hugging them both with babblings of thanksgiving and praise.

Bobby, who stepped forward to shake Cora's hand,

stopped in arrested amazement. "Cora," he said softly, "what in the hell have you been drinking on that boat?" But Cora only blinked at the cameras and said nothing.

Biddle Bonniford Broadhurst strode hastily across the deck, his large, liver-spotted hands wide in welcome, then clasped Ray, Milton, and Bertram Smith in his own huge embrace, beaming back at the cameras. "Come on, Cora," he shouted, "Get over here! You earned it, lady, and I'm going to give it to you!"

Soon the four heroes were separated and adjusted, two on each side of looming B. B. Broadhurst, who fished a large-size certified bank check from his pocket and turned, bowing low and gracefully to Cora, who smiled fearsomely and seized the check. "One million dollars, Cora. Less than a tenth of a percent of Claude's loss potential for us, and more to come," said Broadhurst, making large, expansive gestures. He turned and bowed again to Milton Stein. "And Captain Stein, we received your message loud and clear in Hartford about the Blackbird, and we're going to get you *two* of them."

That was too much for Ray. "Oh hell, B. B.," he snarled, "just give us one and hand the other one to Israel. Then that damn-fool judge, what's his name . . . Farbgold, Silverfarb, Goldenfinger . . . will electrocute those college-punk environmental freaks . . ."

Fortunately, most of this was made confused or inaudible by a combination of Cora's loudest snarls and by both Bobby and B. B. Broadhurst stepping rapidly forward with loud, agitated laughter. Broadhurst waved his arms wildly at the others. "Come on, you giant-killers, get in the picture, all of you!" he roared in all directions.

As they pressed noisily forward, Moke said in Bettina's ear, "Man, I'm really glad to see that old Ray is okay. I figgered he'd been beaned by one of those ice balls when he kissed Milt and Aunt Bertie."

"Oh, give Ray his moment of sweetness, Moke," said a smiling Bettina. "Nobody's completely imperfect. Remember what you said on the way over to Wasque?"

The idea of Ray's sweetness had turned Moke's agile mind in another direction. He leaned back, while B. B. noisily tried to get them adjusted for the TV shots, so that Bobby, Bettina, Nunes, and Professor Worth could hear. "Did you guys ever actually picture Ray and Cora making it together?" he asked in a quiet voice. "I mean totally undressed, on a giant, queen-sized motel bed with a bottle of gin on the nightstand."

So sudden and unlikely was this vision that Bobby, Bettina, Nunes, and the professor simultaneously doubled over in attempts to stifle their uncontrollable laughter. As the TV lights and cameras panned across the assembling group, Walter Nunes's mother, Isobel, sitting proudly in her New Bedford parlor to watch her son honored on TV as one of the tiny team of hurricane busters, was dismayed to see him bent, helpless, in a convulsive laughing fit. "Well, he never did take much of anything seriously," she said apologetically to the other women.

Her next-door neighbor, Rose Meideros, snorted. "So, and what's wrong with enjoying yourself? And look, those two big shots and that old professor are broken up, too."

That observation mollified Isobel Nunes somewhat, but she thoughtfully shook her head. "Still, see how straight, how dignified and proud that big colored boy who works with Walt stands there. He went to Harvard, Walter told me. My, what a difference that makes!"

JACK L. CHALKER